I0891614

Praise for Late Rehearsals

"Allow me to recommend to you the work of Dominic Hoffman. In the most sincere literary praise of my native Chicago: 'This guy writes real good.' Sincerely yours," —**David Mamet**, Pulitzer-prize winning playwright, *Speed the Plow, Glengarry Glen Ross*

"Hoffman's stories have a rare, wonderful light playing through them. Immensely enjoyable." —**Jeff Johnson**, *Tattoo Machine, The Darby Holland Crime Stories*

"I love adventure! Dominic Hoffman's stories deliver multiple exciting adventures. I was along for the ride from beginning to end! And I wanted more." —**Carl Weathers**, Actor/Director, *Rocky, The Mandalorian*

"The world is coming to an end and Dominic Hoffman is giving us the play by play.
His percussive prose dances from the Pacific to the Seine and beyond, where the species of a certain vintage rages against the dying of the night. Read him now while it's too late." —**Roger Guenveur Smith**, Actor/Playwright, *A Huey P. Newton Story, Till, Do the Right Thing*

"From the homeless ghosts of Venice, CA, to the Gauloise-scented banks of the Seine, Dominic Hoffman's tales get us nodding—like we think we know where he's going—then reverse themselves to land us where we never expected to be. His voice is elegant, raw, and authentic. His words will haunt you." —**Michael Schiffer**, Screenwriter, *Colors, Lean on Me, Crimson Tide.*

"The triumph of Hoffman's stories is his ability to create characters you want to be with, and worlds you don't want to leave. These stories are thoughtful, authentic, and very entertaining. The words wrap themselves around your brain, paint vivid pictures and before you realize it, have beguilingly taken you away." —**Timothy Prager**, Screenwriter, *Silent Witness, Waking the Dead, 55 Degrees North*

Late Rehearsals

Dominic Hoffman

RISING ACTION

This book is a work of fiction. Any references to historical events, real people, or real places are used fictitiously. Other names, characters, places, and events are products of the author's imagination, and any resemblance to actual events, places, names, or persons, is entirely coincidental.

Cover Illustration © Nat Mack
Distributed by Simon & Schuster

ISBN: 978-1-998076-46-8
Ebook: 978-1-998076-26-0

FIC029000 FICTION / Short Stories
FIC000000 FICTION / General
FIC049000 FICTION / African American & Black / General

#LateRehearsals

Follow Rising Action on our socials!
Twitter: @RAPubCollective
Instagram: @risingactionpublishingco
Tiktok: @risingactionpublishingco

CONTENTS

Preface	1
Story Story	5
Maurice	27
Smuggling Elegance	31
Paris Graffiti	59
Echoes	73
Car Problems	103
A Trip	111
Naked	137
Love Letter from Venice	145
Passing Through	153
Dark Muse	183
Juveniles	213
Turkey Day	221
Thanks	257
About the Author	259

This book is dedicated to Eleanor Zoe Hoffman ... the best human being I've ever known.

Late

Rehearsals

Preface

How this book came about was largely chance. I have been a writer my entire life, mostly plays, screenplays, and the odd poem (what other kind is there?). However, I've been making my living as an actor on stage and elsewhere. For the last twenty years, I have also been an audiobook narrator. I submitted a few stories to an agent and the result is this collection. Having spent decades working in Los Angeles, I was stunned at the ease and civility of this exchange. I remain mildly astonished to have the opportunity to portion my work publicly after so many years of comical bloodletting in LA.

I'm not sure what connection these stories have with one another. That would certainly be better assessed by the reader. I'm sure my collective occupations (actor/writer/book recorder) have influenced my writing as much as my life experiences. This has made for a gallimaufry of narratives, telling a bunch of stories without trying to prove anything. I consider myself fundamentally a playwright, and that distinction proved the most interesting concept to explore while writing this book. I found commonalities: they're both about craft and sweat and the writer must disguise them both. Short stories and plays also share the battle between love of language and the telling of the story. The main distinction, of course, is that plays are primarily dialogue driven. In any event, I opted for the freedom to look at the world and people I have known, a few stories I have been told, some places I have been, and squeeze them into short story form.

I am fundamentally baffled by the trajectory of the world these days. With climate change leading the way, pandemics, raging wars, the rich eating the poor, and the general inability of people to respect one another, it's difficult to 'get in where you fit in,' to shamelessly quote one of my characters. To speak of these important issues with the deserved seriousness they merit would be cynical and boorish. To gloss over them would be irresponsible. That said, the present state of the world provides unlimited content for artists and comedians. News seems to blunt the intellect and writing fiction seems to me the unwitting antidote. It also allows one to excavate the humor from the madness.

Succinctly ...

I am an unapologetic Francophile so two of the stories are set in Paris. It would take a better writer than myself to explain my infatuation with France and do it justice. Let me simply say my love for the place is limitless.

I snuck into Cuba twice in the late nineties and the cultural upheaval I witnessed had me taking prodigious notes, which became the beginning of a story. I abandoned it. Fast forward to this opportunity to revisit those notes and it turned into the Cuban tale, Smuggling Elegance. Traveling produces epiphanies.

I attended college at UC Santa Cruz and have lived in Venice, California, for a major portion of my life. Both of those places are evidenced here in this collection.

I am personally interested in and motivated by the oral stories to which I have been privy. I have been fearless, or perhaps reckless, in my associations, and have benefited mightily from what I have heard and have stolen what I needed.

That this was written during the pandemic adds a measurable situational element. A story or two deals with COVID peripherally, yet I wonder if they would have been completely different tales had there been no pandemic. I have no idea. But here they are, and my slim hope is that what follows doesn't interrupt anyone's future interest in reading.

A jazz musician was standing on an empty stage fooling around with his horn when a man came up to ask him what he was rehearsing. The musician replied, "Man, you can't rehearse what you ain't invented yet."

That's what writing this felt like to me. Rehearsing the uninvented.

Dominic Hoffman
Mexico City, Jan. 2022

STORY STORY

It was several months into an ambiguous lockdown, and everyone was unwillingly conversant with the mighty COVID-19. The pandemic's very name had a kind of septic poetry to it. An evil, nasty racecar, and to further the metaphor, it moved like one as well. Romantic as an anal blister. The accompanying lockdown proved gentler to my temperament than to many others given the non-stop complaints and challenges I witnessed daily. For me, it meant fewer tourists, calmer beaches, and less bumper to bumper. I live in Venice, California.

I am also accustomed to isolation. Being a writer literally by vocation, I understand enduring or, in my case, luxuriating in quiet; the only sound, peace, which has its own distinctive qualities. The wind rushing through my open kitchen window. An occasional thud from my upstairs neighbor chasing his dog. The distant metallic roar of the ocean. The painful moans of sexual congress emitted from a neighbor's apartment. This being Venice, there was also the more than occasional technicolor scream of insanity from the street below my third-floor window. Daily existence. Nightly occurrence. Familiar distractions of my choosing. Of my choosing.

All parts of Los Angeles were experiencing continuous public protests and acts of defiance. The internet sites were demonstrating vividly how divided we were as a country, and of course, there was madness leaking full bore from the president and his followers. All in all, a magical time for writers. Nothing even the most adventurous writer could fabricate would sound remotely farfetched. Fiction was nowhere near as fictitious as reality. I figured now would be a great time to write a horror tale. Something that would align itself with the present-day horrors of the open wound this pandemic has become. A wound that is not to close any time soon, regardless of our inability to accept its existence. Why not take people's minds off of the virus and scare the shit out them with a ghost story? The timing was perfect. The world was ready to be frightened by something that didn't actually exist. Clearly, this would be a preference. We do appreciate a good pandemic scare, though not while we're in the middle of experiencing one.

I sat at my table with two sharpened number two pencils, two ink pens: black, a yellow legal pad, and my computer open on a blank page. I like to go back and forth between mediums and tools. I don't believe it serves any positive function, other than making me feel warm and fuzzy and productive before I even begin. I immediately considered the ghost of my story, which needed to be something amorphous but frightening in its ambiguity. The real horror had to occur in the reader's imagination. There is nothing so chilling as one's own imagination. So, the real play had to be in the setup. The place was of absolute importance. I live in Venice, a community of contrasts and confusion, which manifests itself in wild and unpredictable human behavior. It's a petri dish of madness and merriment that multiplies like rogue cells. There was no need to place the story elsewhere.

I came up with the ghost prototype quickly. It would be a composite of homeless folks whom I have often seen, intentionally avoided, and placed in my rolodex under scary muthafuckas. The homeless theme was not only topical, but it was also an unavoidable issue for LA residents. People had strong feelings about them. Homeless people were considered something other. They were both foreign and indigenous. They were uncontrollable, in evidence on streets, sidewalks, under bridges, lying in the middle of anything and everything. Blocks of streets were under de facto control by these individuals. I had recently spent a few days strolling dangerously close to some of the homeless encampments. Areas of sidewalks or dead ends were appropriated by tents, bicycles, garbage, cardboard boxes, and panels serving multiple purposes. My research for the story raged right outside my front door.

As for the story... initially, it began itself.

I called him Benedict. Never to his face, of course. His name didn't necessarily fit, but it popped into my mind the first time I caught a glimpse of him and stuck like shit to a shoe. We didn't speak, which was uncommon. I like to at least acknowledge the homeless crew I see on a daily basis. It's safer and an easy way to partially ingratiate yourself into the surrounding culture. I don't like being considered a stranger in my own hood.

Benedict could be found in a different location every day on the beachfront strand. That in itself stood out. Itinerants have a tendency to stake a claim on a patch of beach, sidewalk, or empty storefront. Staying in a small group usually provided a bit of solidarity and protection. Not Benedict. He was always solo. Always in a different place. I assumed it was because he had so many things going against him, even for a homeless person. He was extravagantly filthy. His clothes, such as they were, had the indelible stains of bodily function refuse. Or more succinctly, he looked like he shit from every pore. It was how I knew he was near. His smell was singular.

Benedict sported a blemished beret cocked to the side of his head in what I imagined to be his last act of defiance. He may have been filthy, a bit smelly, he was definitively homeless and destitute, but he was cool. His face reminded me of no one, nowhere. I had never seen a human face as foreign as his. It was more dinosaur than human. A prolonged jaw, sunken eyes, and slashing cheekbones. His lips pulled away from his mouth to reveal gums and teeth, not unlike a cadaver before being infused with formaldehyde. Curiously, his face was the one thing he kept relatively clean. On this particular day, he was sitting on a mound of sand just off the walkway, staring intently at another mound of sand with half of a baby carriage sticking out of it.

I was strolling the strand on my bike. Seeing Benedict, I stopped abruptly, thinking perhaps this would be a good time for us to acknowledge one another. I rolled slowly in his direction, keeping a respectful distance. What I have learned in my twenty-seven years in Venice is that the one thing even the insane respond to is respect. So, there I was, ten feet away, waiting for Benedict to return my stare and complete my random sense of community. I didn't have to wait long.

The sun was blazing. There was a palm-tree-bending-wind, and the sand managed to find both of my eyes, even behind sunglasses. Paranoid about putting my hands to my face, I roughly rubbed my eyes using my shoulders. Vision cleared, I returned to Benedict, who was no longer on the sand mound. I was suddenly assaulted by the smell of putrefaction and smoke. This prefaced my realization that Benedict was standing five feet away. I let out a baby scream, or maybe it was a giant scream that wouldn't release itself. What I know for sure is that I ran into half a dozen people on the strand as I sped away on my bike without looking back at the damage. I was fully a mile away before I stopped.

Real fear is a funny thing. As I was speeding along, attempting to reconcile what had happened, I began to laugh like a madman. It was a sad, conflicted laugh. A laugh of embarrassment. In the parlance of the street, I felt like a little bitch. Still, I was glad I got the fuck out of there. Maybe we aren't all supposed to get along. Maybe there are some people better kept at a distance. Maybe I am not to understand everyone and everything to help make the world better. Maybe I am just full of shit. This was going to be a long bike ride.

My ride skirts the Pacific Ocean. There's an unobstructed view of beautiful blue along the bike path. Pelicans, pigeons, and seagulls traffic the skies. Next to the bike path is the pedestrian lane. Few people pay attention to the logic of such creations. There are often accidents, screaming insults, and sometimes violence, a result of people ignoring the sanctity of bike lanes. I generally judge people by how well they behave on public paths. Those who walk in tandem with others against traffic, ignoring the oncoming cyclists, are the asshats of life. I precede every ride with a calming mantra: "Many people are irresponsible, privileged, delusional portals to a bottomless vortex of anger. Do not lose your temper."

The ride was not very far. Eleven miles, which is only about half of what I normally do. I had a later start than usual. I'm not partial to riding back in the Venice dark as it is fairly peopled with both felons and the fearless when the sun goes down, but there it was. Night. As expected, the homeless tents lining my way home were active. Stolen bikes were being reassembled by flashlight. The air was thick with the smell of pot and the fustiness attached to the criminally unwashed. Conflicts were mounting as I rode up to my apartment, just a half block from crazy central. A police car passed me on the alley. I acknowledged him. He looked right through me. Not an enviable job that. Especially now. Hey, he chose it.

I carried my bike up the stairs and triple-locked it to the staircase. At my door, a few steps away, I froze. Something was wrong. I only had it for an instant, but it was the faint but unmistakable smell of Benedict. I turned and looked down the hallway before entering my apartment. Nothing. I smelled my hands and my shirt for good measure. Nada. Okay, I was imagining it. As I entered my two-room apartment, I heard a loud recognizable voice carry up through my open window. My kitchen faces the alley and the endless row of garbage containers from the various apartments. There is a man who shows up like clockwork, investigating the cans and preaching a sort of free association discourse to the Gods. He's very large and dangerous-looking and but for his situation, would no doubt have made a fine actor. His voice is resonant and as colorful as what he has to say. Tonight, his sermon was a fine garbling of mortality and spaceships. I've lived here long enough to appreciate the madness of such outbursts.

It was dinner time. My kitchen was fully stocked for the apocalypse. I opened the refrigerator and stared at its bounty and considered how many times I'd looked in my fridge that day to view the same exact items. Random thoughts are one of the results of COVID. Spending so much time alone, one of the major battles is turning off one's thinking. Failing to be a practicing Buddhist, my thoughts appear relentlessly, aggressively, and if I'm not careful, insanely. So, after about ten minutes trying to estimate the number of grapes in a huge bag, I closed the refrigerator door and began cooking my dinner. Thirty-five minutes later I was seated eating a bloody steak and some roasted potatoes. With a glass of some funky and fantastic organic red, my windows open to a slight Santa Ana wind, I felt as if I was in Paris for a second.

The evening was uneventful with the exception of a dream about Benedict. The specifics escaped me by morning, but I seemed to recall a brutal fight to the death, unsure of whose death it was. The next morning, I decided to visit the ocean front walk in disguise, which for me meant adorning a tattered hoody and abused jeans. I sat on the impoverished stretch of lawn and sand that separated the tourist walkway from the bike path, and in turn led to the ocean. Hooded and masked, people rode past me avoiding eye contact. I had joined the army of the invisible—the homeless. I realized almost immediately that this anonymity brought with it a certain freedom. Ironically, the air felt cleaner. The colors of my surroundings were more dynamic. I felt like a foreign correspondent on a secret mission. Okay, maybe that's a stretch, but I was immediately energized enough to discreetly seek out Benedict.

Mornings for the homeless are no different than those of us who have beds and walls. Tempo is leisurely. Hair is messy. Many of them have dogs. The canine dispositions match those of their owners. Both are a bit startled by the very presence of day and everyone is looking for food. As I walked by the various encampments, tents, and open-air domiciles, I wondered openly where Benedict would choose to sleep. Certainly, he would find an isolated spot. Perhaps out on the sand near the ocean. What did he eat? How did he eat? I never saw him pawning off the tourists and his demeanor was not overly inviting. I walked on for a good mile until the strand broke up into the less homeless and more privileged, unconscious types. Exercise classes, beach yoga, and exquisitely wrapped spandex asses became prevalent. I watched a group of girls playing volleyball for a while until I realized that even from a distance, my staring presence might frighten. I moved on reluctantly.

Conga drums sounded in the distance. A drummer myself, I followed the beat. The drummers of Venice beach are usually something I avoid as they cater to the community feeling, as opposed to the beat. The Venice drum circle is a highly democratic experience, but it just isn't rhythmic. What I was following was the sound of real congueros playing a complicated rhumba. It was so funky, I forgot about Benedict. I watched a bunch of drummers and a timbale player. Someone was on clave, and another was killing it on a shekere. I was in heaven. I began dancing. A crowd gathered. Others danced. I was invited to play the tumbao, the bass drum. I only had to keep the bottom swinging. Well, hell yes. An hour later, the song ended. I stood up, thanked the players, and decided to return home and eat. In the distance, in the direction of the water, I spotted Benedict. He was seated looking out over the sea. There was someone with him. From my vantage, it appeared to be a naked woman.

I moved as discreetly as possible, tracing a distant parallel line, never looking up. I walked all the way to the water and then behaved as if I was returning from the same. I didn't look up until I was comfortably near, yet far enough away from him and his guest. My first thought before I looked up was, how did this very dodgy homeless man score a woman with breasts that could be detected from a distance? My second thought was, how did I not know she was a mannequin? My discovery was difficult to reconcile. It was a complex feeling of regret and embarrassment. Regret that I was not actually looking at a naked woman, and embarrassment at having coveted a mound of plastic in Benedict's clutch. I walked away, confused, forgetting my main reason for being there was to establish contact with playboy Benedict. I was too disappointed to think straight. It didn't matter. Benedict rose, lifted his plastic princess in the air, whom I now realized was literally bottomless, and headed in my direction. Whether it was embarrassment or confusion, I remained in place, stuck there while Benedict accompanied, slogged through the sand. It's moments like these selfies were made for.

He passed by me close enough to smell, which is redundant, then turned back to glare. I did my best to appear nonchalant, holding my breath, smiling kindly. He turned to his mannequin, planting a more than platonic kiss on her scarred plastic lips, then carried on. I followed apace. This was becoming a mad mystery bereft of plot. I passed another of the homeless disciples, a Black man with wild unruly hair, which animated his maniacal laughter. In a booming crackle of a voice, he said to no one in particular, "Oh my God, it's crazy how much I don't give a fuck!" continuing in unhinged laughter. It stopped me cold. I'm not sure why, but his declaration sounded a malignant truth in the marrow of my soul. It was a revelation of sorts, devoid of any disingenuousness. To state the obvious, his response to the world in general had profoundly surprised him enough to be incapable of containing the mad glee of his arrival at that point. I envied him and wondered if that should be an objective. To arrive at a point in life where it's shocking how little fucks one gives. There was so much horror not to give a fuck about. Benedict was no longer in my sightline. I was tempted to turn and follow no-fucks-to-give-man, then thought better. Random philosophers at the beach are a mainstay.

Now I was four blocks from home with nothing but embarrassment to show for my cultural outing. What new information had I found out about Benedict? Benedict. Why did I name him that? It smelled of Catholicism. My Catholic upbringing surfaces in the strangest moments. I was raised Catholic, went to Catholic schools, and served as an altar boy when the mass was still performed in Latin. At one time, I had designs on becoming a priest. It was a time when all observant Catholics named their children after saints. Mine is Thomas, after Saint

Thomas Aquinas, a philosopher-priest. I have always wondered what real influence my religious upbringing had on me, other than rendering me a staunch atheist. I recall being scared to death of the nuns who taught me. They were, with a couple of exceptions, malignant witch types. Their go-to was always to threaten and then deliver on the threat with a firm ruler. My memory of all the priests was much gentler, kinder, with none of the pedophilic tendencies one might presume.

Saint Benedict was a monk who truly preferred solitude and eventually founded a monastery. My Benedict was a loner even by homeless standards. St. Benedict lived part of his life in a cave. My Benedict lived on the beach. I was trying to draw some type of relationship between the two as I recalled all things religious and slowly make my way back to the apartment. One has to be careful. Religious musings are a candlelit and incense-filled rabbit hole for fallen Catholics. I had to shift gears before the ever-present Catholic guilt kicked in. Besides, I was hungry. Even that reminded me of secretly snacking on unconsecrated hosts in the sacristy after serving a mass.

I turned for a last look at the Venice Beach tableau. A strange example of not-so-still nature. Nature morte without the morte part. Turner skies with clouds bruised in purple and splashed in orange fire. No ships. Today we have only boats. The sea blue water was a Monet palette. Choppy but somehow drama-free. A wind and smell only Michelangelo could express because he possessed both visible and invisible powers. The faces: disfigured, tangled, disturbing, beautiful, and haunting, as if Dali, Francis Bacon, and Picasso came together to speed paint portraits. Modern in every unfortunate sense. Art of and for the masses. "Bitch ass niggahs" was the last pronouncement I heard from someone screaming by on a scooter. Yes, it was time to retreat. I had a ghost story to write.

Arriving at my apartment on the third floor just off the beachfront walk was always calming. With my windows open, I could still hear the Venice din of madness; however, with a distance cushion and three locks on the door, the world changes. I am not homeless. One's appreciation of walls and a roof is never wasted on a Venice local. Once more to the fridge, dear friends, to guiltily explore bounty not afforded the world I had recently departed. A Danish dinner. Smoked salmon, butter pickles, hard cheese, and brown bread sated me. Now...the story.

I obviously had a ghost in mind. Benedict was a perfect candidate, but I couldn't keep him outside. Outside, he remained a safe experiment. Outside I could observe him in public which didn't allow for the element of danger necessary to thrill the punters. I had to bring him in my house, at least metaphorically. The thought of him in my apartment immediately brought his pungent marinade to the forefront of my nostrils.

These were merely random thoughts that can be mistaken for useful attempts to arrive at a starting point. It's important to clear one's head of all useless intellectual meandering before a word is written. It's important to simply be in the moment. I was searching for the moment. Being present is where it's at. I mean, you sit down and you're having food. The taste is supreme. There's a strain of music from upstairs and a screech just outside the window. The stove is on, and the flames lick and rumble softly. A car passes through the alley. The heat goes on, so the radiator speaks. And all of it...all of it is what your life is, and you feel thankful for knowing that. It's not covered up with what you have to do or think you should be doing or what you should have done. It's literally what you are doing and, by extension, who you are. And that has to be enough.

This momentary realization was insufficient to the task at hand, and I was at the point of throwing in the towel. I felt sleepy. I made a promise to myself never again to eat directly before writing, a vow I have made many more times than I have kept. Was it postprandial somnolence or an excuse? As my eyes involuntarily closed, I heard a sound. My windows give out to a busy alley. The building across from mine produces an acoustic pocket, making the sounds from below appear as if they are originating from somewhere inside the apartment. I looked outside to where a man was going through the large dumpster which services the neighboring apartment. I often watch people as they go through the trash, fascinated by their varying degrees of commitment. Some people jump into the dumpster and ferret around as if in a bubble bath, looking for the bar of soap, while others pick through it as someone extracting seeds from a pomegranate. This hooded, darkly cloaked individual was talking to the trash while gently poking at it with a golf club. His tone was hushed—half conspiratorial, half accusatory. One hundred percent crazy. I turned out my lights to obfuscate my glaring outline from above. You never want them to know where you live.

Another man came by with his dog. A muscled pitbull with no leash and a still tail. The man stopped to watch the man in the dumpster. His dog walked to the other side of the man holding the golf club, his tail rising like an angry flagpole. A charged silence grew as the two men acknowledged proximity.

"You find anything?"

No answer.

"That's my dog."

No response.

"He's hungry."

The hooded dumpster man regarded the dog, which had now moved closer. He finally spoke.

"What's his name?"

"Dog."

"Does Dog like music?"

"What?" The dumpster man pointed at Dog with the golf club as he spoke. "Some dogs like music. I had one who liked to listen to country songs. Especially liked Merle Haggard."

Dog man took this information in thoughtfully. "Got any food in there? He ain't particular."

The dumpster man pushed some things around with his golf club. "This here's Millennial trash. Empty Amazon boxes 'n shit. They don't eat, them Millennials. Just play video games. Lotta empties. I'm a pet your dog if you don't mind?"

"Not me you gotta ask."

The pitbull was already growling quietly, a preamble to what I thought was soon to be a vicious mauling. Dumpster man turned toward Dog and began to whistle. I didn't recognize the tune, but his pitch was on point and the sound melodious. He walked right up to Dog and stuck his hand out. Dog took a vicious snap at it, missing by a centimeter.

"I guess Dog says no," Dog's owner lamented. At that exact moment, all three of them focused on something approaching. I heard the faint squeaking of wheels turning. Slowly, Benedict appeared, pushing a pram, his plastic date sticking out, her arms akimbo, a blanket covering her missing half. This was now a lively trifecta, excluding Benedict's object of affection.

There was a hard knock on my door. It was either someone who knew I couldn't hear anything less than a hard pounding from my living room, or it was something worse. I left the window and attended to the door. Cautiously looking through the peephole, I spied the forty-year-old virgin.

Terry Cummings was a knockout. I met her a couple of years prior at the farmers market, where she was giving new meaning to inspecting a head of broccoli. A conversation ensued, as did dinner later that evening. It was the strangest first date of my life. She told me, as she served me an inedible vegan meal, that she was a virgin, but not to worry about it. After that evening, we would get together for almost-sex every couple of months. She truly was a forty-year-old virgin. We did everything but penetration and it was a gloriously unsatisfying but impossible to resist. I let her in.

Her clothing style always accented her physical gifts. They would be impossible to conceal in any event. Whatever she wore would be appropriate attire for any evening at Burning Man. Tonight, it was a psychedelic belly dancer. Terry laid her hand gently on my chest as she silently passed me, kicked off her shoes, and moved purposefully to the other room. I engaged all three locks on the door and followed.

When I arrived in the other room, she was looking out the window, her arms holding onto either side of the window frame, looking from my vantage point as if she were being arrested. I stood behind and appreciated the view. I knew this was her gift to me. Look at me. Look at me. Look at me.

Knowing she would stay there until I interrupted, I spoke, "Are they still here?"

"Who?"

I approached. Everyone had left. I put my arms around her, bit the back of her neck, and then backed away. "There was a meeting of the homeless union out there."

"It's getting so bad in Venice. I took a chance coming here."

"Well...I wasn't expecting you."

Miss Terry finally turned around. It made me gasp. There are some women who have so much power in their person, it's difficult to remain buoyant in their orbit. Far from a classical beauty, she had several inelegant features. A large nose, untrimmed eyebrows, a natural sneer, and a mouth large enough to have its zip code. Together these physical qualities willed themselves into a stunning portrait of woman. She had lived a life of being objectified and her best defense she decided early on, was to transform whatever she had into a weapon. She retreated inside and turned her body into a fine-tuned machine. Terry was a fine, tofu eating, yoga practicing, animal saving, non-drinking, hippie dancing, white girl who had so much going on she certainly didn't need a man. It would take someone of more intelligence or stronger will power than myself not to avail himself to her at a moment's notice. That is, I believe, why she was still a virgin. What's her motivation to be otherwise? When I told her on one sticky afternoon that she should let me be her first, she calmly replied, "What's in it for me?"

Terry inelegantly sat on my nearby couch and stared at me quizzically. "So, what's the great writer doing these days?" I told her I've been trying to write a ghost story.

"Like a movie?"

"No. Like a story."

"What's it about?"

"A ghost."

She laughed and lay back suggestively on the couch. At least I thought it was suggestive. She closed her eyes and waited for me to transport her. I felt naked, which was some kind of reverse projection, as naked was the state in which I presently wanted to see her. What is the story about? Hell, if I knew that in detail, I would have already finished writing it. I watched her adjust herself while I tried to imagine what would be the most interesting thing I could say to incline her to move on to the more physical aspects of our meeting. I was lost momentarily as I observed her steady breast undulations married to her breaths. She lifted her arm and placed it pillow-like under her head. "Well?"

I began by simply explaining how I was searching for an antidote to the nonstop madness of COVID and Trump and humanity in general. I wanted to create a horror diversion. A diversion that was safer simply because it wasn't real. I spoke about Benedict and how the homeless were both sad and scary. I told of my forays into the world of the homeless, and how it was like being on another planet. I explained how, once in my investigations, a man and a woman whom I had given a dollar to asked me to enter their tent. They were excited to show me how well it was decorated. Feeling it would have been unseemly not to accept, I stepped inside. The smell made my insides collapse. Why I recounted this episode is a mystery to me. It was the dead opposite of foreplay. As I lay all of this information out to this woman, whom I only wanted naked and agile, I realized that I had no idea what I was writing about. Not in any solid way, other than wanting to desist from being inundated with the pandemic. She opened her eyes.

"Can I be honest?"

"No," I said, not jokingly.

She stared up at the ceiling as if she had just discovered heaven's portal. "I would write a homeless love story. I mean if you really want to get away from the COVID, you need to make people see goodness. Who needs to be scared? People want safety. People want love. They don't need to be more scared. They need the opposite, whatever that is. Maybe you should visit the couple who invited you into their tent and write about their love story. Love in the midst of homelessness. That's kind of beautiful, don't you think?"

It's always touchy explaining writing that is still in its gestation to someone. It's not that the writing is underdeveloped; it's not even writing yet. Usually, the idea is shared out of vanity: 'I think this is a great idea', or insecurity: 'I wonder if this idea is a load of shit?' Those are noble reasons for sharing compared to mine. I only wanted to commence our virginal exploits. However, she asked the question, and if that was going to be the turnkey to her private vault, I'd share royalties with her. Terry seemed rather pleased with her suggestion and offered me her best eureka gaze. As far as she was concerned, problem solved. I concurred and moved to the couch.

"Thank you, Terry. You're so right. Who needs a ghost story when things are ..."

"Shut up," she interrupted. She laughed and lay her hand in my lap to afford more room. "You don't care about what I think. You just want what you want."

"Not true and true. I do care about what you think, and yes, I do want you. But no, I am not going to befriend some homeless romantics."

And just like that, my priorities had changed. I no longer cared about Benedict or the plight of the homeless. I was indifferent to the story line, vague as it was, or any effort to sit in front of a computer and excavate from my emotional void a frightening tale for a bunch of strangers who may or may not ever read it. I reconciled there and then that my focus on the physical possibilities between Terry and myself was far stronger than any motivation to create. It was a disturbing revelation, but one I had to accept. The parting of Terry's legs could all my questions. Perhaps I wasn't a writer. The only proof I had was that I had been doing it my entire life. I had also been having sex my entire life, with which I was not only more successful, but certainly brought me more pleasure. Maybe it was COVID. In any event, Terry must have understood my private musings. She put her index finger in her mouth and then slowly slipped the same finger into mine. As always, she was queen, and I was subject. It had been months since I had any physical contact with a woman. I had followed COVID safety protocol almost to the letter. There were a few women whom I could call for a bit of midnight persuasion or a spot of afternoon delight, which I did. To a person, they had already found someone to see them through the pandemic. One of them, Connie from Milwaukee, who had the most sexual stamina of any woman I've ever known, felt bad for me and said if I wanted to call later and have Face-Time sex, she would walk me through it. Her words. Walk me through it. It made me feel like a John. I told her no thanks ... but I would accept photos. She hung up.

So, there I was, using Terry's finger as a pacifier on this crazy night after a crazier day, contemplating the possibility of non-penetrative sex as a four-year-old contemplates Christmas morning. Let's open the fucking presents already! There are times in one's life when we know exactly what we should do. Where we are cognizant of both our situation and our options and can act accordingly. This was not one of those times. For me, the possibility of intimacy is almost bigger than the moment itself. I was leaning over Terry, hard as nuclear physics, her eyes sucking every bit of logic from my soul. I was trying to navigate a river of risk, danger and fear that comes with dealing with this particular individual. How much could I let myself go? She had rules and limits, and she was the only one who knew what they were. She came over when I was in the middle of a completely different movie and turned it into a double feature. No, she made whatever I was doing before, no matter its importance, a mere trailer for a film I had no desire to see. It sounds terribly dramatic, but is in fact, understatement.

I became dizzy. My sight was blurry. I thought I might be having a stroke. The air changed and a soft light appeared like a cloud around Terry and me. I felt music. I didn't hear it but actually felt melody throughout my body. Impossible to describe, easy to acknowledge. An unfamiliar but mildly agreeable smell pervaded the slim distance between us. It was as if the molecules that activate olfaction were experimenting. And then everything began spinning around me like the tornado scene in The Wizard of Oz, and bizarrely familiar images slowly passed me. The first one, unfortunately, was the plastic mannequin which stood in for Benedict's girlfriend. There I was with a stiff dick while a bottomless mannequin swirled in my purview. I was falling and flying at the same time. There was a sunset and a raging ocean and seagulls and crows fighting. A picture of a child that kept morphing from a baby to a grown man. I was onto something else before I realized the baby was me. I didn't know if I was participating; I wasn't aware of my physical being and thought perhaps I was dying or had died or wanted to die. There was no sense of time or of my controlling whatever this experience was. It was all too mystifying to be afraid, but I'm sure that's bullshit.

I think I was telling myself not to be afraid, yet I wanted to pray. A sure sign of fear. When all else fails, we find God. I was searching for distance, a distance from whatever was transpiring, looking for a proper place to land. The feeling was not unlike when I tried acid for the first time. I was completely out of control mentally, while at the same time, I was engaged in some parallel perspective that allowed me to at least restrict the madness I was undergoing. There were parallels. I was in a parallel.

Now, only now, I realized I was on my back. I was in bed. My body felt as if someone had borrowed it, done unspeakable things to it, then tenderly sewed it back up, wishing me love and luck. There you go, you're on your way now...

As my vision cleared, I could see monitors. I was breathing haltingly, helped in no little part by the oxygen supplied by the nasal cannula loosely attached to my nose. It felt cold. I felt cold. I tried to say something, but my throat wouldn't respond except with a painful hoarseness. I'm in a fucking hospital. What did that crazy bitch do to me? Did we do the deed? I'd never been with a virgin before. Not completely. Is this what it's like?

A nurse entered briefly, viewed me with concern and left. Momentarily, a doctor entered with the same nurse following him at a professional distance. He was wearing the name tag, Dr. Benedict. I don't know what my facial expression was, but it prompted him to hold up his hand to calm me.

"Please don't try to speak. You've been on a ventilator for a couple of weeks and that tends to make the throat fairly sore. It will get better in a few days. I'm sure you're a little disoriented, as you've also been highly medicated to provide a certain level of comfort. We tested you today and although you have the antibodies, you have received a negative test for the virus. So, it's all good news for you today. Unless there are any further complications, you should be returning home in a day or so. I'll see you in the morning."

The doctor took a quick look at my history the nurse had pulled up on the computer. On his way out, he smiled cordially. "You're a very lucky man. Congratulations." The nurse pushed a half smile in my direction and followed him out. As the door opened, I heard some laughter from a rather busy hallway. Hearing laughter at that moment was jarring, but no more jarring than finding myself in that room. I never liked visiting other people in hospitals, but I preferred it to waking up in one. A doctor friend of mine once told me a hospital is no place to be sick. You get in and then get out to heal elsewhere.

I looked up at a small blackboard on which was written my name and vital signs. There was also the name of the nurse for the evening, Caroline, and of Doctor Benedict. I stared at the blackboard until I my eyes went dry. I fought to stop myself from thinking. I stole a look at the empty bed next to me, ready for the next patient. I gazed at the television, which had a silent Fox News story airing. I immediately turned from that and focused on the blank ceiling above me. For a moment, I was empty of thought, trying my best to clear my mind. I then carefully lifted the blanket, pulling it over my head, and surveyed below.

I couldn't help but wonder if Terry had visited.

Maurice

There is a certain category of friends that is particularly irritating or according to differing tastes, immensely pleasant. I'm talking about those people who anticipate everything. You're about to pay the check, and they've already given their credit card. You're telling a joke, and they anticipate the punchline. You're about to present them with a gift, and suddenly, they offer you a beautifully wrapped package. Maybe to call it a category is too much.

Among my friends, only one was like this. Maurice. It would be difficult to describe him; I've lost memory of him. Tall or short, with fair hair, brown hair.

I can remember him during a demonstration. We were all lined up with our red banners. 1973. Suddenly, Maurice looked up at the sky and said, “Communism is dead.” This was seventeen years before Boris Yeltsin.

In 1980, Ronald Reagan was elected president. Maurice was pacing up and down in front of the television absentmindedly. Then he looked up and said, “Reaganomics is finished.” He made the last prediction while looking at a sky full of clouds.

"Bistadsoni, as a leader, is in pieces."

Bistadsoni? Who the hell is Bistadsoni?

"You'll see." Maurice disappeared.

Before disappearing forever, Maurice's sole infatuation became the sky. He would stare heavenward for hours. He didn't even speak anymore; he would anticipate his own words. He was starting to anticipate his own movements. This was becoming very uncomfortable for him. He would often eat before getting hungry. He would wake up before falling asleep. He would arrive before leaving. The laws of cause and effect were becoming uncertain where Maurice was concerned. Scientists began to take an interest in him, monitoring him closely. Although he seemed perfectly normal, he was on the verge of challenging all the rules of physics.

In a short time, he became a public figure, but he never got excited about all the changes that being Maurice was involuntarily bringing about. Anticipating other people's behavior depressed him, because it meant a long wait.

Finally, the day arrived when he got fed up. Fed up with anticipating the delay in everything; fed up with waiting for the check to arrive; fed up with the lack of sense for common decency. Tired of obeying a government he didn't respect. Maurice dared the ultimate anticipation: he tried to live before being alive. That's when Maurice met God.

It was a friendly encounter, but with a touch of oddity. Anticipating his handshake, God dismissed Maurice. Anticipating the dismissal, Maurice appeared before God for an encounter that, logically, should have been the second encounter, but that Maurice proposed to call 'minus one.' God realized the subject before him was a challenging one. To put him at a disadvantage, God anticipated the time of the encounter, before the existence of mankind. But Maurice anticipated him in his turn, showing up before the existence of God.

The non-being of God and the non-being of Maurice were facing each other. For a second, they had the idea of anticipating each other yet again, but the frightening emptiness that already surrounded them gave them pause. They stared into each other's non-eyes, which is very different from not staring into each other's eyes. God's non-eyes were flashing, and Maurice merely lowered his.

"Why are you challenging me?" asked the non-being of God. "Have you considered how much more powerful than yours, my non-being is? If I don't exist, all mankind is lost, left wandering in a world of darkness. They'll kill, they'll rape, they'll commit the most horrible and crazed deeds. If you don't exist, the most someone will say is he was going to have been such a nice guy."

Maurice replied, "The same cannot be said about you."

The non-being of God got very angry and was strongly tempted to destroy this stupid and presumptuous creature of his. The non-being of Maurice was afraid to disappear beyond the last unknown barrier. A shudder went through him. God looked at Maurice and understood. God smiled. Before hurling him down into the unknown universe of non-memory, God asked he, who had dared to challenge him, to make a last wish.

The non-being of Maurice hesitated for the first time in his non-existence. Then he borrowed a very elegant pen from his non-maker, and in his very personal handwriting, he wrote a NO in the heart of the future of mankind.

Smuggling Elegance

The fourth-floor balcony hung out over the city like a parched tongue. Below, in disarray and disrepair, the city of Havana stretched in the afternoon sun glowing with mean neglect. Building after building in the shape of ill-formed dominoes stood thirsting for paint and plaster. Even in the light of an unforgiving sun, I could see that Havana's architectural genealogy was so elegantly pedigreed that no amount of ruinous abandon could consume all its splendor. Like a good soldier in his last desperate act of defiance, bleeding from all orifices, Havana refuses to fall.

It was only my second day there, but I felt that Cuba had firmly established itself the moment I landed at Havana's airport. From the stories I'd read concerning the 'dreaded Castro regime,' I half expected a Latin boogeyman to lay claim to my soul as soon as I deplaned. I was instead met with a wallop of moisture and the pungent smell of Caribbean earth. After crossing the steamy tarmac, I arrived at the small, stark building that housed customs.

Customs was much smaller than I anticipated, considering the local emigration and immigration complications. President Clinton may have been considered liberal, but he wasn't about to mess with the Cuban sanctions. Because of the decades-old embargo, I traveled from LA to Mexico City to Havana. Here, the rules were set as an officer in a stained-yellow cubicle took my passport and studied it from under a ledge that completely obfuscated my view. I waited silently, hoping he would stamp only the visa and not the passport. He looked up at me intermittently through dark, hapless eyes. I noticed his government khaki shirt was one wash away from being diaphanous. His eyes told me he could send my American imperialist ass back on the plane I came in on if he felt like it. When my non-verbal response demonstrated the appropriate obsequiousness, the officer slipped slowly into a grin and welcomed me to Cuba. He was the boss. I was the visitor. This is Cuba. Move on.

It took one day to find a two-bedroom apartment in central Havana right off the Malecón, the great walkway and adjoining main road which lines the Caribbean. For twenty dollars a day, split two ways, I was introduced to "Cuban life." Dante, my traveling partner and guide, was one of those Spanish-speaking Anglos who is more black beans and rice than he is macaroni and cheese. We met over the internet. He ran an ad in Craigslist:

GOING TO CUBA? I'M YOUR MAN/ BEEN THERE/SEEN THAT/DONE THIS...AND ALL IN SPANISH/ I AM NOT CHEAP/ I AM INVALUABLE.

Five days later, I was standing out on the balcony of my Cuban flat. To my left was the Malecón and directly across from me ran a wall of apartments dotted with balconies similar to mine. With a cold can of the local beer always within reach, I would soon be spending countless hours observing uninhibited Cuban habitation from on high. The balcony became my office, my thermometer, the place where I had my morning coffee, and finally, my clearest memory of Cuba. It was from the stony lip of this perch that I became privy to Cuban life.

The balcony is the social equivalent of the stoop in New York. In similar neighborhoods in Manhattan, you sit out on the apartment steps and watch the Dominican men slapping dominoes on a card table in the middle of the sidewalk, or you watch the white boys in their suits on their cellular phones make deals while coal black Jamaican women pass them by pushing perambulators occupied by snow white babies.

In Havana, you stand on your balcony in a subtle yet bold act of exposure and curiosity. We had rented our place from a local woman, Anna Marie. From what Dante told me, she was the honorary mayor of the neighborhood. From the balcony, one looks into all the neighboring apartments through big, screenless windows and other balconies. Cuban life unfolds in kitchens, in front of TVs, and in single bedrooms where entire families sleep. There's always something to see. One of my favorite things was to wait for Laura, the dark-haired, dark-eyed girl from across the way, to come out onto her balcony to peel potatoes and rearrange chromosomes with her natural beauty.

"I finally got a hold of Papi. We got a car."

I turned from the blinding light of the noon sun to peer into my shaded apartment. After a minor pupil adjustment, I connected the voice with Dante's fluorescent white body, which was presently illuminating the living room. He approached me, underwear-clad, squinting aggressively, when he was smacked backwards into the living room by the sheer volume of heat off the balcony.

"Shit! It's going to be a fucking hot one today, macho. Better break out your number fifteen sun block." Dante snorted, given that I am a Black man of yellow-red-brown complexion.

"He's on his way now?" I yelled at Dante's derriere as he bent over a carrying bag and packed his Super 8 video gear inside it.

"Papi's the man. You'll love him. He always drives me. I made some coffee, want some?"

Dante and I shared the immediate intimacy that only strangers, who by definition have nothing at stake, can afford. There was no competition since we shared no history and consequently, there could be nothing more than mild expectation from either of us. He was my guide. Since I paid him a fee, he had a certain undefined obligation to me, although it was difficult to enforce, since he was the one who spoke Spanish and we were in Cuba, a country he had already visited ten times that year. We both were keenly aware that we were in fact breaking the embargo by patronizing Cuba with our tourist dollars, having snuck into Havana by way of Mexico City. In other words, Dante was completely in control of the situation.

"Does this driver speak any English?" I asked.

"Papi? Not a word. Todo Cubano. I'm tellin' you, you're going to love this guy."

I'm hardly the type of traveler who presumes that wherever I go English will be served as the main course, but the logic of his comment was troubling to me nonetheless. My Spanish was far from nonexistent. That said, Cuban Spanish was incomprehensible to me. Well, at least we had a car. Dante had informed me of the following: we were paying Papi twenty dollars a day, five dollars more than he makes a month, plus petrol, to drive us anywhere in Havana and beyond. I also knew that our mode of transport would be a 1985 piece of shit Russian Lada, a gutless wonder of an automobile that is both loud and slow. Since the car and most other property are state-owned, it was illegal for Papi to drive us around for his own personal gain. But then again, everything in Havana is illegal, so you do it anyway and simply avoid getting caught.

"It's really hot today!" Papi shouted as he pulled up and rolled out of the car. I was on the third-floor balcony and his voice carried like a ball of gravel, alerting many inquisitive neighbors. He said this and everything else in mostly unintelligible Spanish. Papi waved at me knowingly.

"Come on, macho, let's go." Dante appeared on the balcony with me. He shouted a few words of rapid-fire Spanish to Papi, his accent changed. The Spanish he spoke in the Mexico City airport was clearer and slower. What came tumbling out of his mouth now was the Cuban dialect, a fast mumbling of resonant sounds through a barely opened mouth containing very few consonants. Several balconies were now occupied as the neighbors inspected the strangers who were inhabiting Anna Maria's apartment. Laura came back out on her balcony smiling, potato-less. I returned her smile. Then she disappeared.

We bolted blindly down the unlit stairwell where snatches of conversation escaped from underneath the neighboring doors. Cuba was pouring out of everywhere. At the foot of the stairs, I met Papi, a short, animated fire plug of a man with skin the color of roast turkey. He shook my hand firmly, showing his tobacco-stained teeth, and spoke laughingly. I smiled, nodding every time I heard a word or a familiar phrase, then nonchalantly ducked into the open car door.

My first ride through Havana in the backseat of a Lada was not unlike what I imagine riding in a shopping cart over a rutted road would be. In the front seat, Papi and Dante spun Cuban rhythms as if they were in some linguistic competition. They answered one another in mounting tones, like talking drums. There was a clarity in their attitude that made me feel privy to the proceedings. Whatever they were discussing sounded beautiful and passionate to these virgin ears.

Through the open windows, the rush of air entered like soft textured blocks of heat wrapped in faint sounds. Then the aggressive whines of motorcycle engines and autos in need of mufflers spanked my ears and fought back the drowsiness I was feeling from the insufferable heat. We were on our way to a hotel which housed what Dante called 'one of the great cigar rooms in Havana.' On the narrow sidewalks, the foot traffic was moving in slow motion through the heat. Black women glistened as they stood in lines that spilled onto the street, waiting to exchange their coupons for rice and beans, sugar and potatoes. Colorful portraits of Uncle Sam appeared on huge billboards with anti-American slogans. Papi watched me from the rear-view mirror.

"You like Cuba?" he asked in English as thick as his Spanish.

"Claro," I replied. Papi showed me his teeth again, then fired up a commanding-smelling cigarette.

We continued to speed roughly over a potholed street that served as a main artery in this part of the city. On either side, a kaleidoscope of architectural heaven streamed by. The marriage of styles and periods stunned. It confirmed the earlier presence of an international community that was intent on building a whimsical Caribbean paradise. It is practically impossible to find any building that, through either historical dictate or intent, does not presuppose beauty. Indeed, one can travel down any number of streets in Havana and conclude that the only thing these structures have in common is the neglect which, sprinkled on such beauty, resembles an elegant symptom of disease.

After some time, we stopped at our first red light. I saw several newly waxed, perfectly conditioned, vintage Chevys and Plymouths sitting curbside, tireless and on blocks. Papi informed me through Dante's translation that there is no short supply of vintage 1950s autos. Parts to repair these beautiful dinosaurs, however, have been unavailable since the embargo began in 1959, which is the reason we were riding in that piece of shit Russian Lada.

"Check it out, Macho." Dante pointed out the window.

Three women, undressed for the heat, crossed the street. They were all back, leg and midriff in perfect exposure. Varying shades of browns percolated in the sun in three distinctly different dress sizes. Their movement was symphonic as they leisurely pitched themselves into the sea of foot traffic. In that mesmerizing moment, amidst pangs of guilt and desire, I came to a stunning realization. Eight days in Cuba would in no way be enough. The light turned green.

Papi dropped us off around the corner from the hotel's entrance and waited under the shadow of its twelve stories. Just as Dante and I left the liquid heat of outdoors, entering through sliding glass portals into the climatized world of this pretty spiffy hotel, a suited man stopped me rather unpleasantly.

"Qué quieres?"

"Yo quiero un puro," I replied, imitating Papi's accent perfectly. What I lacked in Spanish was bolstered by the equipoise of my Cuban look.

Dante interceded quickly. "He's American. Tell him you're American."

I switched to a New York accent, deadpanning, "I'm American." An obliging smile slid into the suit's mouth. "Enjoy your cigar. Cubans are the best, you know." He stealthily resumed his post next to the palm tree. Out of earshot of the suit, Dante informed me that hotels were off limits to the local Cubans. This was 'strictly a tourist experience.' Suddenly, I felt akin to an Afrikaner hanging out on the streets of Pretoria in the eighties.

We strode across shiny marble floors, past boutiques that sold five-hundred-dollar cigarette lighters and Mont Blanc pens, to an escalator that rose out of shimmering fountains through a jungle of palms. In this monument to capitalism, there were no signs of the austere poverty that hung on the Cuban people like a skin jacket. Water cascaded freely over polished rocks, then fell into the base of an ornate fountain. I recalled how, of the three toilets I had been to in my thirty hours in Cuba, none of them flushed without the aid of a follow-up bucket of water. Dante smiled at my silence.

"Deep, huh?"

"Leagues and leagues."

"Fathoms."

"Which is deeper, fathoms or leagues?" I wondered aloud.

"Cigars." Dante pointed. We pushed through the glass double doors like a couple of thirsty gunfighters. The room was empty, or so we thought until our eyes became adjusted to the scented dark of Casa Habana.

Wood dripped from the pecan-colored ceiling to the worn sienna rugs. Dim candlelight winked at us from each of the discreetly scattered tables. People slowly appeared in focus. Dante and I opted for a couple of stools at the bar.

"What do you think, macho?"

"I think it's fucking dark in here. An elegant place to get a knife in the back."

The bartender approached. Her eyes were darker than the smoke-stained wood in the room and, without preface, locked onto me like gentle handcuffs. In one motion, she placed a plate of nuts, a paper napkin, and a book of matches in front of me. She leaned intimately in my direction. Out of her mouth, a thick, willful tongue presented itself and then melted away. A labial conundrum. She smiled unselfconsciously then spoke.

"What is your pleasure?" Her English was faintly perfumed with Spanish. I was stunned and she allowed for my silence without expression or judgment. I pointed at a case of cigars. She smiled and used her hand to indicate she was referring to a drink. Would I like some rum? That, I understood. It was 11 a.m., probably 90 degrees, and I had yet to eat, having only recently arrived. Why not begin the day with a strong Cuban cigar and some famously potent Cuban rum? I smiled in affirmation. She turned to reach for a bottle.

Cuban women are famous for their beauty, but I was certainly unprepared for her front-to-back revelation. I was so entranced by her rearview, I felt I might be arrested any second for felony objectification. She returned with a Partagas Robusto and a rocks glass darkened by a generous portion of the rich rum. Dark brown seemed to be the theme here. A smiling Dante lit my cigar before lighting his own. There are times in life when you think everything you have done up to that point has been right because it brought you to the present moment. I was in Cuba, being attended to by one of the most beautiful women I'd ever seen, smoking a cigar with a glass of Cuban rum in my hand, and it wasn't even noon.

Dante watched me, unable to contain his wicked smile as he observed my complete surrender to this stranger, this Goddess of the island. "Well, macho, you in love yet?"

My bartender was attending to another customer. Otherwise, I wouldn't have heard a word he had said.

"I like it here," was all I could say.

He responded with a laugh usually reserved for the funniest joke ever told. Initially startling, it brought me back to earth. I realized I was behaving like a child arriving at a McDonald's.

"You have to take it slow at first or you'll burn yourself out. Cuba can do that."

"Let's hope I'm that lucky." I took a long pull from my Robusto and began to settle in as if this was how I lived on the normal.

After the cigar, Dante wanted to visit one of his many friends and I wanted to walk the streets. So, Papi dropped me off on the Malecón, some distance from my apartment, and advised me to simply follow the ocean when I wanted to return home. Simple enough. I exited the loud and slow Russian Lada and began my first walk on the Malecón.

The Caribbean version of the Atlantic crashed against the wall on my left and the city of Havana rose on my right, a perfect initiation to the capital. I knew only a few historical tidbits of this storied city. It was founded in the sixteenth century and eventually replaced Santiago de Cuba's importance as Havana became the most influential port. It was a drop-off for the slaves that were captured, imported, and extradited by the Spanish to this island. I made two related discoveries early on. One, there was a huge Black Latin population. Two, they seemed to be much poorer than their White Latin counterparts. The better jobs had white faces representing them. As always, color mattered. That realization put a hitch in my walk. There were varying shades of Cubans to be sure, but history has a way of revealing the many unavowed truths that lie in the cut.

The sea breeze was welcome on this hot and humid afternoon. The ocean spoke in stops and starts. It sounded like a crash-bang as water first folded over itself and then slammed into the stone wall. The walkway was well attended and, as on most Caribbean isles, the pace was leisurely.

There's an art to walking through a moist wall of heat. All islanders seem to prevail, but it's a technique I've failed to master. I was clearly the only person perspiring mightily while trundling down the street. As per usual, I began to wonder what everyone did when they weren't walking the Malecón. This had become a preoccupation of mine, not unlike my habit of looking up at windows in an apartment building and imagining what's taking place behind a partially open curtain. These are the kinds of thoughts that come to mind in unfamiliar cities. I behave like a quasi-foreign correspondent on a secret mission to invade its culture. Fantasies are cheap and readily available. There is also the added bonus that I am anonymous. I know no one here. No one. That I resemble a Cuban prototype spares me much of the hustle directed at tourists. Dante advised me not to wear any new gear. I brought the oldest and most beat-up Nikes I had and simple one-color T-shirts with no logos. Going without jewelry was not a problem since I never wear the stuff to begin with. I fit into the scenery like a '57 Chevy. I did bring plenty of cash, which I had hidden all around the apartment, so well I feared I might forget where some of it was.

Stopping at a makeshift café on the way home, I bought myself a cone of coconut ice cream. Helado. There were plastic seats out front for paying guests only (a sign made this clear), where I sat and watched the world go by in between licks. I also didn't carry any books from the apartment, as a clear sign of a tourist is someone reading a novel in English. I could hear other Americans being smoothly hustled by a Cuban local a few feet away—a pretty duo of American twenty-somethings being introduced to professional hustlers. The Cuban people have been ostracized for decades and have honed their skills in the art of improvisation in any and every way imaginable. The men also match the women in physical beauty, and I figured this guy might know a little French, as he was currently working on a menage à trois. My money was on him. I smiled as they left in tandem.

The color palette of Cuba is decidedly pastel, from the faded primary colors of buildings to the sky imprinted by both sun and clouds, to the blueness of the ocean, which also adds a gentle soundtrack to these elements. One experiences Cuba more than one views it. As I left my café, I felt pulled into some visceral, waking dream narrated in Spanish. Back across the street on the Malecón, strolling like a local, I realized I was not fully in charge. My heart was open, my mind was clear, and I was experiencing the feeling of life being more than the sum of its parts. I was a participant only in that it was happening *to* me. I was the recipient, not the instigator. Whenever I am in a foreign country, this feeling arises. A certain emotional release valve engages. It's a feeling of human liberation that connects me to every sentient life form. I looked at the stone lip of the barrier wall and could feel its age and see into the life it supported. I could smell history as clearly as I could sniff the salt spray of the sea. The strangers I passed reeked of humanity, and I felt connected. I experienced mental clarity. My emotional palette expanded. It was as if I were gliding through a monumental moment, a fragile presence which produced confused tears. And then it vanished, and I could see my street in the distance marked by a large wall portraiture of a serious Che Guevara. I hung on to the residual sensation until I arrived at my building and walked up the cool, dark, and dank stairway where other smells intermingled with my reverie. The scent of beans cooking and damp wood alternated as I climbed the three floors.

I was pleased that Dante had yet to return. It allowed me to gently reconcile my out-of-body experience. I unpacked, opened a beer, and went out on the balcony. Again, the sun's heat stung me. The view from the balcony more than made up for the thermal discomfort. To my right was a long line of buildings similar only in their disrepair. They were mostly residences and it made me smile to look at them. To my left was a shorter line which ended at the ocean. Directly across from me were balconies and windows which afforded unobstructed views of people's homes, where light and shade revealed people cooking in their kitchens while others lay in their daybeds. The gentle echoes of children playing down on the street below reverberated.

Some of the kids were looking up at me. I got the feeling that everyone in the neighborhood knew Dante and I were the temporary tenants at Anna Maria's apartment. Dante told me people rent their places and then go live with relatives until the lodger leaves. Illegal, of course, but financially sound. I had yet to meet Anna Maria, but I noticed how people in the neighborhood would look at me. Nothing unfriendly about it, simply a quick bit of immediate measuring and analyzing, which was over in an instant.

Looking at the ocean and surveying the ground in between brought me back to my earlier sensation. Feeling one with the neighborhood, with the world, and all that was in it. Then Laura came out to her balcony. Dante had told me about her. A lovely girl who would show up occasionally, either washing clothes in a large tin pan or hanging them to dry on a makeshift clothesline. Today, she was peeling potatoes. A bowl rested between splayed legs as she artfully denuded potatoes the same color as her hands. There was a Zen to her movement. The skins went into the bowl and the potatoes were placed somewhere outside of my vision because of the low wall. From time to time, she would look up at me, but her gaze was distant and told me little. It was as if she were forced to go to the zoo and look at animals she didn't recognize. Where are the tigers? For whatever reason, I was bold enough to continue watching her without invitation.

My gawking was interrupted by a knock. It was Anna Maria. She came to ask about the apartment. Was it to my liking? She reminded me of a cousin from Lake Charles, except she spoke Spanish. Her voice released a trumpet of high notes and happiness, and though her hair was snapped back with rubber bands, her face always seemed to march forward. She added a certain clarity to the afternoon, which was now approaching evening. As I stumbled through my Spanish, she would include a word or two of English. She patted her dress often, not nervously. She was accustomed to always be doing something. Anna Maria spoke randomly, rapidly. The upshot was a discreet inquiry as to my sexual preference. I responded as tactfully as I could. "I am like any other man on the planet, I love beautiful women." At least that is what I think I said. She let me know that not every other man on the planet would agree. We both laughed. Sharing a joke in someone else's language is cool, even if they did all the work. I liked her and hoped she didn't think I was some dipshit privileged American. I brought out another chair. Sitting on the balcony, we shared a few minutes of comfortable silence. Anna Maria exchanged looks with Laura, no longer peeling potatoes but bent over the wall, looking down on the street.

Anna Maria exhaled. "Bueno."

A simple word gifted with nuance. At this moment, it meant goodbye. She took a good look at her house, where she normally sleeps, raises her children, and feeds her husband, then left.

I was sleeping when Dante returned. I woke to hear female voices, still feeling disoriented from the plane, cigar, drink, and Malecón stroll.

"Macho!" Dante called out.

I emerged from the bedroom and found him in the living room making drinks for two locals. They were young and pretty, and they greeted me with smiles.

"It's mojito time," he said as he gave the girls a drink and forced one on me.

"Hello," I think I said to the girls. They answered in Spanish paragraphs, speaking over one another. Dante laughed. I drank. I asked him what was going on.

He pointed. "Elena and Adriana. They live next door to the friend I was visiting and wanted to hang out with a couple of Americans. How fucking cool is that?"

Elena stared at me and launched into what I thought might be a conversation. I quickly realized she was speaking to Dante, though her attention was directed at me. Whatever she said gave Dante a look of concern.

"She says you remind her of her ex-novio, her old boyfriend. Not sure this is going to work out, macho. She does think you're handsome, though."

I wanted to keep my travel high, so I downed my drink, smiled, and returned to my room. Elena didn't seem displeased with my departure. I went back to bed and spent a moment thinking about this slight development. Having this as my first encounter with a Cuban girl was not to my liking. I took solace in the fact that I wasn't the one who initiated it.

Women are always a big part of traveling for me. Why shouldn't they be? They're a big part of being alive. However, meeting women from different countries always proved a reset button for me. A friend once told me he liked dating because you get to start all over. I never got that feeling locally, but if you throw in a different culture and language, if you're not unsettled by being surrounded with the unfamiliar, if you can feel comfortable being vulnerable and no longer in charge because everything is foreign, one is obligated to start from square one. That type of discomfort works for me.

My forehead compressed into a frown. I didn't intend to make too much of what occurred, but the rejection by Elena took me down the rabbit hole of self-appraisal. Maybe it was as she said. I reminded her of someone whom she didn't wish to be reminded. I thought, *damn, that's extra*. I was already conscious of being a stranger in a foreign land. Being American, I always feel as if I'm carrying baggage that doesn't belong to me. Yet, I am American, and as part of a privileged tribe, I suffer from wealth's wounds. We're a huge, powerful country and are option-rich. The dearth of options offered in other countries, Cuba, for example, redirects priorities. Over simplified, I find women from financially underperforming countries more humane and less immediately judgmental of their opposites.

I spend more in a day than these folks make in a month. I had thought a great deal about this before I came to Havana and had some idea of the impossible position in which I had placed myself: a Black man visiting a poverty-stricken country wanting to enjoy himself without demonstrating the same traits as the people he holds in contempt stateside. Good luck with that. And with this uncomfortable realization, I fell into a deep sleep.

Waking up in Cuba was akin to waking up inside a kaleidoscope. My eyes had problems focusing and every time I turned my head, I saw something which didn't quite compute. But the colors were lovely. I had to remind myself that this was my second day. This room was familiar. My vision cleared and slowly my head followed. I was bleeding sweat and had a string of drool connecting my forearm to my mouth. Although I was soaked with my own salt water, I could feel the temperature had dipped. It was almost dusk, and I wondered if Dante was still entertaining.

I walked out into an empty room. There was no sound from Dante's bedroom, so I called out. Everyone was gone—nothing to do but open a beer and revisit the balcony. I brought my notebook. I won't call it a diary, as there was as much fantasy as history between those pages. There were also drawings. I opened to a page of one of my pencil sketches and had no idea what I was looking at. Something abstract, although I'm sure that wasn't my aim. My father was an artist, and I am living proof that on occasion, the apple falls so far from the tree it turns into an armadillo. Unstymied by my lack of talent, I began sketching my memory of Elena. I had to pay her back somehow and perhaps she would return later where I could present her with my portrait of her. I began with her profile, which resembled a boulder with eyes and misshapen mouth. I kept adding to it and before long, I had something that looked like an angry, nuclear test fish, with slight whiskers. I laughed and heard someone else laughing with me. Looking across the chasm, I spied Laura. She was laughing too. I gave her my euphoric smile. She retreated into the house. The door to the apartment opened, and Dante's laughter followed.

"Come on, Macho. I got plans for you tonight."

We were down the stairs and out the door before I could think of any good reason not to follow his crazy ass through the streets of Havana Viejo, the older part of the city. We were going to meet up with Nestor and Férnan. They were cigar smugglers on another level, I was told. Cool dudes. Walking through the city past the bars and plazas and open storefronts that sold odds and ends, Dante observed me with a sly expression. I was his de facto anthropological experiment, and he constantly measured my reactions.

"Like another planet, huh, Macho?"

At the end of the street, two tall men waited. One was built for damage, the other, pure peril. As we approached, they appeared even more dangerous when they smiled. They hugged Dante and laughed at nothing. Dante introduced me. I was welcomed in broken English. We walked. As we passed by the locals, these two were held in deference. I surmised I was hanging out with two pashas. People bowed their heads in our direction and moved out of the way as we passed. The two men took it in stride. They were deep in conversation as we moved down the street, ending up at a building that had never seen its best days. In front of the structure, a man patched up a tire. He stopped work to acknowledge my new friends and then forcefully pushed open a door for us to enter the building.

It took a moment for my eyes to adjust to the darkness of the windowless room. My sight returned just as my sense of smell was pleasantly assaulted by tobacco. There were boxes of cigars stacked floor to ceiling. That pungency, along with the rhythmic Spanish the guys were spinning, carried me through several doorless, half-walled rooms, all of them lined with boxes of cigars. I had so much to say, yet no tools to express myself adequately. Dante caught me mid-thought.

"Pick out what you want. You're limited to ten boxes. Twenty dollars US a box." I could sell any box of cigars I was looking at for at least three hundred dollars back home. Probably closer to four hundred. I could also end up being heavily fined for going to Cuba in the first place. I didn't jump at the offer. We must have passed through a half-dozen identical rooms before we came to a kitchenette. We sat at a table made from a large wooden spool, probably used to store industrial wires, and chose cigars from two mason jars. I picked out a Cohiba Coronas Especiales. Férnan informed me it was the cigar of choice for Fidel. How could I go wrong? A bottle of rum appeared, and I knew I was having a unique Cuban experience. I was mildly attentive during the nonstop conversation between them. Other than marveling at the dramatic rise and fall in pitch or amplitude of volume, I was lost to their conversation. Occasionally, Férnan would glance at me with his smiling, dead eyes.

I would feign being totally enraptured with my cigar and rum, which seemed to pacify him. Nestor mostly smiled and laughed. His size negated any need for him to act threatening. He was gently massive. Anyone approaching him would do so cautiously. I imagined most of his life, he had appropriated courtesy so as not to automatically engender fear.

Dante was making a deal with these guys. The mixture of warmth and serious business was hard to miss. I picked out six boxes and unearthed a hundred and twenty dollars, offering it to Nestor. With the slightest gesture, I realized I was to give the money to Férnan. Férnan pulled out an enormous wad of American dollars and added mine to the bunch. He also paid attention to the fact that I put the rest of my cash back in my sock. Nestor produced a burlap sack and handed it to me. I gently managed the boxes into the sack, and we were on our way out after a brief toast. To La Vida!

We retraced our route back to the apartment. Férnan and Nestor accompanied us part of the way. Even I was viewed with respect in their town. Férnan stopped to let a woman put her arms around him suggestively. Her apparent crush on him was only equal to his indifference towards her. Some women like dangerous men, and Férnan reeked of bad intentions. He kissed her roughly and released her. We all said goodbye.

I was quietly reconciling what had just transpired this past hour when Dante spoke, "You did good, Macho. What do you think?"

"How did they get all those fucking cigars? They had more than a cigar store."

Dante brought his voice down. "Those two are the absolute shit. They've got it all worked out. The police don't even mess with them. And now they know you too." I wasn't sure if that was a good or bad thing.

A wind had picked up. There was still some humidity, but man, the breeze felt nice. The people, la gente, were out in force enjoying the open streets. At a plaza anchored by an old church, artists were packing up their paintings. Festive lights were hung. There were tourists, mainly from Europe, sitting in cafés, drinking mojitos and smoking cigars. Dante told me Italian men fly here just to connect with the women. I looked around and noticed the coupling of white men and women of color.

"You haven't found a novia yet, Macho?"

"I'm just you know ..." I didn't know what to say. Of course, I was interested in every third woman I saw, but I hadn't met anyone other than Elena. Besides, I wasn't the most courageous in the company of strangers whose language I didn't speak. I neglected to admit this to Dante because I knew this was a copout. I speak well enough to at least engage in conversation. I also felt there was something terribly romantic about being with someone with whom you don't share a language. Improvisation is not just something that occurs in the bedroom.

Dante pushed it. "Carmen could hook you up."

Carmen was a woman Dante had been seeing for a couple of years here. A lovely woman who was his main companion on his bi-monthly forays to the island. At least that's what he told me. I didn't answer. One of the things I liked about Dante was how he afforded me silence. The rest of the way home, I experienced that wonderful feeling of simply being alive and involved in life's music. I'm either on the verge of either laughter or tears from nothing, but somehow profoundly focused and grateful for the moment.

When we arrived at the apartment, Laura from across the street walked over to meet us. She spoke, and Dante answered. I watched. After a brief conversation, she marched back. Not once did she acknowledge my presence. Dante disappeared inside without a word, and I followed, exercising extreme patience as we climbed the stairs. We entered and he went directly to the kitchen to extract a couple of beers, handing one to me. He stood in front of me smiling.

"Okay ... what's going on with our neighbor?"

"Secret." He took a big swig and burped fully. "They invited us out tonight. Should be good."

"Who?"

"Férnan and Nestor."

"What about Laura?"

"What about Laura?"

"Come on, man. Quit fucking with me?"

"She just gave me a message from Anna Maria. About the apartment. What time we would like someone to come and clean. You didn't understand any of that? You speak better Spanish in LA."

"It's the accent ... and the mumbling. Everyone talks like they have marbles in their mouths. I like it. It's just that I get lost and am always playing catch up."

Dante went to his computer. "I gotta send some emails. Figure out who's getting what cigars.

"Where are your cigars?"

"Too many boxes to carry. They know what I want. For me, they deliver. It's been a good day, Macho. Be ready by nine."

Nine-thirty sharp, we were dropped off at a club with no marquee. It was a large building in the middle of a field, half an hour's drive from our place. There was a line to get in which stretched almost to the street. Papi pointed before he drove off, and we saw Férnan and Nestor waving us on from a distance. We walked past a line of locals, to a person/ dressed to impress. I took assessment of my linen outfit, which, out of my concern not to resemble a rich tourist, was not my nicest attire. I concluded I might be underdressed. I was punctilious in the wrong direction. Following the two pashas, we went straight into the club. *There's no waiting in line for cigar smugglers,* I thought, exaggerating my notoriety. I was instantly overjoyed that the interior of the club reminded me in no way of the Dominican Republic. I love the DR, but the volume level in their clubs is auditorily crippling. Here, I could actually hear people speaking when they were next to me, and Dante had much to say. He was giving me a blow-by-blow account of every woman here he had at least spoken with. Dante was fearless in approaching women and loved to have a tangential experience with as many as possible.

His axiom was a simple one: "There is success only in numbers, Macho."

The band was hot. In Cuba, that's a redundant observation. The Cuban's musicianship is on another level. It needs to be, as the people live and breathe their music. Everything is connected to rhythm. The dance floor was alive, bodies moving in rough, sexual poetry. The sensual experience is authentic and instinctive. I felt my body moving in different directions effortlessly. I had to dance. Many years ago, I lost my fear of simply getting up and dancing by myself. In my many trips to Europe, I found if you waited until you could find a stranger with whom to dance, you might not ever get on the floor. I walked a few feet away from the table and began. Solo. Mercifully, the one thing I have always been able to do is to express myself through movement, dance or otherwise. It is a pure dialogue with my soul. I don't believe in God, but if someone presented a musical representative of the Holy One, it would find in me a fervent follower. I like many styles of dance and use all of them to arrive at what is authentic to me. Or in more prosaic terms, I try to find the funk in everything.

Férnan was watching me in shock. Cleary it was not something he would ever do ... dance by himself. It would be unmanly and perhaps imply he couldn't get a girl to dance with him. He followed my movement with heavily lidded eyes. I paid attention to him because I figured he was someone who didn't suffer any breach of his own personal etiquette, even something as slight as an American tourist dancing on his own. Eventually, I was having such a good time, two women came and danced in and out of my orbit. I was relieved to see Férnan drop the mad dog look. I mean fuck, I was just dancing.

I returned to the table sweating, glad to be in linen. Férnan had a mojito waiting for me, and one of the most attractive women I'd ever seen sitting next to him. This fucking guy! Are serial killers attractive? I mean, he was not unattractive, but his danger quotient was inexorable. I thanked Férnan for the drink and acknowledged the new woman at our table. She looked to Férnan and he nodded her hello for her. Fine by me.

"Where did you learn to dance, coño?" Coño is slang and is used in various ways, but its literal meaning is the female genitalia.

"Videos ..." I lied. What was I going to tell him? Ballet, jazz, and the street? I was doing my best not to look at his beautiful friend. I thought I'd get up and dance again but was already sweating through my linen. I drank my mojito in silence. People would come to our table and speak briefly and respectfully to Nestor and Férnan. Dante had brought a girl to the table. I assumed it wasn't his friend, Carmen. I watched him as he launched into some diatribe that had the woman laughing. Nestor now had a girl sitting in his lap. I felt like the fly in the buttermilk.

"Eres maricón o que?" Férnan said with a smile. His girlfriend laughed, her tongue hanging out of her mouth.

"No, man. I'm not gay. Damn."

"Que?"

"No, it's just that ... no conozco a nadie ... I don't know anyone." They all laughed at this except Dante who was in verbal overdrive with his new friend. Férnan ordered me another drink. Obviously, I was going to be his joke material. I excused myself and went to the toilet.

Walking through the club was rejuvenating. A sea of mostly black and brown folks communing in rhythm. I didn't really need to use the bathroom, so I just walked around the spacious club several times. There was a simple table and chairs set up. In Cuba, it's about the bare necessities: music, alcohol, and la gente. Nothing unnecessary to attenuate the sheer joy and relief of dancing. The word 'callipygian' came to mind repeatedly as I walked. It was a word that sounded so ill-suited to its definition: 'Relating to or having buttocks that are considered beautifully proportioned.' I don't remember how I found the word, but I remember looking it up and being stunned by how incongruous the sound of it was. All the women were gifted in that respect, and their presentation was as natural as it was compelling. I went to the bathroom if only to forestall returning to comedy time at my expense.

The toilets were outside, a few yards away from the club. It was a beautiful evening, and people were gathered in groups laughing and talking in loud voices. A stifling miasma greeted me upon entering. It smelled as most club bathrooms do except for a slight scent of coconut which made the smell seem to enter through my mouth. Whatever my need, I figured I could hold it. As I reentered the club, a girl snatched my hand and ushered me out to the dance floor. She danced as if possessed and I fell willingly into her spell. A few songs later, she kissed me hard and left. I watched her return to a table of three men. Like I said, Cuba is something that happens to you. My only hope was to hang on.

When I returned to our table, Dante was in full make-out mode with his new friend. Everyone else had vanished. I noticed the bill was still on the table. When Dante detached himself from his girl, he told me the boys had left. We were to pay the bill. Somehow, I was not surprised.

"Don't worry about it, Macho. They're good dudes," he said and returned to his open-mouthed friend.

Eventually, I had Dante call Papi to take me home. Why not? We were both sharing his salary demands, something I should have thought of earlier. The ride back home was calm. The silence was a welcome sound after passing a few hours in a club. I sat in the back seat, windows down, riding through a strange town on a dark night. I could smell the pungent earth and Papi's strong-smelling cigarettes. Wasn't a bad combination. It prompted a childhood memory of riding through the streets of Central California in summer. I remember lying on the floor in the back seat of my father's car, long before seat belts were even an option. I could smell grease from a hamburger stand. I could hear and feel the road as my ear lay on the backseat floor. I could feel the wind tickling even in my low position. Something beautiful and jazzy was playing on my dad's radio and though I couldn't have been more than four or five years old, that moment defined something in me. It was perhaps my first epiphany. I'm not sure what an epiphanic moment would be to a four-year-old, but I suspect it has something to do with growth. It was a moment when I realized all the ways the senses can take in beauty. Fortunately, it was not wasted on this four-year-old—beauty, manifested in a moment of presence. Often, even now, I can recreate it. The feeling. The memory. I was doing so on my way back to the apartment. Grateful for Papi's silence and my ability to be present enough to receive this strange gift, I closed my eyes and contemplated all things beautiful. The portal had opened.

Sometime later, when I lay in my bed half asleep, Dante came home and burst into my room with an uncontrollable urge to discuss his evening's antics with whatever her name was. She did not accompany him home, so I figured a parade of complaints was to follow. He surprised me.

"You know, Macho, just when you think you have a basic understanding of women, they about-face your ass, and you can't help but smile and throw respect at 'em. You know what I mean? You want 'em to like you ... hell, you want 'em to love you, so you got room to move, but they've already gone to another planet, and you just get in your rocket ship and hope you got enough oxygen to keep up. I'm telling you, man, there's enough fiction in one woman to fill a fucking library! This one ... the one I was with tonight ... you saw her, right?"

"I didn't really get to talk with her. Your mouth was covering hers most of the night. She seemed nice," I said.

"I don't know, maybe I fell in love. What do you think?"

"About what?" I replied, not wanting to get into anything too deep with a man who had recently ingested almost a fifth of rum.

"Women, man! What's your take? Is it always like some puzzle we gotta figure out or are we making all this more trouble than it is? I can't call it anymore."

I thought about it for a second. It wasn't that strange a question. I have wondered about women in the same existential way myself. In my most honest moments, I have to admit to a revealing fantasy. I want to travel the world with one woman whom I like as much as I love. No boundaries and no expectations. If I can't have that, I would settle for an adventurous woman to accompany me at every port. Why wish for a loaf of bread when you can wish for the grocery store? That is what came to mind. What I said to Dante was more prosaic.

"Men are basic math. Addition, subtraction, and sometimes division. Women are multi-disciplinary. Astronomy, Astrology, literary fiction, history and of course, anatomy, so I have more difficulties with women than men. Sex has something to do with it or the lack thereof, but something in women just engages the impossible."

"Engages the impossible," he repeated. "I like that. Want a cold beer?"

I shook my head, and he left.

I woke the next morning feeling fresh and joy filled. It was a testament to the happiness waking up in a foreign land brings—nothing to do but enjoy yourself and discover a new everything. I think I was whistling, something I never do. I left my bedroom in my boxer shorts and entered the living room and stopped, stunned, to see Laura from across the way cleaning our apartment. I stood there in disbelief as she came in from the open kitchen, a broom in her hands.

"Hola." Laura said as she calmly looked me up and down. She was wearing shorts, sandals, and a braless T-shirt ornamented in a flower design. Simple, beautiful, and unafraid, she waited for me to say something. I think I replied, "Yes." I couldn't move. I stood there hoping, wishing, praying we could stay locked in this moment. I so desperately wanted to say something meaningful to her. To somehow tell her I would love to walk around the city with her, and then. And then ...

"Hablas inglés?" I finally said.

"Pequeño." She added, "Habla." She corrected me.

She returned to restoring our house to order, listening to me narrate as she did her job. I told her a part of my life story. Where I was born, how many brothers and sisters I had, and how much I hated the embargo. I even apologized for America's treatment of Cuba. She continued working, from time to time giving me what I interpreted as encouragement to continue. I told her how I loved coming out to the balcony and watching her do whatever she was doing at the time. I told her about the club last night and the cigar adventure. I think she chuckled. I know you're not supposed to tell beautiful women that they're beautiful. It's something they hear all the time. But I couldn't help it. I told Laura I would kick a dragon's ass for her, figuring that would be tough for her to translate. I said if there was any place she wanted to go, anything she wanted to see, anywhere she wanted to eat, I wanted to take her there. Now she was washing dishes, and I had run out of things to say. I gave her one last long look and went out on the balcony.

The heat and humidity were now welcome friends. It snapped me out of whatever frame of mind I was in, then sent me into a fit of self-appraisal. I felt embarrassed. I was practicing the same privilege I despised in others. She was poor. I was rich (by her standards). She was working and I was attempting to subtly use my status to seduce, conquer, influence, or whatever verb implies imperceptibly advancing on a woman. In international relations, it's called soft power. More often than not, money is involved.

I watched Laura through the glass doors, busily cleaning the apartment. I imagined Anna Maria and her family bunking up somewhere so she could rent her place to me. Out on the balcony, the sun sizzled. The faint crash of the Atlantic on the walls of the Malecón sounded a distant lullaby. The earthy Caribbean scent of Cuba was overwhelming. America was as far away as reconciliation.

Paris Graffiti

I missed the smell of Gauloises. As a cigarette it was unsmokeable. However, the perfume it expelled was beautifully odious. I was strolling Rue Charlot and feeling the night surrounding me like a smokeless vapor. No smell of Gauloises, but I liked remembering the smell. I was pondering my senseless love for all things French when the aggressive whine of a motorcycle interrupted my reverie. The driver, his face covered in a black-on-black casque, looked back at me. Perhaps he thought I was a terrorist. It seems like a leap, but that happened a lot in Paris. Unfriendly stares in random situations. When people stare at me, I always imagine the worst. My default status. That I was carrying a large, bulging, black garbage bag in each hand at two in the morning could have prompted any number of suspicions. That and the fact that I was the same color as an Egyptian or an Algerian or anyone suspiciously brown in color.

I was here on the streets of Paris slinging filled garbage bags in the early morning as a favor to my friend, Larry Green, a five-foot ten block of black granite whose entire existence was predicated upon thievery and violence. Violence being his preference. What mystified me about Larry

Green was that one look at him was sufficient to inform you that he was a mound of danger devoid of subtlety. Nonetheless, he was often challenged—"disrespected" was how he would always put it—and that mistake was always adjudicated by abuse in the extreme. How we became friends is a story I will take to the grave. Hopefully, later rather than sooner.

I came to the end of the street, scanned the next corner and saw I had reached my destination. Number 5 Rue Charlot. I had to drop both bags to put on my reading glasses, put in the code, and enter. Flicking on the hall light, an unremarkable winding wooden staircase appeared. No elevator, of course, so I climbed the four flights, the smells changing on each landing. The stairs were unvarnished hollow boards that announced one's arrival with each step. Not a stairway which afforded surprise. I arrived at an apartment door and extracted Larry Green's handwritten instructions.

Knock twice. Wait. Ring the doorbell once.

His handwriting was nearly calligraphic in its beauty. It was hard to reconcile his gnarled killer hands producing such languid lettering. I knocked twice, pushed the buzzer as I'd been told, and waited. Nothing. There was writing on the back of the page.

If no one answers, use the key in the envelope I gave you and let yourself in. Call me from inside the apartment.

What was originally a simple late-night delivery of unspecified items was gaining speed. Inside the apartment, I cautiously felt for a light switch. I found a dimmer on low, which I turned to bright, and the inner sanctum revealed itself to be a large studio. Whomever lived there had the decorating taste of a funeral director. Everything was black. Unlit dark candles were in abundance and there was the faint sickening smell of incense. I had no desire to meet the occupant of this place.

I called Larry Green, who answered immediately.

"Talk to me."

"Nobody's here."

There was a pause. "You sure?"

I realized I had yet to check the bathroom. I did so. It was empty and a bit funky. "Yeah, nobody."

Another pause. "I'm coming through."

"You coming now?"

"Just stay there, muthufucka."

The phone went dead. I wasn't offended. That was Larry Green. He called everyone muthafucka. It was late and I was hungry, so I checked the fridge. Empty, but the malodor of an ancient cheese remained. I looked back over at the couch where I had dropped the delivery. Two black garbage bags on a black couch in a black room. Not a good omen. I sat in between the two bags with my arms around them like baggy girlfriends, which reminded me I was to have a lunch date in a few hours with a Moroccan girl of unimaginable dimensions. I needed sleep. I needed food. I was also dying to see what was inside the bags. They were secured by only a couple of twisties. It would be easy enough. How would he know? Two knocks and one long buzzer immediately put everything in context. I rose but hesitated before answering the door. There were no written instructions for this situation.

There was a peephole, something I never liked to use. I'd seen too many movies where there was the barrel of a gun on the other side of the door. I looked anyway. The convergence of an unlit stairway and Larry Green's midnight skin revealed merely a shadow of a shadow. I opened the door. He came in quickly, smiling.

"Couldn't see my black ass, could you? Hungry?" He handed me a bag. "From my Lebanese boy. He don't fuck around with them chicken

... whatchamacallits." He clocked the two bags and headed to them directly.

"You look inside?"

"Nope."

"You weren't curious?"

"Nope."

"I woulda looked."

"You're Larry Green."

"All day long."

He untwisted one of the bags, opened it, and smiled his million-dollar smile. Then he frowned.

"Muthafucka was supposed to be here."

I was busy devouring what seemed to be a Lebanese burrito. "We good?"

"Nah, we ain't good." He opened the other bag. "Muthafucka was supposed to be here."

"No, I mean am I good?"

He reached into one of the bags and extracted a stack of fifty-Euro notes, which he threw at me. Larry Green was always generous to me, but this was another level.

"You know what I like about Paris? Muthafucka can walk around Paris with two garbage bags filled with cash and people pay more attention to his shoes. I gotta check my messages." He attended to his phone as if I was no longer in the room. I finished my burrito like a starving goat, even though the roof of my mouth felt as if it was dissolving from the hot sauce. I quietly watched him listening to his messages. What else could I do? It would have been bad form to begin counting the money in front of him. From my mental calculations, my options had just expanded exponentially this trip. Oysters and champagne for lunch with my Moroccan beauty. Perhaps a bottle of Cedric Bouchard champagne. He got off the phone.

"You know what I don't love about Paris? They got a fucked-up idea about personal space. Like the way they play chicken walking down the street, daring you not to move outta their way. I'm learning patience, little brother. Patience and forgiveness." He paused and looked around the room with feigned interest.

"I need you to stick around. I gotta make a run and I can't carry this shit through the streets of Paris."

"But you just said—"

Larry Green interrupted. "A normal person can walk around with two bags of cash. Larry Green can't do that shit."

I knew he was right. Larry Green had as many friends as he did enemies and sometimes, given the circumstances, they were interchangeable. He had also just handed me a playground of Euros for babysitting a couple of garbage bags. That was the positive side of the ledger. The flip side of this equation was a bit like *Dante's Inferno*—a journey into hell. Larry Green could be the Virgil character who showed you the madness of the place and provided you with the wisdom to navigate the terrain. He could also be Charon, the skipper of the boat, depositing you into the depths of hell itself. I knew I was still in the outer circle of hell, and that was where I wanted to stay. Besides, I was already in love with a Moroccan woman with whom I had yet to have a date.

Whatever I thought was of little significance as Larry Green had already left me standing in the doorway, pondering how he made it down those hollow stairs without making a sound. It appeared as though I was stuck in this mausoleum turned bank, so I did what any logical person would do. I counted my money. Thirty-five hundred euros. Obviously, they weren't all fifty-euro notes. Still, this was a new level in our relationship.

I had known Larry Green from my San Francisco days. He was a bodyguard to a character named Prince Baron, who was neither a prince nor a baron. What the Baron was, was a kaleidoscope of criminality, his angle changing with whatever was required of him in the moment. He was morally ambidextrous in the extreme. What he didn't do was violence. So, he hired Larry Green five minutes after I had introduced them. It was a very profitable relationship that ended abruptly some months later. One day, Prince Baron failed to show up for his morning coffee at Dante Café and was never heard from again. Rumor had it that Larry Green had terminated him and then quickly relieved the Baron of his ill-gotten proceeds. I disbelieve part of that supposition. Not the money part. Larry Green always knew where the money was. I don't believe he would have done anything untoward to his employer as Larry Green enjoyed a very beneficial relationship in that regard. Prince Baron, on the other hand, took too many chances and pissed off too many people. Any number of self-inflicted wounds could have permanently compromised the Baron. Even Larry Green couldn't save the Baron from himself. In any event, Larry Green suddenly had a nice bit of cash. That's where I come in. What I do is simple. I introduce people. Specifically, I introduce people who have money to people who don't have money. I try to make sure those who don't have money have everything else. Connections, product, ideas, or information that is worth investment to someone. I extract a percentage from both borrower and lender, so I make out all right. An example of which: Larry Green, who made a small fortune investing early in the marijuana market thanks to me. It was one introduction and just on the south side of legal.

I opened the windows that gave out to the quiet street below. Directly across, there were banks of windows which had flower boxes that had been strung haphazardly from tiny balconies. I was hit by block of cool air which instantly rendered me present. My concerns dissolved into a smile until I saw the remnant of a slivered moon and remembered someone telling me Mars or Mercury or some planet was in retrograde. I didn't know shit about astrology, but I knew that couldn't be good. A woman came out on her balcony directly across from me. She spotted my friendly smile in her direction. What she returned was a brief blank stare, then she immediately closed her windows. The doorbell rang. No knock. I froze. I turned to see the handle of the door move ever so slightly.

"Who is it?" shot out of my mouth.

"Je cherche Larry Green."

"I don't speak French," I lied.

"Larry Green."

"No Larry Green here." Silence. I looked through the peephole. He was gone. This person had the same skill set Larry Green had when it came to navigating a creaky stairway. He had vanished without a sound.

Thirty minutes later, I was walking down my street, garbage bags in tow, checking every few seconds to make sure I wasn't being followed. I had a small loft in the République, so the walk was short. Paris at 4 a.m. is a thing of quiet beauty. Even pigeons eventually have to sleep. A family of gypsies was camped out on the sidewalk just before my building. I had to navigate sleeping children, their toys, assorted bags and pillows, and the children's extended family. I handed a five Euro note to a young child with eyes the size and color of an old penny. As I walked away from a "merci beaucoup" chorus, I was wondering if I had just set a precedent.

Entering my apartment always made me smile. It was small with angles everywhere, but it was more than serviceable and had a great bed. Some things are more important than others. My door had three locks on it, and I engaged all of them. This was a first. My feeling of security in Paris is normally absolute. I remember one day coming out of my flat and out of the corner of my eye, I thought I saw a black and white, an American police car. My blood froze. I immediately became aware of the level of stress I had normalized living in the States. I had accepted an underlying fear of unexpected danger: unprovoked, illogical, yet frighteningly real. I was also cognizant of the fact that I have never experienced that paranoia in France. Unless, of course, I imagined an American police car somehow appearing on the Paris streets. But here, now, as I engaged three locks on my Paris apartment door and fingered my new stack of euros, I felt an unmistakable twinge of danger.

Being in possession of two garbage bags of money will have that effect. I have dealt with moral outliers my entire life. Normalcy was never a virtue I required in an acquaintance or a friend. And as far as morality was concerned, I mean, really ... there are extremes of course, but the middle ground is judged case by case. Larry Green would be considered an amoral man by many. To me, he was an honorable individual who lived in a world of extremes. It was the danger that surrounded him that was my present concern. He led with money and its pursuit. In that, he was undeniably conventional, and in that world, anything was possible. My goal in these situations is simply to begin the dance. I never want to remain for last call. Following this rule, I should have dropped the bags off, returned to my cozy studio apartment, put one lock on the door, and slept with dreams of Morocco. This was not to be the case. I was stuck with two bags, which surely had an unholy history. I'd had a momentary stay in a deathly black apartment, been visited by a shadow, fled from said apartment, and there was no Larry Green.

I sent him a text immediately after the stranger had disappeared down the stairs. Larry Green was **averse** to texts except in the case of an emergency. My minor missive to him was simple and I'd hoped, worthy of his immediate attention.

Unknown visitor came to the door/He left/Me too.

I was too nervous to sleep. I decided to take a walk. It might not have been the smartest thing to do at that moment, but it was all that I could come up with. I was out the door, decidedly unconcerned about imaginary consequences. I had my phone. I was in Paris on vacation. Hopefully I had a date with Yasmine from Morocco in a few hours. Life was good, if someone didn't try to kill me in the interim.

It was now five a.m. The streets of Paris were still calm except for the pigeons who were preparing for a banner summer day of tourist leftovers. I walked down a wide street with mature trees and stone sidewalks and headed in the direction of the Seine. For me, few things in life were more calming than walking across the Seine on one of the many bridges. I made good time. It was still dark in the City of Lights. Ironically, it's called the city of lights because of the dark. It was one of the first European cities during the age of Enlightenment to install gas lights to illuminate the streets and major monuments. Now, the lamps have been rewired, mostly electric, but they add a nice romantic flow to the city's monumental beauty. I followed some steps down to the edge of the river and sat on the bank watching the shimmering reflection of dark and light become a modern moving canvas. Without the garbage bags on my person, I felt at peace. Still no word from Larry Green, so it wasn't long before I began imagining someone in my apartment removing said items and leaving nothing more than foul footprints on my freshly cleaned floor. Shoes were not allowed in my apartment, a habit I began years ago in New York. I doubted that any burglar would be considerate enough to remove their shoes before relieving me of my bags of euros. What had I gotten myself into? I had only been in Paris for two days and I was in two bags of trouble before my jet lag had expired. That is what I was thinking when a hand landed on my shoulder. My body instinctively attempted to levitate but was held down by the grip of my unseen assailant. I summoned every bit of my fear to successfully pull away, hitting the back of my head on the stone walkway. I scrambled a few feet away and stood up in an offensive crouch like they do in the movies, my hands at the ready. Larry Green doubled over in laughter. He had the laugh of a child, joy-filled and unaffected. Immediately, I was at ease, although my expression belied that sentiment.

"What the fuck!" was all I could say. His hands were on his knees, and he was having difficulty catching his breath in between fits of laughter. I've always been impressed with people whose laughter could exit from the lining of their soul. I almost instantly trust anyone who can make themselves that available to joy. He gave me his Colgate smile and then sat next to me, staring out at the river as if it was the first time he had seen water. A full five minutes passed in silence. Paris has that effect. Something about the city silences the mind and body. I snuck a look at Larry Green's profile while he was fixated on the water. It was quite beautiful. A sociopath at rest. I thought he would have made a good subject for Rodin, if Rodin had sculpted homicidal African Americans. I could see the moment had ended when his eyebrows joined. "People are fucked up, you know?

I didn't answer because I knew it wasn't really a question. I knew this was merely a prelude. He would continue at his own pace.

"I try to be a man about myself… not just my business. Ya feel me? Say what you mean. Keep your word. Mind your own business. Don't go making enemies cuz they damn sure gonna present themselves without your help. Don't fuck your friends is what I'm saying. But some muthafuckas ... man, they just bring out the lethal in me."

He took a momentary pause. I thought he might have been lost in the moment again. Then he changed gears.

"Don't worry 'bout the visitor you had. He ain't gonna be making no more house calls."

He then turned to me expectantly.

"I appreciate that," I responded simply.

"Paris." He laughed. "I can see why you like this place."

"You do?"

"I'm feeling it too. It's like this fairy tale. For adults. Castles 'n shit." He pulled out his phone, read something, and his peaceful reverie ended abruptly. "Muthafuckas ... how long you here for?"

"I got two weeks."

He stood up and took another look at the river. Just then, a péniche floated by with a couple on deck embracing in a daybed.

"Look at dat shit." He chuckled. "Man ...white folks got it good." He began walking away. Without turning back, he rumbled in my direction, "Keep your shit tight, young Negro. Keep it tight."

I watched as Larry Green moved away slowly, demonstrating some French swagger on the banks of the Seine. An image, until this moment, I could never have imagined. I had never noticed until now, but Larry Green was slightly bowlegged.

I pulled myself away from the bank and walked to a bench situated directly behind me and stretched out. I was too tired to go any farther than that. A slight nugget had formed on the back of my head from the fall, so I lay down on my side like a clochard. This was something else I would never do in the States. I fell asleep instantly.

Grateful for the power nap and thankful no one pissed on me while I slept, I was opening my apartment door three hours later. The gypsies had moved on, the sun was out, and Larry Green had made an appearance. Life was suddenly bright. My happiness was short-lived when I noticed the bags had disappeared. There was a note in their place. Even from a distance, I could discern the easily recognizable calligraphy of Larry Green. He had written something on the back of a NYC Chinese takeout menu.

The euros were counterfeit. Muthufuckas. I took care of the bags. Best to burn it. Handle your shit. See you when I see you. You know how we do. Fix your fridge ...

Fix my fridge? What was wrong with my fridge? I opened the door to my stunted appliance. Two bottles of expensive champagne sat on the top shelf. Larry Green intentionally left the price tags on them. There was also a small white bag on which he had written: *REAL*. Inside the bag was a stack of euros bound by a rubber band. All of them were fifty-euro notes. Everything seemed to have worked out peacefully. No bleeding bodies. No introduction to the French police. I was almost disappointed. Almost.

I began thinking about how the world had changed dramatically in the last ten or twelve years—specifically, our notions and acceptance of violence. As I sat in my apartment in the middle of Paris, having recently slept on the banks of the Seine, it was my exposure to violence that was still working on me. I was imagining what could have happened. Out of habit, I turned on my computer to discover there were two mass shootings in the United States. Two. Within hours of each other. Recently I had been putting myself to sleep by watching series and episodics, all of them ending in body counts. I never turned on my Paris TV for fear of being presented with a ringside seat to any number of wars transpiring globally. I thought about how children and adults were addicted to video games in which the only strategy was of destruction and self-preservation. And then there was Larry Green and me. Nothing had happened. I lost a bit of sleep. I received a chicken McNugget on the back of my head courtesy of my fall. But it could have been worse. Much worse. It could have turned into an episode of tv I had been watching.

I closed my laptop and went to my tiny balcony. The nine a.m. sun had washed the wall of the apartment facing me, giving the building a bright glow. On one of the glass doors, I saw my reflection in a floor-to-ceiling window. An uncensored reflection of myself. It produced the most normal of responses: I laughed.

ECHOeS

It was my son's eighteenth birthday, and we were engaged in a lively discussion concerning his plans for college over a meal of lobster lasagna. It was my specialty and his favorite dish, which was the reason I brought up the topic this evening. I had calculated all the positives aligning in my favor: a great meal, his birthday gift of five hundred bucks, and my allowing him to have a glass or two of some terrific red wine from the Rhone Valley, though he was neither age-appropriate nor had he the palate to appreciate it. We had a solid relationship grounded in a lovely father-son bond, which had recently developed some fissures he had attributed simply to his being older. I blamed it on the internet. In any event, he told me he wasn't sure he wanted to follow in my illustrious footsteps, enlisting in four more years of classroom, having just completed twelve years of the same. Tonight, it was my intent to fully impress upon him the unexpected wonders provided by a university landscape.

The dinner worked its magic, and the money did what money always does. I believe he was loosened up from the wine as well, which made me happy. If only two glasses of red wine had that effect on him, I could have confidence he wasn't much of a drinker. He refused the offer of a third glass. The conversation was varied and hit upon the quotidian themes, current politics, world views, personal expectations and growth, and of course, women. I even managed to get him talking about his favorite books to move us closer in the direction of the subject at hand. It was a completely civil discourse until he jumped to where he knew this conversation was leading. He laid down his fork, wiped his mouth with his napkin, and fixed me with his eyes. There is something about the way your child can look at you and effortlessly undress your soul. I felt helpless and I knew he was loading up to say something either profoundly disturbing or uniquely exalting. I was already treading cautiously with my son, as boundless love with no safe frontier available rendered me vulnerable and I recognized he was now as serious as I was. I waited patiently for him to unload.

He began, "College is outdated. I don't mean learning. I mean, how learning's taught. You're a writer and you were trained on stuff that was centuries old, and nothing has changed. Now it's remote this, and crypto/NFT that. History is redefined and reinterpreted, which is interesting, but not in a university environment. My culture is so far removed from yours, Dad. I don't want to make this long and contentious. I just believe current academics is applying an outdated solution to a brand-new problem. Tell me what I'm going to get out of university that I couldn't get elsewhere. Something? Anything? If you can do that, I might have to look at it from a different angle. You know?"

My son has always been thoughtful in the extreme and impulsive in the extreme. It was a marriage of the immoderate I'd grown to appreciate in him. He certainly wasn't wrong. The world he had been given was not one even I could understand. I tapped out for the evening as far as that conversation was concerned. We continued the night peacefully with my tacit acceptance that he was going to do whatever the fuck he wanted to do. I also figured the matter wasn't completely closed. I knew I could regroup and revisit it on another occasion. I needed to sit with his question for a while. It was worth consideration. What would he get out of college that he couldn't discover elsewhere? His question was legit. At that moment, I had no answer.

The next few days, I spent trying to come up with a solid reason for him to choose college from solid reasoning. I began seriously revisiting my college years. I'm sentimental by nature and I have amassed an encyclopedic collection of my past in various forms. I have photos, letters, matchbooks, diaries, and all things related to my past life in its various stages. I opened a couple of boxes clearly marked college and immersed myself in a time gone by. My memory was immediately fired by an hour spent rereading some of the many diaries I had produced. Simply listening to how I spoke about my experience gave me chills. Certainly not for the quality of the writing, but what I read was truthful and fearless, and marked by love—friends, women, experiences, and yes, even books. Like I said, I am sentimental by nature and thought if only my son could feel what I was feeling in that moment as I reacquainted myself with my younger self, he would understand at least the social value of college. I was convinced it was the social value he was concerned with more than the volume of work or responsibility. He was living in the same virtual world all his friends were and it was difficult for them to imagine something outside of those confines. Something like real life. At that moment, I didn't know if I was going to find anything relevant to him, something persuasive or meaningful in any way. What I did realize was that I had a personal need to return to my first year in college, as even now I was wondering how it all came about. I sat in the attic for hours.

Then days. It was outfitted as an office and was a perfect place to spread my life out on the floor and try to put the puzzle together.

The Catalyst was a music venue. A music venue was any place which could feature a band and have an open floor large enough to accommodate a pot smoking audience. Dancing usually ensued. In Santa Cruz, dancing was more an exercise in freedom than paying any attention to rhythm. At least that's what it was in the mid-70s, when I was a freshman at UC Santa Cruz. How that came to be was by sheer chance. I wandered into a minority recruiting office at a community college and found myself signing up for a field trip to the university. It was a lark. I was tired of working in a clothing store selling polyester shirts and bump-toed shoes and had a couple of days off. I decided to drive up to Santa Cruz for the day on the following weekend.

Fresno, California, where I had grown up amid farmers, Armenians, and pretty girls sporting daisy dukes, was falling into my rear view. I had the adolescent's aching desire to experience anything other than what was happening now. To be truthful, I was living an accommodating life in that sweltering central California town. I subsisted on a very manageable diet of work, clubs, acquiring new albums, hanging out with friends, and fantasizing about being rich. I'm not sure what else I was looking for, but I was curious about the things and places I had read about. My major saving grace was the appetite for reading my parents instilled in me, though I couldn't possibly realize its importance at the time. Like most kids my age, I thought I knew everything without knowing shit about anything.

I was to show up at the university, where I was to be met by a counselor and given an introductory tour of the campus. I set out on a leisurely drive to Santa Cruz from Fresno, a route for some reason I had never taken before. It turned out to be quite memorable. On the road there, I came to the bracing realization that my life was on autopilot. No direction. No goal. No thing. It was an epiphany. Random, like all epiphanies, except for the fact that in youth, they take on the severity of Moses discovering the tablets of commandments. It was both a momentous and terrifying moment. An uncommon sense of displacement snuck up on me. It would evolve as the journey progressed. It was a near out-of-body experience. This was not a part of the experience I would share with my son lest he think I was under the influence of some psychedelic. That, of course, would happen in college shortly. This was the late seventies.

Eventually, I fell into a tranquil state of presence. I passed through large scale farming regions ingesting the alternating smells of fresh soil and cattle emission. I was smelling them for what seemed the first time, though they were familiar scents, having grown up in mostly farm country. Geographically challenged since birth, and bereft of Google Maps, I took several wrong turns. Eventually, I found myself immersed in a forest of redwoods where time and temperature transformed into something alternately solid and animated. It completely seduced me. Again, I settled into some altered state. All these trees whipping past me, unbothered by my presence, untethered to urbanity, produced a feeling of utter calm. My entire body smiled. I had no experience with that kind of solitude—that audible silence. Fresno was not a big city, but it was all things urbane to me. Being surrounded by redwoods and the smell of pines was transformative. If there is a time in one's life where everything changes in a moment, this was it. The deep green color and the fresh smell of oxygenated earth took away my fulcrum. I found it difficult to reconcile; my breath caught somewhere between heaven and earth. So simple, nature, yet I was overwhelmed. I'm revisited by that feeling to this day by seemingly simple shows of nature.

After an hour or so of this meditative engagement, I found myself at the entrance to the university, a long, impressive drive up a hill, the balance of the city and the ocean falling off to my right. The campus was relatively new and built on two thousand acres of redwoods, with the school visible in small bites. The ecological objective was for the physical campus to be hidden in the splendor of its natural beauty of place. It accomplished that objective so thoroughly that I had trouble finding my building in this woody forest. UCSC was spread out, containing several colleges broadly representing different disciplines. No one was happy with the tumultuous political activity on the UC Berkeley campus at that time and perhaps this was the Regent's answer to all their disruptive protests. UC Santa Cruz was the newest college, and it was not by accident that they decentralized it by separating it into miniature colleges. Perhaps they hoped this action would make it more difficult to unite and eventually to create what the Regents desired, a more peaceful path to learning. The Vietnam War was over in name, and this could be a fresh start.

I met with the counselor from Fresno and three other would-be students in a cafeteria on one of the several campuses. It was impossible to be unimpressed by the sheer magnitude of the place, except for the fact that the cafeteria smelled of stale bread and Lysol, there was glory in its positioning amid the woods. Floor-to-ceiling windows put me right in the heart of nature. I had not seen anything like this before and its effortless splendor humbled and embarrassed me. I felt naive for being unaware that places like this even existed. I would describe my upbringing as richly poor. We didn't have money, but we had the goods of life. Being introduced to so many things outside of my personal sphere really drove home my cultural and geographical shortfall. More proof I needed to leave Fresno pronto. Truth be told, one must be taught that they are wanting. Like Hamlet, I could be bound in a nutshell ... were it not for I have heard there's better stuff. In any event, I was sold on the campus. We had a quick tour, and I returned to Fresno the same day, not wanting to spend money on a hotel which was beyond my means.

Somehow, I was accepted to the university and my situation was buttressed by a small scholarship and countless student loans. That fall, I loaded up my Volkswagen bug with my clothes and albums and started a new life.

This trip, I was prepared for the magical woods and winding roads. I drank it all in like Jesus' wine. I took some side roads to enter deeper into the greenness, taking possession of what was now my neighborhood. I was not as virginal in my impressions as I was on the initial visit, but for the remainder of my four years at school, I never ceased to be overwhelmed by its natural beauty. I spent an hour driving around the campus until I accidentally found my dorm, which sat on a hill like a white plaster jewel stuck on the finger of the forest. I parked, and loaded down with suitcase and boxes, found my dorm room and was excitedly met by my roommate, Fernando. He was a big Mexican guy from the neighboring city of Watsonville, a farming town known for, among other produce, strawberries and broccoli.

"Hey, man. Welcome to Santa Cruz. Need any help with your stuff?"

He was as large as he was friendly. His smile and candor were by turns unnerving and ingratiating. Fernando was a gentle giant of the first order, and I wanted to get the fuck out of there immediately. I'd had roommates in Fresno, but they were chosen by me. In this big, sweet stranger and this minuscule room, I saw an immediate precursor to an unending invasion of privacy. I remember during our initial conversation, I spoke of women exclusively, sprinkling in the word 'pussy' liberally. I wanted to get the temperature of his sexual inclinations from the jump. I shared explicit personal exploits I'd had in my hometown, sparing no sordid detail. He listened carefully as an eager science student. I thought he might pull out a pad and take notes. Appearing neither shocked nor disgusted, I was happily relieved and took him for a virgin. It was in fact Fernando who hipped me to the aforementioned Catalyst, informing me that's where all the women in town foraged. He couldn't say from personal experience, as he was a mere eighteen years into this world. I had possessed a convincing fake ID for a couple of years, which made me a veteran of those establishments. And so, it began.

The first few days at school consisted of introductions to the campus and what was expected of us as new students. I was still reeling from the university setting. It was a full press body and soul acclimation of new sensations and all those awkward feelings one has when experiencing overwhelming newness. I found the campus itself to be a playground for a student, a wonderland of trails and vistas, concealed spots for romantic mayhem. At this point in my life, I was only interested in two things: women and reading. This campus would do nicely for both. I soon discovered there was also a troubling nature to the place. The setting had a comprehensive silence about it. A disturbing echoless void, I would notice many a late night while taking the odd walk through the hilly trails. It could seem a little creepy, as often the only sound one could hear was the fog settling on loose branches or the wind whispering in tongues. Before Santa Cruz, silence was not a phenomenon I had ever needed to manage. I had recently seen the film, *The Exorcist*, and was still spooked by its music, which occasionally replayed in my subconscious. The penumbra detected in lighted fog I experienced on those sparsely lit trails mimicked the image of the priest arriving at the demon's house. It would take me some time before I would be conversant with a silence of this magnitude. The other reason I had yet to leave the campus was because I was intimidated by the workload. I had serious work to do.

They had a class called the Core Course, obligatory for all freshmen. It featured a daunting reading list of about twenty major works: literary, political, philosophical, from Marx to Hemingway to a bunch of other fabled dead white guys. And this was only one of the five classes in which I was enrolled in their short quarter system. Trying to get a head start on the required reading, I spent most of my time away from my room, bundled up on a couch in their impressive library.

Libraries have always been a sanctuary for me. It's a comfortable place to read, almost willing the occupant to invest their entire soul in the pages of a book and fall into the depths of that world. It was also my favorite place to meet girls. You don't meet too many of the intellectually deprived there; nonetheless, the difficulty quotient in them increases substantially, buoyed by intellectual backup. I found a comfortable corner surrounded by windows which gave me a view of the hearts of trees from my third-floor vantage. I spent long hours studying both the books and whatever women were in my proximity. It became clear I was always overdressed for this place. This was a hippy community, and to look as if you cared about your clothing style was anathema at worst, and pretentious at best, to this student body. Eventually, I would go with only jeans, a T-shirt, and tennis shoes, but I had come from working in the clothing industry, so it was going to take some time for me to stylistically downgrade appreciably. I was also begrudgingly learning how to appreciate the smell of patchouli oil. I was fairly sickened by it generally until one evening at the library a woman came in and shared my table. Her approach was preceded by a redolent wave of patchouli, strong enough to stagger. I was about to leave in dramatic fashion until she removed her big, shapeless sweater, revealing a sheer shirt, unbuttoned for comfort. She was bra-less and in possession of a staggering example of womanhood beyond her young years and ability to realize their effect. I felt the lights in the library brighten, or maybe it was my pupils dilating in a dance of joy. Finally, proximity! I hadn't even spoken to a girl those first few days for fear they might intuit my carnal intent. In Fresno, the dynamic of male/female discourse was mutually accepted and shared. I had felt none of the sensuality or possibility of the same since I had arrived on campus. It certainly made it easier to study, but that was only half of my personal equation. Without thinking about it this way, kissing, flirting, touching, and its aftermath were all part of my idea of normal communication. I had to speak to her. This was going to be my first attempt at breaching the culture of counterculture, as it were, and I was in bad need of a diversion. I was already distraught from the book I was reading, *Huckleberry Finn*. It was not one of my favorites among America's classics and I was dreading the future philosophical talks in class regarding slavery and the Jim character amidst a class of exclusively white students. I was dissecting a long passage of the text, predicting how white people might frame the friendship of Huck and Jim, while essentially planning my opening dialogue with this girl whose physical proportions stopped time. She was paying me absolutely no attention and it was easy for me to sneak the occasional glance in her direction. From her vantage, I might as well have been an empty chair. I decided to interrupt the library's quietude. It was perhaps not the strongest opening.

"You a freshman too?"

She didn't quite look at me as much as she vaguely considered my existence. "Sophomore," she whispered.

"What are you studying?" I lowered my voice to match hers.

"Double major. Women's Studies and Environmental Infrastructures."

"Wow. Impressive."

She watched me, not quite satisfied with my response, waiting for me to amend it. I smiled at her out of embarrassment, attempting to hang in there with a shred of dignity. Her eyes never left me as she jiggled a bit in her seat for comfort, stretched backward, featuring her God-given accessories, inhaled deeply, then fell back into her studies. She had moved on without informing me. I wanted to stand up and applaud. Seriously, I was mightily impressed by her composure. Her sense of confidence and equanimity was equal to her rousing patchouli effluvium. I had much to learn. Clearly, the library was the best setting for this lesson. I continued watching her. What more could I lose? The old joke came to mind: 'I suppose a fuck is out of the question?' I returned to the dreaded slave narrative, feeling a bit like Big Jim must have felt. Powerless.

I went to bed wondering why I hadn't gone off the hill and into town to the famed Catalyst. I had work to do but damn, school was to begin in earnest in a couple of days and I had yet to investigate the city. The school was known as 'the City on the Hill' to non-students because it was distinct from the rest of the town by way of proximity and vibe. UCSC was its own planet, even though you could ride a skateboard downhill a couple of miles, ending up downtown in less than half an hour without ever pushing off. It was time to go into town and see what was on the rail for the lizard. I was making a grand attempt, but I was pitifully unprepared for college discipline. I knew the classes which mostly involved reading books were not going to be a problem. Writing papers was also something I could handle as I was conversant in bullshitting at length on paper. It was the mandatory second language class that worried me. That, and the dreaded science 101. At the risk of getting ahead of myself,

I failed French 1 and barely passed my science course despite concocting an elaborate and spectacularly unsuccessful attempt to cheat on the final exam. The other reason I stayed put on campus was my fear of being disappointed in my choice of coming here. I had already been there a few days, had the lay of the land, and realized without effort it might be too pastoral for my tastes. Fresno would never be considered a thriving metropolis, but it was New York City compared to this snail-paced place. To bring it into context, the school mascot was, in fact, the banana slug. Reasons to terminate my time here were slowly piling up. To begin with, I wasn't sure I could handle the silent structure of the university environment. To add to that, I was ill-suited to the routine of monastic discipline. I hadn't met any girl of interest one way or the other, and I imagine this was a mutual feeling. I was also severely challenged by the fashion police, and if my encounter with the girl in the library was any indication of my ability to communicate with the opposite sex, I could only look forward to being masturbatorily ambidextrous. It was time to get off the hill and acquaint myself with some non-scholastic life before either my brain or my balls imploded.

And so, it was on the last weekend before the first day of my proper education, my very first Friday evening in Sant Cruz, I drove down to the main drag, parked, and walked a bit in the downtown area. I had dropped off a couple of hitchhikers I picked up along the way and drove in circles for a while to air out the patchouli scent stuck to my clothes before heading into the Catalyst. I guess one would call the downtown area charming. It was a mix of the organic and the processed. Birkenstocks and realtors. There was, however, life there. Bell bottoms and beads. Long hair and paisley pants. This was a moneyed hippy town. I had no problem with that manifestation. It made people gentler, more inclined to accept someone like me, whoever that was.

I strolled over to the club and stood briefly and excitedly in a short queue, breathing in a sweet and fishy ocean breeze. In Fresno, I was a regular at several nightclubs, and not solely for the obvious reasons. I loved to dance. Some people can draw. Some can dance. I certainly couldn't draw, but I had a natural relationship with rhythm and its physical expression. That women were attracted to a good dancer was a benefit which never ceased to pay dividends. I paid my two-dollar entrance fee and walked inside.

It was a cavernous space, darkly lit, sweltering, and quite full. My pupils slowly dilated to accommodate the lack of illumination, but not before my olfactory senses kicked in. Human musk was pungent, at once foreboding and inviting. *Well, alright,* I thought. I clocked the bar at the other end of the building and slowly navigated through a sea of bodies and a wall of voices and music fighting for dominance. Yep, this was exactly the prescription this patient was hoping for: dark possibilities and mysterious options. I knew no one in the room, so whatever ended up happening would have had that lovely anonymous quality to it. I could be responsibly irresponsible. I needed to nurse a beer. It was de rigueur to have a drink in one's hand while sussing things out in a club. There I stood at the end of the bar waiting to order, a light contact film of perspiration already appearing above my top lip. They had a full bar, though the barkeep was toiling to keep up with the draft beer orders. It took a while to be served as he had to change two exhausted barrels. As I stood there trying not to judge the rhythm-proof dancer in front of me, I wondered how many in this crush of people attended my school. Would any of them be in one of my classes? Am I going to meet my college running buddy or my asshole nemesis in this musty place? Was the girl who was wearing what looked like chopsticks in her earlobes going to be my first college crush? I had already decided on trying to find one person to be with at least through the first quarter. There was way too much work to spend time dancing, romancing, and prancing through the numbers game. If I spent too much time in conquest, surely, I would flunk out in the first quarter. Finally, my beer arrived. My first college beer. Like I said, I'm sentimental. The beer was cold and helped to nullify the strong body odor permeating the place. I surmised rightly it was a smell for which I would have to develop a tolerance for, if not an appreciation.

The music was good. For me, that meant it was funky in the non-body odor sense. It moved me, so I moved. I found myself dancing in place. It wasn't long before a woman danced her way over to me, her movements like that of a drunken snake. I was wondering if I was supposed to answer her in kind, which was impossible. I was severely culturally challenged when it came to moving like white people moved. She came close enough to smell her sweat, which was sweet and musky. She took both of my hands and led me out to the middle of the dance floor, where she got one of her girlfriends to dance with us in some unholy circle. Well, okay. We danced in our little spheres to some Tower of Power, all the while I was fixated on how successfully they both could challenge these obvious rhythms. When the song ended, they stopped and looked at me, hugged me, and gingerly put their hands on my face. Then they laughed and left me in the middle of the dance floor. Whatever that was, it was light-years better than my library experience. I went back to the bar to look for my beer which someone else was now drinking. Lesson learned. All I remembered about the two girls was that they were short and lusty, but obviously not for me.

I spent an hour dancing by myself. Occasionally, someone would join my orbit, fix me with some incomprehensible stare and move on. I was drenched and completely satisfied. Perhaps not completely, but this was my first night out. My expectations were slight. As I made my way to the door, someone touched me on my shoulder. It was one of the girls I had danced with, her friend standing behind her, smiling strangely. My first thought was that there was no school tomorrow. My second thought, wouldn't a menage à trois be a celebratory opening to the school year?

I ended up loading them both into my car and driving them to their home. They turned out to be roommates and living in a little apartment at the end of a street near the freeway. They were both nurses, or at least were in school to be such and I felt a little more comfortable knowing they were conversant with health issues. We sat in my Volkswagen in front of their apartment for a good while, finally introducing ourselves and talking about life and shit. They were funny and nice. All I could think about was how I was going to discreetly finesse the condoms from my glove compartment. And then it began.

Sophie, in the backseat, reached around and began to massage my shoulders. This seemed to interest Mara, sitting in the passenger seat, as much as it did me. Conversation halted. Mara boosted herself over me using the gearshift as support and began kissing me. This strangely acceptable interlude went on for some time. Mara and Sophie then changed positions and now I was being erotically assaulted by Sophie with Mara in the backseat coaching her on. Without thinking this at the time, I was involved in some type of tag team erotica. It ended as abruptly as it began. The two of them silently signaled one another that it was time to go inside. They ended the evening by delivering a chaste kiss, not to me, but to one another. As I watched their egress, I slowly realized I must have been in shock not to be pleading my case to continue. They fumbled for their keys at the door, laughing, and waved me off before disappearing inside. I sat in the car, a ten-pound bag of mixed emotions. I considered knocking on the door like the big bad wolf. Instead, I simply checked on the condoms in the glove box. There was no reason to do this other than to extend the previous moment. I glanced at the lonely three-pack I always carried with me and accepted my situation without having any idea what had just transpired. I didn't even get their phone number.

My first week of school was a blur. I lost one of my classes due to late registration. The class was already full when I arrived, and I had to submit to a rather embarrassing exchange with the professor in front of a packed classroom. I exchanged this Shakespeare class for one in Economics. This was not going to bode well. I was as interested in Economics as I was in Ancient Lavatory Architecture, which I believe had been offered as a class. To add more shit to the circus, my French class was daunting. In reality, there is no such thing as beginning French in college. My presence was the lone example of a French neophyte. Everyone else was clearly advanced. This was a slumming class for the rest of them, probably taking it to pad their GPA or to manage an easy four-unit respite. I spent most of my time smiling unconsciously at the attractive professor as she regarded me with unfriendly pity. I would indeed fail her class. The only saving grace was that I would meet my college best friend in French class. He, too, would fail.

Les Steiner was a handsome, wild looking Jewish kid from San Francisco, with a big head of curly hair which entered the room before he did. A wanna be writer, he was sharp of mind and quick to laugh. He also had a bit of criminality in his DNA, which always appealed to me. Nothing serious, together we functioned more along the lines of Butch Cassidy and Sundance. They were criminals who robbed banks but would never hurt anyone. The myth even says they were loved by the people and boy did we want to be loved. We even figured out a way to rob a bank, eventually drawing up plans. It was back when people made night deposits and cameras were rare. We were going to line an outside night deposit opening with a garbage bag, deeply recessed so no one would realize they were filling our empty bag. We were to come in the early morning, pull up the bag, then return home, counting our spoils. Fortunately, we never put this idea into practice, though we never ran out of schemes. Les was more centered than I was, witnessed by the fact he had a girlfriend to whom he was wholly committed. I found him pure in that sense. Something for me to aspire to, or not. To his credit, he never judged me for my insatiable appetite and appreciation of the opposite sex. He turned out to be my coeval in all things except my pursuit of women.

Les was the only person to whom I could shamelessly recount the story of the coven of kissers from my first evening at the Catalyst. His response was a laugh so extended I thought I might have a career in stand-up. I told him that I hungrily returned to their tiny place the following night where a big hairy guy answered the door. He said he had no idea who the fuck I was talking about, then invited me in for a bong hit. I remember Les pulling out his pad and paper, taking notes. He did this a great deal when we were together, and I can claim partial ownership for a half dozen short stories he wrote during that first quarter. I read a bunch of his work. I knew he was talented as a writer, but what came through most clearly was that it was the work of someone who housed two warring factions always in conflict, criminality and purity. He was as iniquitous, ungodly, and depraved as he was pure of heart and morally forthright. When I met his girlfriend, Sarah, I realized where part of his purity originated. Sarah Gross had piercing blue eyes and an expression that one could easily imagine set in stained glass high above a church altar. To add to her angelic proportions, her voice was slight, and musical as a dulcimer. When Les was in her proximity, I could see how much influence she had over his feral proclivities. She lent certain probity to his malfeasance. He always accused her of making him want to be better. His entire body exhaled when he sat next to her. I would spend some time with them together and it was a humbling thing to witness that kind of connection. Her influence on me was less obvious. Her goodness fired in me the imaginings of sleeping with the Virgin Mary. In any event, Les played a large part in my college life and helped me remain a student.

I was now a few days into assessing my college life and though I had unearthed many discursive memories, I was nowhere nearer answering my son's question regarding school and life comparisons. My son was coming over tonight with his new girlfriend, or at least new to me as I wasn't aware of his previous one, and I had no new ammunition. Just then, I opened an envelope and found my grades from my freshman year. They were narrative evaluations, clearly written appraisals of the students according to the professor's vagaries. I felt a wound opening. Students were allowed to choose how they wished to be graded, whether by written evaluations or letter grades. Like an idiot, I chose the former. There was nowhere to hide with the evaluations, and several professors revealed their malevolent personas in their evaluations of certain students. I read a few of them and immediately thought better of sharing this portion of my university experience with my son. There were some good ones, but the first one I read reminded me why I should have chosen letter grades. It went as follows:

"Mr. Clark is not without talent, of this, I'm sure. Unfortunately, he mostly demonstrated this talent in class discussions wherein he would be unable to resist positing the inanest interpretations of whatever the reading material was, albeit in a terribly creative way. I felt he was more interested in being unique than in discovering fresh ways to discuss literature. His papers, which were almost always turned in late, were of interest in the same way as seeing the aftermath of a nuclear explosion is interesting. One is only left with the question of how on earth this came to be? I do foresee Mr. Clark continuing in his quest to reassess literary icons (He has a penchant for deconstructing them, to their immense dismantling.) and perhaps he will find an audience to alternately abuse and confuse. I wish him well and hope he can rid himself of some of his anger. It affects his writing in ways in which I am sure he is unaware."

This fuckhead ... Professor Marcus. I had almost forgotten about him. Reading this now, I was sure if I had chosen a letter grade, it would either have been an A or an F. Either way, it would have been a more welcome outcome as I would have been spared the evaluation vitriol from that racist, egotistical, odious fuck. No, after seeing this appraisal of my work, I knew it would be too disingenuous to cherry-pick from the others on my son's behalf. I angrily put all the evaluations back in the box and went to prepare dinner for my son and his new shorty. Professor Marcus ... that fuckwad.

Dinner was lovely, chiefly on account of his girlfriend, Aida, being a complex, imperturbable thing of beauty. She had an unforced joy about her which never outshone the fierce intellect she used at will. I remember one of the first things she said to me about my son was that 'he was a willing student of the absurd.' I thought it a brave statement to say to a father, one with which I agreed completely. I thought she was the kind of girl I was never lucky enough to meet in college, and I wondered if that was because things *had* changed so much since my university days. I wondered if my son might have been right when he constantly informed me that I couldn't understand the way things are 'these days.' I watched them interact and realized the film of age had kept me at a distance from their communication, even at the dinner table. Something was going on between them, like a silent foreign language I could neither translate nor factor into my speculation. I developed a bit more faith in my son for having chosen her as his mate, however temporarily.

Aida was in her sophomore year at college and was still unsure of which path to take. She had no clear major and said, almost defiantly, that, 'It didn't matter as long as I have control over what I've learned.' My son and I have an intellectual relationship and shorthand which can be daunting to a stranger. Not that the content is so elevated, but our communications are spirited and stout, no matter who's in the room. Aida was cut from the same cloth in that she never masked her dynamism. She spoke her mind at length, but her weapon was suasion, not coercion. I asked her about school, and she answered with a mouthful of salmon ...

"It's all about how you spend your time. That about sums it up for me. The world is so crazy right now, we have to act like this is business as usual while we course through absolute insanity. It's headlines and sound bites and #MeToo and BLM and ANTIFA and politicians who practice criminality as an art form. School just seems to be a safe haven for me until I can figure out how I can recalibrate. I'm still looking at life in terms of its beauty and possibilities. I guess if I could start all over it would be in music. So maybe what I'm trying to find in school is the entry point to life's musical analogy. Music is kind of the key. I guess what I'm really saying is I have no idea what is happening, but I refuse to expect the worst. This salmon is heaven. Is that coriander?"

I'm sure she had no idea how attractive she was when she simply spoke her mind. I could see my son's pride in his choice of companions. I could faintly hear his thoughts, "See, Dad, I know what the fuck I'm doing.' My reply would still have been "No. What I do see is that you are fortunate enough to be around someone who has made the right choices through careful consideration. That doesn't mean you get to jump on that bus. We all have a tariff to pay." These were not thoughts

I could share at the moment, or perhaps at all. We said our goodbyes and I surmised they were heading back for a more intimate setting. As embarrassing as it sounds, I was tempted to call someone with whom I might cosign the evening as well. A bit like when one person yawns, I suppose. Instead, realizing I needed to do more research to unearth another angle, I returned to my attic and memories of a time past. At this point, I was no longer sure for whose benefit this was. I was rather enjoying this trip to the unrepeatable, sadly enjoying the journey. It firmly instilled the smell of mortality in my person, another sentiment that continuously called for attention. I realize I'm in the fourth quarter of my life. But I always have possession of the ball.

School gradually became more interesting to me thanks in large measure to my TA's: teaching assistants who were assigned to professors as they burnished their doctorates. Most of them were bright and energetic. Being not so far removed from their students age-wise, they still had a grasp of what we were going through and had consequently shown some empathy for us poor, lost, pursuers of knowledge. In other words, they had a sense of humor about it all and it made for less boring classes. One of my TAs exhibited a welcome strain of transgression like my own. Les and I shared a class in PHD candidate Paul Lehman's section. It was almost a convocation of concealed criminality. Paul would have hated that sentence. Too easy. Paul was a true poet and profound thinker when it came to literature. I learned a great deal about writing from that guy and if it doesn't show, he's not to blame. He was on another plane when it came to analytical, theoretical, or conceptual processing, and most of the time, I would just be hanging on for a rare moment of comprehension. Still, he was so cool and unassuming it was always an enjoyable hour and a half traffic. Make no mistake, his scholarship in no way diminished his recondite criminality and as the classes went on, we became as entertaining to him for our intellectual lawlessness as he was in helping us to keep these thoughts merely intellectual. If that makes any sense. In any event, we got along like a cocaine addict and a rolled dollar bill. He was also my first personal example of how intelligence could be an aphrodisiac. Like I said, he was a poet. And all poets keep Eros in their back pocket. He represented a friendly flame to many of the women in class and I doubt all of them took his William Blake class simply for the poetry. Some of them discussed his sultry presence with me (if I'm remembering correctly) and I felt uncomfortable, a tad emasculated. I felt as if they were sharing secrets with their gay best friend. I'm sure Paul would have some arcane literary term for that feeling, which would only solidify it poetically. In thinking about this, I believe it can serve as a motivator for my son to go to school. I could attack it from the point of view that by not going to college, he is limiting himself to the less intelligent pool of possible companionship. Nobody wants a dummy. So, noted.

Another of my favorite TAs worth mentioning was Tom Antonelli, a short New Yorker who taught literature with the energy of a football commentator. He was a huge sports fan of all teams, New York, and somehow effortlessly merged Chaucer with an excitement usually reserved for sporting events. His literary scrutiny of The Canterbury Tales was revelatory. Who knew a Middle English poet could be so entertaining? In most classes, Tom would recite several of his favorite passages from memory, revealing his love for the material as much as his talent as an actor. He had a rare talent for reading Middle English melodically. Our relationship with him was limited to our class time since he lacked the requisite lawless tendencies necessary to include him in our off-campus scenarios. I still follow his literary achievements online. I remember he gave me an evaluation at the end of the quarter that ended with the sentence: "Matthew's predatory approach to literature is singular and he, with the right guidance, might bring something authentic to the world of literature if he chooses to continue with his writing." He was manifestly incorrect in his prediction, but I will always love him for thinking it feasible.

Time was getting tight for me. My son was now working full time at a popular clothing store and fulfilling his Gen Z quota, which was simply to be wearing the flyest shit possible. On the one hand, this was good. I knew the gig would eventually bore him to distraction. On the other hand, he could be persuaded to move in whatever direction his associates were headed. I'm a big believer that we are influenced mightily by our surroundings, which was the main reason I wanted him in college. The university environment fueled endless possibilities and connectivity. The well was deeper, and not to put too fine a point on it, for the most part, it was fueled by people who had read a book or two. So far, observing my initial days in school, the meager advice I had to offer up was that he should associate with like-minded criminals—we'll call it 'criminal light'—but I had found nothing really to convince him school was in any way superior to his current choices or lack thereof. I had been through a box of photos and felt all warm and gooey about the people in the photos who were now some thirty years older. And what of them? Were they successful graduates? Pursuing their dreams gestated from the table of education? Or were they serial killers, drug dealers, and child molesters? Or worse, life coaches, lawyers and venture capitalists? There was still work to be done.

The next evening, I retired to my attic with my laptop at around seven in the evening. I had also digested half of a marijuana brownie to help slide me into a more layered reminiscence. It worked to a point. Opening boxes eventually turned into an indolent sport. There I was enjoying the smell of the old papers I had written by typewriter thirty-some years ago. A typewriter! I spent the next half an hour wondering what happened to that antique machine, and another half hour in appreciation of its retirement and replacement by a computer. Things moved slowly until I came upon a shoebox of letters written to me in that golden epoch. Love letters made up most of the contents and I was shaken by the emotional output witnessed in some of those missives. Some made me out to be an estimable and intimate confidante, while others sounded like warrants were soon to be issued. I was fairly under the guidance of THC, so I responded with laughter at even the most embarrassing of communications. My curiosity regarding a few of these erstwhile lovers was occasioned bereft of common sense, which compelled me to see if I could get in touch with one or two of them.

Aware of name changes as well as every other type of change, I put a few names on Facebook to see what popped up. Surprisingly, I found the one girl about whom I was probably the most curious. Her name was Andrea, and I remember not being interested in her as a freshman. By the time she was a junior, she had grown into a rare beauty pursued by students and teachers alike. Not exactly a frog turned princess, but my God, how mightily she had changed in two years. I found her sister online, who remembered me fondly enough to give me Andrea's phone number. It was before ten in the evening, and she picked up after the second ring. I recognized her voice, which was a mixture of liquid music and burnished wood. I smiled and wondered if she could sense it. I was awkward in my attempt to explain why I was trying to get in touch with her now, tonight, this many years later. She didn't seem to mind, and we caught up leisurely and I thought rather effortlessly. Twenty minutes went by (though I can't be sure, as I was high), and not wanting to overextend my visit, I launched into a pithy apology for being so stupid as to ignore her during her freshman year. I could not have been more self-deprecating, and I thought, charming. There was a moment of silence. I was sure I could hear her smile. She said goodbye, nice to catch up, then asked me in her mellifluous voice not to contact her again. I wasn't sure what response I expected after all these years, but it wasn't that. The conversation necessitated a return to more pleasant college memories.

It was now becoming rainy and chilly in Santa Cruz and the campus took on a mystical feeling. The sound of rain through a forest of redwoods is a soft entry into another dimension. Part of the quiet grandeur of the university was in walking the intertwining dirt paths which laced the campus. One glides through terrain, fragrant with nature, to arrive at an interior space, the classroom, warmed by intelligence and challenge. Entering a class on a rainy morning after a stroll through nature's drama produced a happy sadness in me, which I can revisit to this day when it is grey and rainy. On this eventful day, in one of my Lit classes we had a guest speaker, a well-known poet who had a strange mystical bent to go along with his ability to connect a perverse sense of humor in wordy calisthenics. If this sounds incomprehensible, it perfectly fits his poetic production. One of my friends in the class was a walking brain trust named Brandon. He was socially inept, unkempt, and didn't care what anyone thought about it. As the guest poet was reading some of his work and launching into explanations of its origin, I could see Brandon slowly becoming bored. He was not in any way demonstrative by nature, more a rather quiet, brooding person who must have had a difficult time containing all that intellect. I never knew how we became friends. I was hopelessly mentally inferior to Brandon. I imagine I provided him with the occasional laugh. At any rate, he began groaning during the poet's clarification of his work. He had his head in his hands as if he was truly suffering from the words coming out of the poet's mouth. The poet stopped mid-sentence and asked Brandon if he was ill. Brandon, without looking up, replied desultorily that ... "this is the kind of pretentious poetic deconstruction best suited to cocktail parties with professors vying for tenure." The entire class was now focused on Brandon. I was the only one smiling, almost laughing.

Remembering this now, it was a moment I would have liked to share with my son. I feel my son looks at university as a trap, a place where you are no longer able to challenge and defy. A place where one sits, opens their skulls, and allows a steady effusion of other people's opinions to be jettisoned into their consciousness. Youth, on the other hand, is nothing if not rebellious. It's a time when the word no becomes a mighty weapon against anything you wish not to have in your orbit, and youth has a very small orbit. But here, Brandon was showing such revolt, such rebellion in the face of a heralded poet and a class of peers, and doing it without a gun, a spray can, or an act of violence. He was using his brain and the knowledge he had gleaned from the hours of work he had put in to arrive at his opinion. He was arguably the most well-read person I knew, and that was enough for him. For my son, it would have been a lesson in preparation. If you know what you are talking about, you are always free to challenge with impunity. The only rejoinder the poet had was to offer Brandon the opportunity to vacate his class if he found it of such little interest. Brandon stuck a cigarette in his mouth— even he didn't know how cool that was—and left.

I spoke with him after class in the nearby coffee shop. I came in and interrupted his reading of a copy of Norman O. Brown's, Life Against Death. He and I were smiling, though obviously for different reasons. He apologized for interrupting class. It was all above my head, but I told him I thoroughly enjoyed his outburst. He said he wanted to put a bullet in his head listening to all that poetic drivel, and I'm not sure that was an overstatement. He looked down at his book and softly contributed, "This is pretty good stuff." We remained friends throughout my freshman year. At the school quarter's end, we met. I found out he had received an A in that class, not that he gave a shit. I had to muscle it out of him. I believe he left Santa Cruz after that year, and I never saw him again. The strange thing is that I believe my son would have mirrored Brandon on a smaller scale had my son dispensed with his love affair with indolence. My son has a scary intellect, which he only shows when he's angry. Vacuous people often are flush with confidence, while bright ones frequently live in punishing self-doubt. Maybe I'm reaching a bit with my son, but my memories of Brandon reinforced my wish for my son to pursue a college experience and inspired me to keep digging. We had another dinner planned in a couple of days and I was scheduled to present my closing arguments. I, too, would take a page from Brandon's book and be prepared. A few more boxes needed to be opened.

Pictures, pictures, pictures. This was no doubt going to be my favorite reveal, a box brimming with photographs, a visual history of my college days. Memory is a powerful faculty, but with visual aids, it can be overwhelming. I sat transfixed, studying these images before me. My father was a photographer, among other things, and all his children inherited his love of taking pictures. I was not bad at framing my subjects, which added to the emotional impression I received from the hundreds of reproductions. Looking at physical prints is a markedly different experience from running through digital examples of the same. That they were photos of my entire college experience, freshman through senior year, turned out to be a bonus.

I saw my progression of friends. I could appreciate my advanced, though still youthful, aging process. I noticed subject matter changing regarding what I felt was worthwhile. I was provided context. The only constant I could discern was that there was almost always an element of captured beauty. Whether it was a girl or an ocean view, beauty in some regard was the touchstone. If it didn't fall within that parameter, it was humorous like the shot of a man pissing on a pigeon. Humor has its beauty, too. I didn't know at the time what good this would be to my son, but I was an emotional wellspring half an hour in. Hindsight is less manageable and more sensually robust than present experiences. As you are viewing something which already has happened, you are inundated with context, manipulated by a time which no longer exists, and defeated by the inability to change anything about it. It is a precious defeat. There were glossy Polaroids of exuberant classmates, thrilled with being young and alive. I could smell their invincibility. I could see what an untroubled face looked like. I must have spent a fortune of my meager funds on developing these photos. People popped up I had completely unremembered. I was somewhat surprised at the dearth of nude photos of bygone paramours. I have certainly changed in that respect. The element of captured beauty, friends, places, situations, and the sheer emotional magic contained in these photographic echoes impacted me mightily. I wanted to burn these images into my soul so I could call upon them whenever the need arose. This gave me a moment of startling self-reflection. I no longer have that feeling of invincibility, though I am probably as happy now as I have ever been in life, and still occasionally flirt with the idea that anything is possible. Perhaps that says my look forward is not as buoyant as my love-tinged memories, so I prefer to remember when ...

Trying to stay on point through my weed haze, I applied some of this to my son. He is young. His past is abundantly truncated. He simply doesn't possess the same open world I was fortunate enough to inherit and then savor while growing up. Of course, I can't expect the same reaction to his dissimilar upbringing. His world changes every week and without the benefit of the innocence of hope and love I took for granted throughout most of my life. To quote my son once more: These are different times.

When my son came to dinner next, he was without his girlfriend. Mid-meal, I learned their relationship was on pause, but their friendship remained fire. He looked well. I tried my best not to keep staring at him in open admiration and love but failed to the point where he felt the need to ask me if anything was wrong. I wanted to tell him that every fucking thing was wrong. Death. Getting older. Not being able to help my child in any useful way. The lack of intelligence and grace visible in the human community. The fact we are killing the earth with impunity. So many things that could be set right with a bit of thoughtfulness, yet we are obligated to watch this pursuit of self-destruction as almost an Olympic event. Fortunately, I was no longer in a weed haze and did not say what I was contemplating. Instead, I pulled out a box from underneath the dinner table and gave it to him. It was a camera.

Car Problems

Their first and only rendezvous took place long before dating apps. It occurred during the era of full-on dating, when there was no need for an embellished resume or the obligatory preferences exchange. All those particulars were to be settled in a face-to-face with your person of choice. It was a golden time when one was given no information regarding the intended partner in advance. You were forced to simply contact them, arrange a date and meeting place, then mix it up like two prize fighters of love. Skill levels would become apparent accordingly and shape the structure of the date. At least that's how Mac saw it. Dating was not only a quest for the holy grail of intimate possibilities, but a mental and physical scrimmage of humans at their most vulnerable. He wished it were an Olympic sport.

He had met Sarantinia at a coffee shop while she was on a break from working at a nearby upscale clothing store. Normally, he asked anyone he met to repeat their name, a useful habit which allowed him a higher predictability of remembering it. There was no need in this case. Her name was perfect. It was so ridiculous an appellation, there was great humor to be found in saying it. Sarantinia. He wondered if her parents were searching for a first name with the most inordinate number of vowels. Mercifully, she told him to address her as Tina.

Tina was a catch, at least physically. She sported a fastidiously cropped afro, framing a face which was inviting in the extreme. Something about her features cried communion. She had beauty, yes, but she was also gifted with uncommonly interesting characteristics. Her face was led by lips fully developed, and for some reason, always moist without cosmetic aid. Her eyes were raw lapis in color. Blue with streaks of something, or maybe it is how he imagined them. He was never certain. He knew the word lapis itself was of supposed Persian origins, meaning sky/heaven, so it fit. Contrasted with the skin the color of a freshly rolled cigar, she stunned on approach. She also boasted a Negro nose, large enough to be a conversation piece, yet delicately contoured. Her shallow dimples put the finishing touches on a visage as interesting as it was appreciable. She was so physically significant in his mind that he found half a dozen ways to visit her on the job without making a purchase. She once commended him on that feat.

Mac Bassman was a Black man who identified with an unresolved, unidentifiable, self-invented culture. He felt himself beyond someone who claimed to merely be international. Interstellar would be a more appropriate moniker for Mac. Undoubtedly ethnocentric, he was unafraid to regularly challenge even his own community. He criticized Obama when he was president for reasons he posed as obvious. Much of the Black community found this an unforgivable betrayal. He couldn't give a fuck. Mac had a gay brother and a slew of friends of the same persuasion whom he loved, yet still he accused the gay community in general of being racist toward its tanned brethren. These were considered outlaw thoughts. Again, he didn't give a fuck. He had been a professional waiter much of his adult life and had seen the public in all its manifestations.

It turned out to be a formidable social education. He was convinced people were at their most starkly revealing at the dinner table. It was in a moment of comfort and joy where diners regurgitated their real selves in direct proportion to the amount and quality of the food they were ingesting. The consequent revelations were endless.

It was on or about the sixth visit he found the testicular fortitude to invite her out. To his absolute surprise, her response was enthusiastically in the affirmative.

"Fun Fun, Fun," was her precise reply. He in turn had two immediate thoughts. *What a sweetheart this girl is ...* being his first and, *I can't wait to see her naked ...* was second. This was a time before Wokeness as well as the dating apps came into being. In retrospect, his behavior those days could now be considered offensive or sexist, or according to some, indictable. He'd never broached physical boundaries, but what he then considered were his language skills would now be mightily questioned in many communities. It was in fact a recent online date gone unhinged that sent him back down memory lane to the good old days of unrestricted conversations between grownups. He didn't want to think about that date. It would require too much time and probably CGI effects as well.

The date was set, preceded by only a brief phone call. She had given him her home address and consented to the agreed upon time. This made him happy. Always better to pick the girl up at her house. More personal, trusting. Meeting at the venue implied formality, no continuation. Greet, eat, and retreat. The date was in two days' time. Mac spent those two days working on his abdominal muscles in order to wear his favorite skintight shirt. One of his friends saw him wearing it and jokingly inquired how long had he been shopping at Baby Gap. Mac didn't give a fuck what his no-six-pack-having-friend thought. His aim was to balance the physical with the mental, showing up with both barrels loaded. If she wanted him for his hard body, so be it. If she were sapiosexual, bring on the books, art, poetry, or history. Mac was nothing if not fluid. Though not fluid in today's sense.

Following his workouts, he meditated. He'd always been into the practice, as it was something he learned early in life. He was advised it would warm up his chi. He wasn't sure what that meant, but it sounded relevant at the time, and he knew whatever it did it couldn't hurt. Mac prepared for a date as a professional athlete would for a playoff game. The more prepared he was, the better he would perform. This was not only axiomatic, but there was also a history behind these actions. He had once spent an entire week prepping for a date, even having his cards read and following all the Zodiac suggestions. His date showed up with two of her female coworkers. Suffice it to say, the evening was memorable.

Mac was unique in many ways, but his car purchase was a standout in that category. His 1987 Toyota had recently died, no doubt from too much servicing. Mac had a mechanic who never found a problem he couldn't make worse. The mechanic was, however, inexpensive and always available. He needed a car immediately. Riding the bus in LA was little more than being an unwilling participant in some shady social experiment. He always kept a screwdriver with him for protection. As luck would have it, a friend of his was returning to London after having spent a year in the States and had offered him a deal on her car. It was a six-year-old Toyota with less than fifty thousand miles on it, and handsomely affordable. He had not seen the car, but at that price, with that mileage, who cares? She was trustworthy. He wrote a check, then showed up at the house to pick up the car. He had to take a bus for what he hoped would be the last time and was subjected to three transfers. He missed his stop twice. Yes, he needed a car today. When the bus pulled up at a corner in mid-city, he turned and said goodbye to the conductor.

The driver waited in angry silence for Mac to get off the bus so he could close the doors.

As Mac walked down the block, he could see Jill coming to greet him in the distance. They'd had a sporadic but torrid affair throughout most of her stay. They were the poster children for friends with benefits. Jill hooked his arm and began talking about all the changes she would have to make after finding the cheapest and most indirect flight back home. She was English-funny, all irony and sublime innuendo in a slightly cockney accent. As they walked, Mac realized how much he would miss her presence. When they came to a stop in front of a very nice home Mac complimented her on her living situation. He told her she was living better than he was, to which she replied:

"I don't live here; it's simply where I found a parking space." She then moved to a parked car. It was subdued yellow in color, with large black polka dots.

Mac had been stunned before by an automobile's look, but usually for reasons of excellence or rarity. A Maybach or a vintage Ferrari would do the trick. This used polka-dot Toyota made him catch his breath. Jill presented it with pride, opening the door and extolling its clean interior, failing to notice Mac's eyebrows meeting his hairline.

"What the fuck is this?" Mac, not being English, did not share her subtlety. Jill tittered. She was unshakable, another thing Mac would miss when she left.

"I thought you might be too precious to drive a car like this. No worries. I have someone else who wants to buy it."

Mac didn't waste a second before whipping out his checkbook and sealing the deal right then. It was a busy day for Jill, and she had much to prepare before her flight. They kissed, she gave him all the necessities, and left him with his new purchase, walking to her apartment complex a block away. He stood looking at his new vehicle, instantly detecting his next move. He would go straight away to have it painted. His faithful mechanic also did paint and body work. Getting rid of polka-dots was not exacting labor.

Once on the freeway, he smiled. Not only was the car in excellent driving shape, but it had surprising giddy-up. It also attracted attention. A black BMW drove past him with the driver staring at Mac and shaking his head in pity. This was quickly followed by a Mercedes keeping even with him on his right. The driver stared at him with something other than sympathy before speeding off to safety. Mac took the next off-ramp in the direction of his home. There would be no paint job today or in the future. He decided if he could disturb the sensibilities of a class of privileged dolts, it was worth the occasional glancing judgements. He drove the car for seven years. He then sold it to a successful house painter ... and that's the story of Mac's car. Now back to his date with Sarantinia.

When Mac arrived at Tina's apartment, she was waiting out front. This was indeed a first and it almost sent him into shock. He had trained himself in the art of waiting. Mac believed that girls, women, all of them, shared the same tardiness gene. It took him years to find a place of calm during the ceremonial waiting period. Initially, he took it as a personal affront to be made to wait for an extended period after clearly agreeing on the time and place. He would be quietly enraged. Having spent hours or in some cases days to prepare for his date, to be greeted with such a show of indifference would set him off internally. The waiting was always followed by the cloudy period of Mac badly attempting to behave as if nothing had transpired because ... well ... that was exactly how his date was behaving. As if it didn't matter that he'd been outside waiting for half an hour. If the wait were longer than half an hour, screaming would be involved. Just Mac screaming at the top of his compass, windows rolled up and music blasting. This would usually help. It would also throw him completely off his game, and he had to think of shit like puppies and babies to calm the fuck down.

He walked up to meet her. She was smiling and silent. Mac followed suit. It was important to share her vibe initially. Don't disturb her groove, whatever it was. These were Player 101 rules. They walked down the sidewalk happily in shared silence. Mac, already imagining romance, dance and chance. He stopped to open her car door and found her still walking. Tina finally halted a few feet ahead of his car, keeping her back to him. After some time, in a barely audible voice tinged with sadness, she asked him if that was really his car. He answered her by inserting the key and opening the door. She did not move. Mac studied her back, admiring its form and her just-for-him dress. His mood was shifting between being flummoxed and pissed off. He still held hope. He decided to break a major Player 101 rule. Skip the small-talk and hit the truth hard enough so it can only be answered with a yes or no. No room for bullshit improvisational disingenuous claptrap.

"Are you no longer interested in me because I drive a car with polka-dots?"

Tina did not answer. Tina did not move. Tina remained fixed on the walkway, not unlike the palm tree which was presently providing her shade. Mac closed her car door, went around to his side, and slowly got in the car. His movement was mechanical. He sat in the driver's seat for a few surreal moments, wondering what Tina was thinking. He engaged the ignition. Did she move? No. It was wishful thinking. As he pulled away, he tried desperately and succeeded momentarily to resist watching her from his rearview mirror. At the end of the block, he gave a quick look. She was still standing in place. Mac wondered if he should have stuck to the rules of Player 101. Sometimes it's hard not to give a fuck.

A Trip

Virgil King woke up at six a.m. every Saturday morning without fail. Nor clock. His eyes would peel open slowly as light asserted itself, and a troubled smile would appear as a subtle slice across an otherwise inert face. He would not rise immediately but find one of his strewn pillows and hold it tightly, imagining a girlfriend. Or even an ex-girlfriend. The point was always to imagine someone there willing, needing to be hugged. It had been over a year since a real person was a stand-in for the pillow and this morning, he was extra loving with his goose down. Saturday was his secret special day.

It was an early October morning in Los Angeles and the advent of fall had lied again. He unembraced the pillow and consulted his phone to see it was sixty-nine degrees on its way to eighty-four later in the day. Perfect. Coffee, and of course, the first song. Bounding out of bed, his entire being was now unfolded into a person. As soon as he reached the kitchen two rooms away, he pressed the random button on his technified stereo and waited for its musical instruction. This was his moment, the beginning of the ritual. It only took two bars to recognize the song, and Virgil was caked with goosebumps as he prepared his breakfast.

Steely Dan's "Deacon Blues" played while he made his coffee and toast. He spread almond butter and honey rhythmically on his toast and drifted. Yes, he thought, call me Deacon Blues, though it was a bit early in the day to be blue. He remembered the first time he'd heard the song. He was somewhere around seventeen, too young to have experienced anything remotely warranting sadness of any depth, but there he was locked in its power, feeling a melancholy so profound it was too beautiful not to acknowledge. Then, as now, he was transported by words he understood and a saxophone line that shot through him, leaving him short of breath. What to make of this now, though? What instruction for the day? He didn't have to answer immediately. His ritual was regulated, but broad in terms of specifics. Throughout any given Saturday, the random song he played had to influence his actions until he opted for the next song. This would last until the end of day, sunset. A nod to his romantic nature. The response to each song could be as simple as spending quality time with a memory or two, or as complicated as committing a serious breach of character on behalf of its musical feeling. It was not without its element of danger, as he had become aware in the two weeks since he began.

How this behavior came about was rather prosaic. There was no poetic life revelation, no come-to-Jesus or Satan moment, no desire for a life change per se. Virgil simply wanted to shake things up a little bit and found the profusion of narcissistic offerings over the internet too soul demoralizing. He tried dating sites with a mind to enlarge the overly familiar dating experience, and thereby life's intimacies, but abandoned those sites. Let's just say the resumés and photos were far from accurate This new venture into the melodic came about one day while sitting in a bar drinking absinthe. Whatever playlist this place had, every song deeply affected him and put him in the crosshairs of his own life. He couldn't shake the idea that music left a residual effect, one which he was probably wasting entirely. Virgil decided to invest in that feeling. To be completely conscious of music. To be a true acolyte of song. To follow the muse, as it were. To live ... musically. Finally, why the fuck not? The world seemed to be anything but musical at present. What's to lose?

He was now in the shower, smiling. Alabama was called the Crimson Tide". Virgil was a sports fan who hated the University of Alabama, as Alabama always won. The song is clearly for the underdog. He came to the realization that was the point. When he dried off, he needed to get on his bike and ride. It would all sort itself out one way or another cyclically.

Virgil rode up to a music shop where he stopped to look at the profusion of hanging guitars in the window. It reminded him of a similar shop in Paris named Orpheus, after the ancient Greek musician and poet. The shop in Paris was on a short but lovely street which traversed Pont Louis-Philippe, leading onto the Île Saint-Louis. It had a large picture window showcasing a cluster of instruments, more recognizable to Mozart than to any present-day passerby. Virgil did recognize a harpsichord. It was magnificent. The dozens and dozens of times he passed it on his daily route, there were few times he wouldn't stop to revere these musical artworks. Having traveled to Paris the previous year, he'd been visibly shaken to see the shop, after decades of existence, had been replaced by yet another high end but unimaginative stationery store. The other thought that came careening from his past was about the guitar his mother had bought him at great sacrifice. He was eleven and undergoing his first attempt at learning to play an instrument. He took guitar lessons from a Japanese man, Larry Ida, once a week. Virgil lacked discipline, and a year after its purchase, his guitar sat against the wall, a burnished dust collector. In Deacon Blues, the song talks about learning how to play the saxophone ... and drink scotch whiskey all night long. That sounded about right to Virgil in that moment. His last musing was how his teacher taught him to remember the notes for the guitar strings: EADGBE ... Every Ant Digs Great Big Elephants.

Satisfied with the homage and attention paid to Deacon's Blues, it was time for another song. Virgil jumped into the bike lane, barely missing an opening car door, put his earphones on, and pushed a button. He was transported instantly to a dusty football stadium and, an outdoor concert. It was a hot summer day and he and his two friends, Pete and Mickey, were traversing the crowded field of attendees furtively passing a joint amongst themselves. He smiled at the memory that one could buy a four-finger lid of marijuana for ten dollars and share several joints without needing medical assistance. The boys were pleasantly elevated and happy, happy, happy when the band took the stage. As War opened with its most popular song, "All Day Music," the young Virgil was thrown into a moment of youthful splendor. His world was pleasantly being deconstructed. He felt his neck roasting in the sun. His body was light, empty. He became a conduit to the universe. The Vietnam War faded into memory. He and his friends were of draft age, but that hadn't mattered. They were invincible and tied into something far more rapturous. The title of the song was not lost on them. It was exactly what they imagined a life should be ... all day music. They moved with the melody; beatific smiles plastered on these three musketeers as they unconsciously expressed rare gratitude for being alive. As all three of them shared this moment, they searched one another's faces for approbation. Pete was first to speak.

"Dynamite like a laser beam." They both turned to Pete. These were the nonsensical outbursts Pete could contribute without provocation. Of the three, he was the most untethered, socially. Mickey liked Pete, though he often got on Mickey's nerves. Like when Pete made comments like, dynamite like a laser beam. Mickey turned to Virgil and simply said …

"Your friend, Petey …" They laughed uncontrollably at nothing and everything.

The song played on, the perfect backdrop to the pageant of young girls scattered everywhere, abundant in their abundance. It was a time of diverse self-expression and sexual liberation, which distinguishes itself from today in that innocence remained achievable. Even the three boys' rabid expressions were attenuated by the fact that given the opportunity, their physical actions, would have been tame. It was all in the appreciation of proximity.

Virgil remembered Mona Triss, a spectacular example of God's aesthetic. Mona defied practical description. Her excellence could only be honored in metaphor. She helped decorate the world. Her presence was a public service. Virgil could remember what she wore on that steamy sunny day. Jean shorts cut high enough to invoke a stop gap in a fellow's existence. He once spoke at length with her, Virgil did. He remembered being embarrassed, wondering if she could tell his toes were curled up in pain the entire conversation. This was a memory of a girl he saw briefly a few times in his life. She would be close to fifty by now. This concert was also singular for being the first time Virgil could access true presence. He found himself standing inside the music. He felt the glory of the sun. He felt intense friendship. All of this happened in a moment where he experienced the balance of his youth while still enjoying it. Perhaps more importantly, he realized life was often accompanied by a soundtrack.

The bike ride had produced a powerful thirst in Virgil. He stopped to get a beer and savor that familiar flavor of hops, which invoked a connection between then and now. Standing outside at one of the makeshift COVID bars, he sipped his ale slowly, not wanting to disturb his present vibe. It was painfully pure. Suddenly, he was saddened. Virgil could no longer recall his friend Mickey's face. He'd heard recently that Mickey had gone away. He had passed. It wasn't verified, but Virgil believed it was true and as such, it was hard to reconcile. He began considering mortality, something only worthwhile when it provides perspective ... life is precious, get on with it merrily. He knew it was time for another song but was reticent to push the play button. The last thing he wanted to hear at this moment was some sad song to hurl him into a disturbing reflection or a troubling acknowledgment of wasted opportunity. He wanted charm and laughter. His normal disposition was, in fact, deeply rooted in life's merriment. His improvisation skills were shit in sadness but give him the possibility of cheer and he could generate a giggle in a demon.

There was a woman across from him nursing some complicated concoction favored by the new class of bartenders—many liquors and herbs and flavors to go along with a price upwards of twenty dollars.

"What is that? You're drinking?" He wanted to keep his inquiry simple and devoid of misunderstanding. She allowed him a lovely smile, which seemed equal parts sadness.

"I ... forgot what he called it. Heaven something. It's nice. There's rum in it. What are you listening to? I was watching your face change back and forth. A favorite song?"

Now Virgil returned her lovely, sad smile. He was momentarily lost in her eyes and thought she could be the prototype for the Isley Brothers song, "Brown Eyed Girl." Virgil spoke, uncensored vulnerability tumbled out of his mouth.

"When you listen to music, what do you think happens to you? I mean songs that, you know, move you a lot. Like songs you will always listen to because they ... you know ..."

He stopped. Brown Eyed Girl's eyes widened, fully dilated, her head turned to one side. The alchemy of a woman looking at him in that way, an impenetrable response to his seemingly innocuous question, gave Virgil pause. He tried to hang in there as she remained fixed in her expression. He wondered if she thought him deranged for asking a question not normally posed by a stranger. Why would anyone invade a place so private without an appropriate introduction? Perhaps she was right. Virgil would never find out, as she pulled out her cell to retrieve a call and he was no longer on her radar. At least he was familiar with that action.

His glass as empty as his current expectations, he was fortified for whatever musical interlude was to follow. Virgil paid the bill and left, but not before observing Brown Eyed Girl a last time. Yes, she likely figured him a candidate for madness.

Virgil was now near the Expo line on the presently useful Metro train. He decided to hop on it with his bike and get off at the beach, the last stop being downtown Santa Monica. He was in luck. He found a seat near the door where he could sit comfortably and keep one hand on his bike. Music would have to wait. The LA Metro necessitated focus. He seldom took the train, finding it a bit minacious. It was not only public transport, it was also a rendezvous point for criminals of the unimaginable type. Being well-traveled and dependent on mass transit in a variety of countries and languages, the LA Metro Line was the one he felt held the most occasion for menace. When he began taking it in its advent, there was no security to speak of. The first time he used it, he was assaulted quietly by a fragrant four-hundred-pound man whispering in his ear from the seat behind. The second time, he was followed by what he assumed was a criminally insane person of unknown gender through four cars. Four cars, because Virgil kept changing them in an unsuccessful effort to land in one with a security officer. Virgil ended up shouting and pulling out his Swiss Army knife, which ultimately had the desired effect. He avoided taking the train for a couple of years after that stretch but used it occasionally only out of absolute necessity.

Traveling from the westside to the eastside or vice versa during rush hour, the train couldn't be beat. Still, felons remained particularly attracted to it. It was like a human Whole Foods to them. A variety of organic produce, ripe for the picking. That much had not changed. A man directly opposite him seemed overly involved with his nose and its prodigious contents, which he pulled out often to inspect. There was also a smiling woman humming the theme song from something like Nightmare on Elm Street.

It was moments like these that rendered Virgil abysmally forlorn. He couldn't contemplate how the world could continue with so many living outside the paradigm of humanity, or was that all humanity was? Layer after human layer of the inexplicable. As he sometimes reduced life to a musical metaphor, he found much of humanity rhythm-filled but bereft of melody. We were all a discordant community held together by a default minor chord. An excremental symphony in which everyone had a solo. He counted down the stops—twelve more to go. The train was now so full he had to abandon his seat. His hands were resting on his handlebars when he noticed someone else's hand fondling his bicycle seat less than a foot away. Ten more stops. He noticed something else. Somehow, there was always someone of interest floating in this sea of reprobates. A striking Asian woman stood nearby. She was conspicuous in attire, wearing a short jacket with colors so vibrant they seemed alive. The liveliness of her chosen color palette made Virgil smile in appreciation. The woman, however, was unsmiling, preoccupied with the strangers crowded around her. Virgil could sense the anguish buried beneath all her splendor and noticed how focused women can be when they want to disappear. He felt confident he could observe her freely as she was clearly no longer there. Virgil's sister once explained it as 'going to her safe place.' Suddenly, the woman caught him in her gaze. There was so much more and less than he could accommodate in her scrutiny. It was the look of a sniper who sits locked in their own private lacuna until the decisive moment. They finally arrived at the terminal. Santa Monica Beach.

Exiting the train was not unlike unruly livestock abandoning freight: nose to ass disembarkment, pushing and shoving into the light and fresh air; the usual busy weekend at the beach. Virgil engaged his music. He was in need of something to cut into this jagged reality. It was time to slip into a parallel universe, or at least feel that less dementia existed in his fellow man. There was a slight lag preceding the music, which amped up his anxiety. Whatever the song was going to be, he would fully submit. The crowd moved like a gust of locusts in the direction of the beach. Virgil leisurely rode his bike in the opposite direction into the city. He would traverse the neighborhoods before entertaining the weekend mosh pit of a beach. No Third Street Promenade for him—he wanted streets where people lived, not a mall with endless commercial offerings. He rode up Colorado and turned north on one of the higher-numbered streets. It was a good choice. He ended up on an avenue (it was too grand to be labeled a street) lined with giant Ficus and Magnolia trees. But where was the music? He pulled over to consult his source and realized he'd accidentally pushed pause. He took that, and almost everything else on this Saturday, as a sign. Stop. Look around at your environment. Take it in for what it is, because it is everything. Now proceed. He engaged his music once more.

A musical electronic line pulsated unevenly, resembling a Moog or an enhanced keyboard. It was pleasantly spooky and appropriate to the canopy of leaves hovering above. Their colors deepened as a high-hat announced the drums in a rhythm which spoke directly to movement. He bobbed his head, and realizing the artist's name was Ultra Naté, produced a sly smile. Music's main power is that it produces the ineffable. Far beyond the powers of description, music lands breathtaking contact with sensation. Virgil was gliding powerfully. He was now two people in separate worlds. One part of him was on his bike, fabricating wind and visualizing random thoughts. The other part was experiencing pure wonder at the feeling of it all. He did not, nor could he reconcile the two. It was momentary, but what a moment. As he came out of this welcome cloud, he recalled the song in its entirety. "Twisted" was the story of a woman lamenting over being hopelessly in love. Twisted. How could he pay homage to this tune? He was certainly not in that state personally. It had been some time since he had been twisted in love, and he was not looking forward to its reappearance. Today was a glorious day. He was riding down a street lined with houses he wished he could inhabit. Revisiting a troubled heart was wholly counterproductive, besides being no fun at all. Music plays by its own rules and the rule of his special Saturday was that he couldn't change the rules. He had to make something out of it, or what was the point?

He changed gears. A woman appeared at the top of the road with her dog. Virgil stopped to let her cross, making something dramatic of the effort. Obviously, it was not dramatic enough, as the woman failed to acknowledge him. He watched her until she landed safely across the street. The song was now deep into the love lyrics. Ultra Naté was singing about her inability to get this guy out of her mind. Against all his wishes, Virgil helplessly reminisced about a similar situation. He hadn't thought about this woman in some time, and the feelings he had for her still disallowed him from saying her name. Or even thinking it. He opened himself up and began to emote freely about the time two years ago when he fell for the wrong person. It was a relationship he could neither resolve nor bring into a present state of harmony logically. It was in fact when he realized looking for logic in love was incompatible with happiness. They loved each other. They even liked one another. There was much they shared along with a healthy portion of discord, just enough to keep the bond fiery. Still, it didn't manifest itself in anything other than an uncomfortable conclusion. He remembered sharing his story with a friend who recounted a tale of his own. His friend's story made Virgil's grumblings seem an innocuous paragraph in a thousand-page novel. It provided Virgil with needed context, but not an ounce of relief. And so, he got over it the way most people get over heartbreak, with labored movement and residual drama appearing periodically. The song ended. Thank God. And it began so promising ...

As he continued his visit through the community of the entitled he longed to be a part of, Virgil recalled a visit by a friend from France. Virgil took him on a walking tour of these neighborhoods. His friend, Jules, remarked on how wealthy the people must be to live there. Not being judgmental, but something other than appreciation was implied. They were walking through the lower Brentwood area, before the houses became chateaux.

Jules walked in silence and purpose for some time until he remarked with obvious pain, "You should move to France. You don't belong here." Virgil convulsed with laughter.

Reassessing heartbreak was one of Virgil's least favorite activities. He couldn't see the point. Nothing helpful ever came from it. If he was being honest, he was not often its victim. If he was being completely honest, he would have to admit to being its instigator on more than one occasion. This was probably why he had been single for some time.

That and the difficulty he found in locating someone with whom he would miss if they were no longer there. He was a romantic and believed comprehensively that love should not be composed of effort. Difficulty, yes. But getting out of bed on a sleepy morning is difficult. That said, the difficulty of unwillingly rising from bed never interrupts the habit or makes one question the action. A relationship which always requires effort, Virgil felt, was more job-like than kinship.

He had now ridden north to San Vicente, where the homes became Napoleonic in opulence. He decided not to play any music. The obvious soundtrack to this leg of the trip should be opera with an over-the-top aria. Nothing less would do justice here. There was no opera on his playlist. Something he needed to correct. Even the massive old-growth trees were operatic. Suddenly, nature began to irritate him. Normally a lover of trees, especially those which looked positively prehistoric, he viewed these as slightly complicit in this embarrassment of wealth—this ludicrous show of well-being. The trees seemed to validate it by default. This dramatic excess truly bothered him because it fired his entire being with the desire to live there, followed by guilt for having this desire. Yes, he wanted to live there, or there, or there, and he viewed these mini forests accusatorially. The trees supported these rich fucks with all their magnificence. Their shade. Their roots exposed like legs of calcified mammoths, their voluptuous leaf-covered arms stretched in power and dignity, and for what? To validate the success of a robber baron who had appropriated from others in direct proportion to his wealth. In his unexpected anger, he stopped, straddling his bike in front of one of those stately affairs with an acre of green before the front door could be breached. What was happening? Was he getting an erection? Is this what certain women feel in the presence of the unlimited power of money? Of means? The literal coinage of desire. As he reached for his music, a brown man who would have been mistaken for a homeless person, if without his gardening tools appeared. The man saw Virgil and smiled briefly. It was the exact counterbalance Virgil required. The gardener began attending to the massive roots in what appeared to be a gentle massaging of the tree's antediluvian skin. Somehow this action was the antidote to all Virgil's anxiety. The gardener belonged. More than the house or the ornate brick wall that shot out from the sides of this fortress. This lone gardener seemed organic to the portrait. Symbiotic. Instantly, all became well with the world. Virgil pressed play

Jazz. Well, okay, Virgil thought. No lyrics to confuse or interrupt the vibe, he could interpret at will. He remembered neither the song nor the artist and wondered why he had added this to the playlist. He decided to listen before consulting the who and what of his selection. It was trumpet-based, the instrument some say is closest to the human voice. It was music to languish in, buoyant then receding. Jazz has that special flavor. It changes directions at will. The freedom of jazz itself was always a beautiful mystery to Virgil. It required close listening but not necessarily comprehension. A friend of his explained this succinctly when, after a concert, a man came up to this musician friend and made the unasked-for declaration, "You jazz guys. You have so much freedom."

To which the saxophonist replied, "There's no freedom in freedom. There's only freedom in structure."

Virgil consulted his playlist. The song was performed by Theo Crocker, a musician whom Virgil had recently discovered. By jazz standards, it was a truncated tune and was almost completed by the time he discovered its title: "Subconscious Flirtations and Titillations." He repeated the title aloud several times, and not simply because the suffixes felt good in his mouth. Subconscious flirtations and titillations were part of his habitual existence. He knew right then and there he would need to leave these tree-filled, empty streets and join the madding crowd. He turned up Montana Avenue, locked his bike to a parking meter out of spite, and continued on foot.

Montana Avenue is a richly middle-class street wholly bereft of a homeless population, a precise reflection of California living for those who can. And on Montana Avenue there were obvious objects of flirtation and titillation. Boutiques, restaurants, and women, a solid trifecta capable of launching his subconscious into overdrive. He found a bench. Virgil was practiced in the art of people watching. Rule number one, remain stationary as opposed to joining the throng, as eventually everyone will pass you by. People watching was a definitively static sport. He didn't have to wait long. A redhead was unsuccessfully maneuvering some shopping bags and showing a keen sense of inability to carry more than one thing at a time. That she was a redhead, Virgil took as a sign he identified as luck. In his personal experience, redheads were not only rare but also famously sensual when given the opportunity. He felt comfortable exploiting stereotypes as he was subject to so many of them himself. He had earned the right. Virgil rose gallantly to her aid. He didn't inquire or hesitate, but he adjusted her and her bags like a social chiropractor. She silently thanked him and proceeded on, no doubt to extend her purchasing power. He admired her retreat and imagined her naked appearance in his bed. A redhead, in bed, well fed, he said. She brought out the Dr. Seuss in him. Subconscious and facile. Jazz, in the key of life minor.

A parking meter attendant was ticketing a car at the very meter where Virgil's bike was attached. Virgil approached, then decided to wait on the bench for the attendant to move. The attendant seemed aware of Virgil but did not appear to be in the moving vein. He was punching in the coordinates on his mini machine of billing, from time to time looking up at Virgil, expressionless. A bus approached and filled the air with angry noise molecules, followed by a motorcycle with an adulterated exhaust system, followed by a door slamming and concluding with the annoying yelp of a nearby canine. None of this was lost on Virgil. If ever there was a soundscape for imminent violence, he was experiencing it then. The energy between the parking meter guy and Virgil was passively charged. Never had a parking ticket taken so long to register. The word, asshole, in all its aggressiveness, was forming in the back of his throat. More precisely, it was This asshole. Virgil began hearing whacking and thwacking, visualizing these words in color like in the old Batman series. Kapow! The parking attendant finally placed the ticket on the windshield, ambling away to his double-parked kiddie car. He then drove away, the new sheriff in town. The high whine from his car also registered badly with Virgil. That moment could have become a ferocious storm of consequences had the current song been something from, say, Megadeth. This being the reason why he seldom downloaded any music too warlike. That, and he had little interest in Megadeth. He could not help but acknowledge the concurrence of violent emotions and machines. He threw a nod to the completely unverifiable idea that most violent influences come from the sound of man-made objects. Whereas nature, even in its most dramatically aggressive state, can produce surprise and wonder.

There was still much to gain from this environment as very real music was now emanating from life. An elderly man appeared on the bench, sitting next to Virgil and bringing with him his own soundtrack. The man's breathing was heavy and phlegmatic. When he rubbed his hands together, the sandpaper tones of dry skin meeting dry skin sounded. The man pulled down his COVID mask to expectorate. He hawked up a good one and let it fly with surprising force and stunted musicality. This action also produced a resounding fart and Virgil imagined him following up with a burp to achieve a hat-trick. Alas he had no such luck witnessing an even more impressive display of public bodily functions. The old man seemed simply exhausted by it all. He pulled his mask up and finally turned his watery eyes to acknowledge Virgil. Virgil always had a soft spot for the elderly and for babies. For selfish reasons, he made sure they were both in his personal orbit. He could extract wisdom from one and rekindle naiveté and presence from the other. COVID had hardened that resolve. He knew that the poor and non-whites were to be last on the list of COVID relief. That was America. What shocked him thoroughly was the way even the white elderly were not prioritized with regard to relief or protection. It was the same 'let them die' mentality usually reserved for poor dark people. If they were going to play Darwin with even their own people, hope in humanity was going to be hard to manage.

Virgil and the old man were locked upon one another in silence, neither one turning away, Virgil admittedly less comfortable than his counterpart.

"What type of music are you listening to?" the man inquired, his voice strong and unapologetic. Virgil launched into his entire back story. He explained how he wanted to get closer to music, to perhaps get inside of music and see how that would influence his actions, his thoughts, maybe his life. The old man listened patiently with no change of expression other than the occasional quick intake of breath. Virgil often engaged in conversation with elderly strangers. There was always much to be gained from them by way of knowledge and experience. He also related to and was conversant with a certain element of loneliness, which is a common affair for them. Talking with others reminded them they were still alive and remained possessed of vibrancy. Virgil's grandmother was pushing ninety and there was nothing she liked better than to be lodged in a room full of conversationalists.

After hearing what to Virgil was a hapless presentation of his musical odyssey, the man turned away in thought before responding, "That's some strategy you got there." There was an elongated pause. "And all that did was bring you here to this bench in Santa Monica?" He took in the general area before continuing, "Music is a lot like a woman ... beautiful but ... all those layers. You got to be careful not to get too lost in the melody. You can only listen to the same song so many times before everything goes south. I married four times. Almost five, but I realized somethin' or other. Same song, ya see? You married?"

"No."

"Cuz it all ends, you know? I had some beauties, and I had a few ducks too. It's all the same. Unless you marry a fat girl. Probably the most easygoing of em all. That one loved me the most. That's for sure." He paused to reminisce. He then proceeded in many directions. "I'm partial to piano music. What do they say ... tickling the ivories. Women change everything but themselves. I don't know, maybe if I was born liking the fellas, it would have been less difficult. But that's still a little disgusting for me to even think about. I'm old, so I can say that. If that's your preference, no offense. Nothing against it. None of my business where a man sticks his business."

A car pulled up and stopped in front of the bench with the motor running. The window rolled down and a young Latina woman smiled at the old man politely.

The man turned to Virgil before rising. "The secret is never to give everything. Never. Cuz then you got nothin left for yourself ... and listen to piano music. It tells the most truth." He got into the car. The wind had picked up and brought a Santa Ana warmth with it. The parking meter man rode by once more, this time glaring at Virgil. What was his problem? It was unnerving to go from this sweetly wise old man to an angry purveyor of parking tickets. So many movies are going on at the same time. Life's nuances sometimes are not so nuanced. Virgil was aware he was now grounded in his own universe. His entire life was in improvisational mode. He started walking with the crowd.

A whistling wind played forcefully in the background before it abruptly changed to something more open-mouthed and violent. This was compelling music. He marched fearlessly into the gust, feeling a sudden sense of joy. For no reason, he allowed a stupidly wide grin to fix his face. Those who passed seemed mindful of his presence. This was a feeling similar to when a hallucinogen was being absorbed in his system, a sudden subtraction and then an addition to his reality appeared without preamble. He lost his sense of gravity while deeply feeling every step taken. He was now peopled. Snatches of conversations were appearing and disappearing in small boxes. Thoughts occurred. All things could be explained. Anything could be explained. No. No. No. That's not right. All things are spatial if not special. What? What? What nonsense was he deliberating at this moment? He didn't care. He knew whatever state he was in wouldn't last and he was determined to make the fucking best of it. He chose to free-fall. Virgil saw a woman walking a dog and wondered if there were ever any dinosaurs that could have been suitable as pets? If so, they would have probably been hairless. Virgil was far from hairless. He possessed a thick basket of curls on his head. Hair was very important to him, but then he wasn't a dinosaur. There were more people now and he was effortlessly vigilant. He was clear, acknowledging the great deal of life surrounding him. A life observed. His hair launched in the wind, and for a moment, he imagined he was wearing a wig and touched it for comfort.

This is great. Life is spectacular. A woman told him recently that his love was king. How can you not feel good about that, even though she mentioned it as she was leaving him for another king. The consolation prize. He thought of the old man. He fantasized the man was playing the piano, his Latina assistant singing something torchy, drinking mescal in a room draped in paintings of naufrages, shipwrecks. This made sense. He had recently been to an exhibition of masters' painting shipwrecks and wild seas. In retrospect, Virgil felt gratitude for being capable of putting himself deeply into the life of a painting. Museums were his fetish and his most comfortable room. There was never a need for music in a museum. A museum was visual music. While at the shipwreck exhibition, he experienced the rocky waves. He inhaled salt ocean. He heard the screams slice the air as people abandoned ship. All this motivated from glops of oil on a canvas. Maybe museums made him high. He certainly felt high right now. He had recently read that peyote has been used for almost six thousand years by Native Americans in Mexico. But Virgil hadn't taken any peyote. He had somehow reached a natural high.

A woman stood with him on the corner, waiting for a traffic light to turn. She had one of those Rolls Royce perambulators. It had its convertible top open wide despite the wind. Virgil openly studied its occupant. This baby was of interest because it had that tortoise gene. It was born old-looking. It already appeared to have had a difficult life. The light turned green, and no one moved. The mother seemed to be awaiting a compliment or at least an acknowledgment of the miracle she had produced. The smile which remained fixed on Virgil did not satisfy her.

"Eat shit. Eat very much shit. You got that?" Two young men in almost-suits were smoking and insulting one another directly behind him. When they passed, a wave of smoke perfumed the air with a lovely staleness. Virgil was an ex-smoker who still cheated when necessary. An ex-smoker can never be neutral about being around cigarettes, like an ex-alcoholic can never be neutral in the presence of liquor. He savored the fumes left in their wake. Lovely, that. For Virgil, a cup of coffee and a cigarette in the morning was the second greatest break of day activity, second only to sex. He felt obligated to mutter to no one in particular ... "I'll tell you who got it right ... cigarette companies. You never hear about anyone returning a pack of cigarettes, do you?" Now he wanted a cigarette. Apparently, he was slowly abandoning his natural high. He checked the time on his phone. Yes, he was definitely losing this marvelous feeling. When one is high, there is no such thing as time. That is one of the chief attractions of being in that magical state. Time disappears and responsibility becomes relative. There is nowhere to be because you are already there. Now he was wondering where he should go next. He was wondering if he should play another song. This was a different kind of wonder he was accessing. A wonder bereft of wonder. He stopped abruptly and tried to manifest enough presence to be taken once more into the dimension of sound. To be serenaded by the natural chorus of vitality. To hear feelingly and be transported between now and then. It simply was not to be. With momentary sadness and then gainful resolve he fingered his music selection. Whatever came next, he would cooperate with abandon. He was ready for whatever.

Shit! No, not now. What the fuck? What the fuck? Fuck! How the hell had that song been added to his playlist? It wasn't even a song. It was a poem he had written to which he had added music. Besides being horribly accompanied by a jangled melody he'd appropriated from a computer program, it was something he had written in a state of galvanized rage. He took a deep breath as he felt the words, his words, invade him to the core.

"Let's kill them all and sing a song/there's nothing left to lose." His smile vanished and was replaced with bedlam. A now ferocious wind could not frustrate his need to perspire profusely. He considered going back for his bike but questioned whether he had enough focus to navigate traffic. His neck muscles tightened, and his walk stiffened. Could others see this transformation? Would he be confronted and forced to respond? "Revenge never dies/it regenerates." Not only was it a violent poem, but it was also unmistakably bad. Why hadn't he deleted it? This one bled anger. He was embarrassed by it. Embarrassed by the exposed hatred, it released line after line. Embarrassed by the crushing language it used. "… unworthy of being called unworthy … and yet you bargain forgiveness …" He desperately wished he could laugh at this ridiculous attempt at balladry. There was no effort to follow any metrical scheme, rhyming came and went, and if there was any consistent theme, it was to show raw anger bent in every direction. A dog began barking at a nearby skateboarder. Virgil wanted to boot the dog and dropkick the skateboarder. He was tempted to snatch the leash, lassoing the dog into the street where it would violently meet with the skateboarder. Hopefully, they would continue a vicious fight to the death. He played the whole scene out in his mind, or at least he hoped it was in his mind. Virgil's smile resurfaced. Fuck it. A deal is a deal. A song is a song. Let it all play out. He no longer felt any kinship with his fellow pedestrians. He was as sickened by the obese man waddling past him as he was by the young waif wearing too much makeup. And look at this sorry sight whose head resembled a misshapen, rotted pumpkin. The sidewalks were filled with rejects, samples of human maladies, unaware of their afflictions. It was overwhelming. He needed to stop and sit. He squatted on an empty bench at a bus stop and sat with his hands folded in his lap, snakes strangling one another. He closed his eyes. The poem had ended, though the last line circled his brain. "Where your nothing becomes something in reverse." Good Lord! He was desperate to erase this entry, but officiating his playlist in any way would be a breach of gamesmanship.

"Virgil!"

A voice interrupted his reverie and opened his eyes. A friend approached. Was she a friend? He remained in a vortex of anger, though now slightly modified. He still felt breached. Virgil was disinclined to communicate. He had no idea what would come out of his mouth. Amber stood in front of him while Virgil elected to remain seated. She wore jeans and a trendy T-shirt.

"You looked like you were sleeping."

No. He was now wholly awake, but reluctant to make sense just yet. Amber was not someone who required engagement. She could carry an entire conversation by herself, which is what she did. She began recounting a great evening she had had with some mutual friends. She thought she would have run into him at the festivities, blah blah blah, but she knew sooner or later they would meet to clear the air. Amber was referring to their last meeting a year ago, when they were both naked and embroiled in an argument that superseded, then nullified the intended amorous event. They hadn't spoken since. Now here she was standing in front of him like Eve in the famous Garden, tempting him with her tree of apples. He decided he would bite. He owed it to the playlist ...amber

"I was thinking you owed me an apology, Amber. We ate a nice dinner. Paid for by me. We drank two bottles of fucking exceptional wine. Went to my place, where I gave you a full body massage and read poetry to you. We kissed like rabid minks. You tore my clothes off me and then proceeded to take issue with a comment I made a week prior. You took fucking issue with me wanting to hold Obama accountable for some of the bullshit that he was responsible for. I mean who gives a shit? Obama certainly doesn't. He's making millions on the lecture circuit and is a saint in the public eye. I don't even remember how or why ... I certainly didn't bring that shit up. Then you just left me, with two hundred dollars credited to my visa card. And for what? For Obama? You owe me an apology.

That is what he wanted to say. What he said was ...

"You look great. It's been a while, and I can't say I was happy with our last meeting. Probably my fault. Sometimes things get twisted. It happens like that with texts, and I guess it can happen when you're literally naked and vulnerable in bed. I wrote a poem about it, which I think you might like. Anyway, I'm sorry, Amber. I think about you a lot."

Virgil had not written a poem about that night, though he would be happy to do so if it would gain him entry. He thought of a song fitting this situation, "Give Me Just a Little More Time" by The Chairmen of the Board. When Amber told him they had missed their chance, the song became Carol King's "It's Too Late." Two miserable '70s songs was the only music that came to mind. She walked away talking into her phone. The wind died down.

This was his third Saturday following the playlist. The first attempt produced mostly smiles and recollections of past grievances or loves. (The experiment was fully embryonic; nothing real was at stake.) He was intimately experiencing random music yet failing to ignite any profound response. It made him wistful. It was fun. It was new. That was about it. Last Saturday was his second go-around. Most of the music which came up on that day was current hip hop. The only thing he felt motivated to do with any honesty was to get off his bike and dance full out, wherever he happened to be. It was a little more daring, and though dancing just off a freeway entrance certainly attracted an audience, there was no noticeable change in his persona, no providential clues of where he might be heading. He wondered if this idea was taking him anywhere. He did almost get his ass beaten after verbally appreciating a woman, but in responding to rap, that was to be expected.

Today was different. The music played Virgil as much as it played itself. He had to acknowledge something he'd always suspected; music was not only the superior sound source, but its most influential. It had power enough to alter his personal dynamic with a key change. A chordal progression could touch upon some hidden love. Any given melody might excite a moment of déjà vu visceral enough to make him feel deep sadness for its passing or lend an unequaled elation for having had the experience. Ultimately, he had arrived at a more profound sense of confusion. That he expected some comprehensive understanding of this experience was only natural. He had put in time and energy that could have gone into something else. What that something else was he wasn't sure of. In backtracking, this effort was merely to offset the daily data that poured out of life like an open fire hydrant. He had been flooded with information and opinions and images in all parts of his waking life. Everyone had. The entire consciousness of the world was floating on a virtual sea. The avalanche of material and metadata was changing who we were without anyone seeming to notice or care. Virgil noticed. Virgil cared. Virgil also felt the same impotence everyone else felt. Whatever he did would be ineffectual against this leviathan called progress. So, Virgil turned to music. His drug of choice. And here he was, close to end of day, back on his bike, navigating the literal winds of change.

He rode leisurely to the beach. Still no music. He was thoroughly exhausted by its portents. The ocean provided its own song. A supreme composition of movement, relentlessly punctuated by crashing cymbals. It was music without repetition even though it lived on replay. Every wave will be different. It will vary in pitch and length and volume. Every time the signature was temporary. Beneath its surface, a grand invisible orchestra secretly conducted this symphony. Themes will collide, scores will be constantly written and rewritten by what lies unseen beneath. It's music which can be savored but never fathomed. This is what Virgil pined for—a rendering of his soul in the face of undeniable beauty. The ocean was not only self-referential, but it also represented humans in the most positive light. It was a record of time itself and a gift to the imagination. It was the original source of man, and it hasn't changed since belching us out of its watery cavity eons ago. It was why, for most of his life, he chose to live near water.

He rode up on his bike and spied the sea from a timbered bluff, away from human distraction. Close enough to smell. Loud enough to hear. The sea was doing its chameleon thing as the sun touched the waters, staining it in different hues. He left his bike unlocked on the ground and stood on the edge of the bluff.

As he looked down over the cliff, he saw a new ocean and a sea of people and lives lived and dogs pissing on trash cans he saw lit candles on dinner tables and balloons rising and darkness hiding in a lighted tunnel and open letters waiting to be read he saw fires burning in a forest of ancient trees and naked bodies twisted in love and beatings of old men for the wrong reasons and women hanging out wet clothes in damp weather and he saw roads being built and children running to school and the stained glass windows of cathedrals and rivers flowing he saw a woman crying on a bus and a man laughing at himself while holding his belly and money exchanging gloved hands he saw someone wearing headphones dancing. He saw a plastic bag circling in the wind and a pregnant girl stretching nearby he saw colors and shapes and began to see sounds though he couldn't be sure. He saw words mutating and he saw his life unwinding as he drifted closer and closer to the ground. And when he landed, when he landed, when he landed, there was no music. There was no sound. There was one last thought.

This didn't hurt at all.

Naked

He was someplace unfamiliar. Clearly, he had slept well. Well enough to lose any cognitive attachment and any ability to identify the who, what, where, when, and why of his present situation. This was not quite true. He did know who he was. He was Lionel Madison. What he was doing in this queen-sized bed with powder blue sheets—he couldn't say. He gathered himself up on his elbows, surprisingly calm given the circumstances. It was a strange bedroom, and, for no discernible reason, he was slightly relieved that he wasn't in a hotel room. Or dead. In that instant, he heard footsteps that he felt sure would provide some much-needed clarity. His attention moved to the door just as it opened.

"No!" Did he shout this, or was it simply his body screaming in defense? The duvet flew off and his naked body stared back at the man standing in the doorway holding two cups of coffee.

"Creams bad. I gave you one sugar," the stranger announced with a familiarity which failed miserably to console Lionel. The man sat on the bed and handed Lionel the coffee.

"It's hot."

Reflexively, and without covering himself, Lionel took the cup, immediately spilling part of its contents just north of his frightened manhood. He pulled the duvet up to his chest as the stranger calmly retrieved the cup. The man rose and left the room. Lionel, quietly yelping, inspected his burn. It was welting and red and mitigated an immediate search for his clothing.

He checked his surroundings. Mid-morning light streamed through the sheer curtains, providing a view of a spacious, minimally adorned room and a floor bereft of clothing. Nice place. Totally unfamiliar, but nice. Lionel rose quickly from the bed to further investigate. The closet was filled mercifully with women's clothes. Good news. Or not. Perhaps Lionel was dealing with a cross-dresser. He took the duvet from the bed and wrapped himself in it, resembling, he thought, some gay pasha. Options were limited. He went out the same door as the coffee man.

A hallway, with doors on either side, led to an open room in the distance. He played the safe bet and waddled straight down the hallway to what turned out to be a living room.

This person has money. The room was large enough for a grand piano, which sat in the corner, gleaming ominously in black sheen. An enormous Persian rug was the centerpiece of elegant furniture rich in fabric but poor in comfort. The backs of the couches were low slung. The ceiling was high and from its apex hung a dimmed chandelier. Lionel had seen places decorated like this in magazines—stylish abodes of the rich. A big floor-to-ceiling picture window informed him that he was near the ocean. He could see a patch of ocean through a line of trees that stood tall like pretty prison bars.

Don't go there, he thought. He asked himself the basic questions.

Who? Me.

Where? Near the ocean.

When? He saw a clock—11:45 a.m. Three out of five questions answered. It was 'the what' and 'the why' which tormented him presently. Lionel wondered if the 'what's' and the "whys' were the most important part of any equation. Strange thoughts arrive in strange circumstances. He thought briefly of the television show he saw the other night, where a forensics team sprayed a can of aerosol to detect semen stains. The room turned out to be covered in semen. A beautiful room, with beautiful furniture. A room like this one. Glowing in semen like a sixties black light room.

Lionel wandered into the kitchen just off the living room. In the middle of this chef's paradise sat an island of gray slate. Fruits, breads and condiments, butter, several jams, and a bowl of honey were professionally arranged at one end of the gray slab. A window looked out over a flower and vegetable garden. A European person. Maybe French. Definitely not English. He sat in a furiously uncomfortable highchair, still in his duvet, and ingested copiously. If this turned out badly, he might be forced to run a great distance. His body would require sustenance. He ate with vigor until he spotted a jar of dog treats next to a pot of utensils. A dog. Perhaps a dog with allergies, since his smell had not yet been detected. Perhaps the dog is out at the groomers—a nice poodle, loud but harmless. Of course, pit bulls also enjoy the odd doggie treat when not growling from the end of a steel chain.

Think like Jason Bourne. Where are the knives? He opened a drawer. Voila. That it was the first drawer he opened made him feel he was making progress, even though he had no clue as to what end he was progressing. Lionel selected a steak knife. Short, but sharp and easily concealed. *A good call.* he surmised. A few more grapes (God, they were delicious), then he'd locate coffee man.

Grasping a hold of the duvet with one hand and subtly brandishing the knife with the other, he walked back up the hallway to doors number one, two, and three. One by one, he tried them. Locked, in tandem. Panic began to rise slowly. Strangely, but not subtly, his panic manifested itself in a sudden and powerful urge to move his bowels. He moved quickly back into the bedroom. A master bedroom must come equipped with a master bath.

Sitting on a porcelain toilet, slightly relieved, Lionel studied the shower next to him. It was beveled and stained and colored, but completely diaphanous. Quite beautiful. Some people have laughable amounts of money. He tried the lock on the door, which he could reach without moving from his throne. It was functional. He flushed, rose from the toilet, and after slowly deciphering the modernist fixtures, turned on the shower. After all, if they, he, she, really wanted to stab him, they could have done so while he slept.

He was seduced momentarily by the shower. It was lovely. Where did they get that shower head? The perfect water pressure? The soap? Everything. How is this shit even possible? The rich person's water seemed to reduce the swelling of his burn, which earlier had begun to throb. As he exited and dried off with the softest towels ever pressed to his person, he remembered his cell phone was in his pants. At the same time, he heard a dog barking just outside the bathroom door.

"Hello?" This time Lionel knew it was his own voice. It was loud and still reverberating off the bathroom walls.

"Hello. Is anybody there?" The dog stopped barking. Lionel unlocked the door slowly. He took a breath, picked up his knife, and slid the door slightly open. He could see the Australian Shepherd standing in the middle of the room, a beautiful creature, white with irregular brown patches, its eyes cobalt and alert. Its tail, however, was still as a broken clock. Dog and man exchanged curious looks. Lionel opened the door a bit wider. The dog didn't move.

"Hello, baby. Ats a good boy. Yes, you're a good boy, aren't you?" The dog looked on Lionel with what seemed like disgust. Yes, it was clear the canine felt Lionel wasn't worth his energy. The shepherd rose and walked slowly out of the room. Lionel listened closely to its egress down the hall, then bolted out of the bathroom, across the bed to the bedroom door, slamming it shut.

"Fuck!" This, too, he was sure he had said because it was such a primal utterance that his throat ached immediately thereafter. Phone. He could call his cell phone and listen for it to ring and locate his pants in the process. There was a phone by the bed. He figured he could put the knife down long enough to make a phone call. He dialed and left the receiver on the bed as he picked the knife back up and listened intently for his cell phone to announce itself. After a full minute, it occurred to him how quiet the house was. It also occurred to him that neither his cell phone nor his pants were in the room.

Lionel returned to the bathroom. The mirror was still shower-steam frosted. He used a corner of the duvet to wipe clear the condensation from its face. It was then Lionel was positive he screamed. It was a long vocal exhalation that ended only because, and not until, his breath ran out. His mouth remained agape and formed a cruel O. The duvet fell to the ground as both hands rose slowly to caress his freshly shaved pate. He was not completely shaven. His otherwise clean, pink scalp was lined from ear to ear with a thin line of hair. A sideways Mohawk, if you will. He backed away from the mirror, an involuntary motion that proved unfortunate as it gave him a complete, uncensored view of his present condition. He was indisputably a naked man, sporting a thin black rainbow on his newly shaven head, with an angry red burn separating his navel from his manhood, adrift in a stranger's fancy house. He could also add that there was an overly friendly, coffee-bearing man who had disappeared somewhere in the house as thoroughly as Lionel's memory.

Lionel could acknowledge these truths. They were self-evident. He was, however, not obliged to accept them. Again, he was left with: 'What would Jason Bourne do?' By now, Jason Bourne would have killed both man and dog. He would have somehow found a girl amidst all of that closeted lingerie and would be sleeping, happily spent, following a nice bit of athletic copulation. This, of course, would have all been done with dramatic music playing in the background. The music was his least favorite part of the Bourne equation, but the moment he imagined it, piano music did indeed begin to emanate from the other side of the door. Lionel confronted the closet again, tearing through all the frilly lingerie, the lace underwear on hangers, the blouses and matching bras, the dresses which accented less than more, searching frantically for something, anything he would be able to run in. At the same time, he had begun to feel a burning sensation in his stomach. He panicked. The food. I've been poisoned. The music stopped on a crescendo that hung in the air, unrecognizable and unpleasant. He discovered a pair of lime green sweatpants and matching sweatshirt. He dressed quickly. There wasn't much to put on. It was ill-fitting, but better than rampant nudity, or a big hairy man in rich hooker attire.

He returned to the bathroom for no other reason than to delay his fate with coffee, man, biscuit dog, and perhaps the phantom of the opera pianist. The image in the mirror froze him. He looked like a fat, lime green popsicle, until you got to his head. In full view, he simply looked insane. Lionel thought that he heard the mirror laughing. This has to stop now. He looked far too ridiculous now to summon the name of

Jason Bourne. He was on his own. The good news was that his stomach discomfort had passed for the moment. It was time to act.

He opened the door and walked slowly down the hallway, striking out with the sharp end of his knife at any imagined attackers. He stabbed and stabbed and stabbed. If air could bleed, he could be sure it now was hemorrhaging. The lime green sweatsuit began to give off a sweet smell, which was a product of his rampant perspiration mixed with a woman's (he'd hoped) leftover perfume. It had been worn recently. That he was now concerned about the relative cleanliness of his getaway outfit troubled him even more. What was going on in his head? He had a few quick thoughts tumbling out of him at the same time. Had he been drugged? Did it fucking matter? Where was the door? Where was the fucking door? There it is.

As he crossed the threshold of the living room, the dog passed in front of him nonchalantly. Lionel proceeded slowly to the door, eyeballing the dog as it relieved itself mightily on the beautiful Persian rug. Lionel opened the front door. Blinding sun washed over his retinas, and then everything went black.

There was a smell of bacon. Lionel loved bacon. It was, yes, the smell of bacon that woke him out of his slumber. His eyelids parted in slow motion. Filtered light, then shapes, then colors, followed by a realization of place. Lionel recognized his bedroom. He was indeed in his bed. He was wearing the silk pajamas an old girlfriend had gifted him. She'd told him they cost three hundred dollars when she presented them. He didn't think much of it at the time. No big fucking deal. She was rich. He would have preferred the money. Now, however, these silk pajamas represented all that was good in the world. That, and the smell of bacon. He rose out of his twin bed, stretched, and went into the bathroom. Everything was just how he remembered.

Everything was the same, except for his sideways mohawk.

Love Letter from Venice

"As a rule, broken hearts are most deeply felt in the evening. The sky is dark, but no longer magnificent nor mysterious. The days are somehow manageable, but dusk fuels the worst of one's imagination. For those in love, however, evening is the defining time. The days are fine, long and languid, yet it is when darkness descends that the lover really soars."

At least that is what Caleb had scribbled in his diary while his lady slept peacefully by his side, drooling on his chest. Caleb had spent the last few days planning how to tell his girlfriend that she was all the light he desired in the Venice night. However, as he wondered at the string of saliva slowly pooling on his pec, he knew that now was not the time to share this revelation. It had been one of those nights where they were on intimacy overdrive, excavating each other's anatomical geography until they collapsed spent, happily exhausted. After a night like that, it would have been easy to pledge his undying love to this lovely naked woman. This friend and lover. This woman who would make him smile whenever she entered a room. He'd entertained the phrase, undying love. Not only did it have the faint smell of morbidity to it, but it was a term used in bad poetry and worse television shows. Forever was also a long time to consider. Forever, like death and taxes. Forever, as in untreatable cancer. This was the train of thought he followed when he imagined the length and breadth of monogamy. Far from being a player (an expression he hated), he felt monogamy was not a character trait to which one should aspire. To finalize one's options. To limit possibilities regardless of the changes in circumstances? To, in effect, make curiosity ineffectual? This made no sense. Animals didn't make this mistake except in rare cases, and who wanted to follow the example of a stiff-assed penguin when you can emulate the majesty of a lion? This inner monologue was becoming burdensome. Reconciling the emotional with the intellectual was exacting and exhausting work. Caleb needed to sleep. His lady was partially lit by a full moon leaking through the curtains. A living painting. Moments like these made forever seem doable. He observed her gently breathing and, mirroring it, slowly dissolved into a sleep.

Caleb was a waiter. He toiled three evenings a week working the tables at a distinctive restaurant taking orders from strangers, accommodating the whims of their palettes, choosing the right bottle of Burgundy for the delicate Kobe ribeye, making sure glasses were filled and the meal moved along leisurely, professionally, without ever being too chummy. Caleb never made the mistake of a silly introduction: "Hello, my name is Caleb, and I will be serving you this evening." He was clever enough to realize his customers didn't want to know about him except in so far as he would be invisibly useful in arranging their meal in comfort and without added distraction. Caleb was comfortable with this customer/waiter relationship, as he felt that a meal with someone you love is one of the most civilized and romantic pleasures attainable. Tomorrow night was his girlfriend's birthday, and having made reservations at their favorite restaurant, he hoped in twenty-four hours to be enjoying the same service he was now providing. It would be a moment of pure perfection. A long leisurely dinner, wine and dessert, lovers' conversation and the painfully pleasurable silences that only paramours who appreciate love's privilege can comprehend. And then, he would be able to tell her.

But first, he had to get through tonight. It was a busy restaurant evening. His section was filled with couples in varying degrees of involvement. As waiting tables was not often the most intellectually engaging of employment, he liked to try and figure out each couple's story to pass the time. He'd imagine how long had they been together. Is this a first date? Are they lying to one another? What hobbies did they share? Did they have sex before they arrived, or will they proceed directly to their bedroom after that crème brûlé and last sip of port? Waiting tables was his way of doing his bit for social anthropology. Seeing people in an intimate setting and observing the life that oozes out of them. As each course was served and the contents of the wine bottle diminished, he could witness an entire life unfold.

The city itself, Venice, was also a great catalyst for personal revelations. He noticed that a certain pride of place accompanies the Venice locals when they show up at their favorite restaurant. The comfort level is immediate, and since the presence of writers, poets, painters, and musicians is always high, a certain benign snobbery and feeling of human accomplishment are also present at most dinner tables. Then there were the people who drove in from Van Nuys or Hollywood or Silverlake or wherever. They come to Venice to soak up some of the local color. Easily identifiable folks and no less joyous than the locals, their gratification is, however, slightly dissimilar. They seem to be happy to come into town, partake in the company of the natives, securely observe foreign habits from a distance, and retreat. Returning to their municipalities, where they can feel like locals, too. It's how people roll in LA. They visit other enclaves but are fiercely loyal to their separate communities.

On this splendid moonlit evening with the Santa Ana winds recklessly throwing the scent of jasmine everywhere, one couple caught Caleb's attention and commanded his interest the entire night. Indeed, he was so taken by them, he didn't find the need to play amateur clairvoyant with any of his other tables. It also forced him to work harder. He had to ensure everyone else had what was needed in order to spend as much time in proximity to his duet of choice. The man and woman who captivated his attention this evening were seated in the prized window seat. A nice move. The light provided by the single candle on the table and the golden spill of the moon gave them an angelic illumination. It was a flattering light on a couple who were already blessed with an abundance of physical charm. Not merely attractive, they were interesting to view, and both of their faces were friendly maps to familiar emotions. He registered the woman's beauty initially, then focused on the man as was his way whenever he saw a woman of interest. He was always compelled to see what kind of person could make an extraordinary woman surrender. The man wore a white linen shirt, out of which emerged a lion's head and a mane of hair to match. A head that would have been considered too large for someone else, he seemed to control it effortlessly, haphazardly moving it around for emphasis while his hair followed lazily afterwards. His eyes were alert, even reading the menu, Caleb could see this was a man of action, someone who didn't just look at things; this was someone who ingested and synthesized whatever came into view. His hands were large and expressive, a trait that Caleb's own girlfriend admired very much. Seeing this man's hands, Caleb felt a momentary pang of envy. Jealousy pops up in the weirdest places. I need to work on that, Caleb realized. The woman possessed a face that demanded attention. Her nose was the first thing he noticed. It jutted out from the rest of her face in bold relief as if to say: "I am big, look at me." Her forehead was high, and perhaps a bit flat, and her eyes were two glassy scoops of chocolate sorbet, that he knew, given the appropriate bidding, could either freeze or melt. Under the ledge of her nose was an asymmetrical mouth, alarming even as her full lips tried to compensate for the distraction. A stream of jet-black hair fell over the shoulders of her wine-colored dress. Hers was a compelling physical vernacular. A crazy mess of warring symmetry. All in all, she stunned. They ordered. A salad of goat cheese and greens with pomegranate seeds. Porcini mushroom ravioli with shaved white truffles. A bottle of Gigondas. Lovely. And so, it began.

Chefs are a weird lot, part prima donna, part genius, all manual labor, but more painter than mechanic. On a night when Caleb needed tranquility in the kitchen, the chef was serving up attitude with every dish. The one thing a waiter tries to avoid is kitchen drama. Don't piss off the chef, tip your bussers generously, and make sure the food comes out hot. Simple rules that, when ignored, infect the evening with unwanted anxiety and compromise the very thing you work for—tips. The chef was French, which wasn't the problem. Caleb spoke wonderful French. He knew his wines and was no stranger to the kitchen. But the heat of the kitchen, the speed in which one was forced to operate, the stress that builds from standing on your feet, trying to keep focused on the details, can rob a chef of his logic, especially when it came to dealing with a waiter. Presently, Jean Pierre was screaming at Caleb for returning a steak to the grill. The customer asked for it to be well done and it came out a bit too rouge. Well done? It is nearly impossible for a French chef to obey this command, seeing as the French feel the best way to destroy a good piece of meat is to cook it anywhere past medium rare. Caleb apologized to Jean Pierre profusely, agreeing with him that his customer was an ignorant American pig who belonged at an In and Out, or a Sizzler. But the apology didn't take, and Caleb was to spend the rest of the evening attempting to avoid eye contact with Jean Pierre.

The moonlit couple was ready to order their second course by the time Caleb was through insufficiently placating Jean Pierre. Now came the almighty entree, where serious discussions and sensual interaction take place amid mouthfuls of gastronomy. Caleb had been monitoring the two closely between chef tantrums and customer beckoning. The couple's conversation had been sparse. All subtext. Body talk. Braille, for the sighted. He noticed she would not finger the stem of her wineglass, an action Caleb always felt suggestive of imminent desire. Instead, her hands lay folded in her lap when not attending to the silverware. Her date crossed and uncrossed his arms, leaned forward to make a point, changed his mind, then would silently fold and unfold his napkin in frustrated origami.

Rare tuna steak with a mango and avocado chutney was his order. She would like the pigeon with potato, turnip puree and petits legumes. Lovely. He placed the order and watched them secretly.

"Pick up your fucking plat, connard!" Jean Pierre shouted at Caleb, sufficiently jarring him back to reality. When Caleb delivered the entrees to his couple, the woman allowed a sad smile to pass between her and Caleb. The man remained infatuated with his napkin. Outside the window, a large palm frond scratched across the sidewalk as the winds picked up. Trees were blowing madly. Nature's invisible power was at work. Right outside their window. Did they see it? The restaurant door flew open. Some of Caleb's regulars came in, loud and gregarious, anticipating a formidable meal and their favorite waiter to entertain them. Caleb did so, leaving the couple to pick through their food. When he returned, their plates were empty and their table possessed the solemnity of two beautiful tolling bells that were somehow rendered mute.

He wanted to shout, "Stop! Stop it. Kiss. What else is there to do? Don't write your epitaph at this meal. Not at my table." What Caleb said was quite different: "Would you like some more wine?"

After a pregnant silence, the man replied, "Maybe dessert. You have sweet wines, don't you?" Ahh, there was still hope, Caleb strongly felt.

He delivered their chocolate soufflé with subtle aplomb. Two glasses of a lovely Banyuls appeared in curved miniature glasses. "On the house," Caleb announced hopefully, then returned to his friend's table. When he passed by their table sometime later, the chocolate soufflé had a spoon stuck in its very heart, chocolate oozing from its hot brown center, the whipped cream running over the side of the dish onto the tablecloth. The couple was gone. Caleb spent a moment observing the injured soufflé on the middle of the table, conspicuously ignored. The wineglasses had been emptied and only its amber residue remained. Caleb had not yet left the check, but there were two hundred-dollar bills along with a fifty, left in plain view. About ninety dollars more than the bill came to. Caleb went outside to thank them. They had vanished into the night. He went outside and spoke to the valet, who remembered them leaving in separate cars. This was simply too much.

Caleb unearthed his cell phone and dialed frantically. Time passed. He spoke haltingly, "Hello baby, I love you in ways I can't explain right now, but by tomorrow, I promise I'll find the words. I promise ... be sure to look at the moon tonight. It's everything." He emphatically pocketed his phone and gazed up at the moon. Caleb inhaled the salty air and went back inside, leaving behind the rough romantic wind, the Venice night, and the two homeless men who were privy to his phone call staring at him, smiling and smoking.

Passing Through

Stanis Powers woke up on the eve of his sixtieth birthday, disgruntled and more than slightly depressed. Even with the knowledge he was to be the fêted at a 'surprise' birthday party the next night, the only thing the occasion gave rise to was the leading edge of a panic attack. He needed coffee, and perhaps a spiritual colonoscopy. Birthdays were admittedly rare things, annual events which engender completely different feelings dependent upon what side of the ledger one is on. In childhood, they are joyous occasions where one can anticipate presents and the feeling of being unique from anyone else in the world. They are mitigated celebrations of self for a twenty-four-hour period, the likes of which will not be repeated for another three hundred and sixty-five days. The next birthday can't come soon enough. Indeed, a child would gladly sacrifice the next nearly four hundred days to repeat these festivities, if given the opportunity. So much for youth ...

On this early morning, Stanis ambled into his kitchen and began his daily and beloved process of grinding beans. Making and then ingesting a cup of strong coffee was more an act of magic than routine. There was enough sorcery in that black liquid to cause clarity. And today was clearly his last day of being in his fifties. Stanis had spent the previous week going over and over what he considered the consequences of such a momentous occurrence. Unable to arrive at any conclusion, much less some reconciliation, he settled for logic. It was normal. Everyone ages. Nothing to be done.

He glanced out the kitchen window and spied two young men running. Stanis was a runner who recently had to change to biking because of the pain in his knees after logging his few miles. He watched the two runners as they went by, laughing and moving at a quick pace. Good runners. Young runners. One day, they too will have to move on to less impactful exercise. But not today. Fuckers! He imagined lacing up his running shoes, hitting the beach, and running until he collapsed. He settled for drinking his coffee and eating a Danish.

The Gods had aligned to provide him with a beautifully sunny day, and he intended to make the most of it. This day, he would live as if he were to die on the morrow. No computer. No phone calls or texts. No car. A day of being present with the world and whatever it had to bring. An appreciation of all things real. His shower was a revelation. He stood in front of his door-sized mirror in the hallway afterwards and admired his naked form. The body of a man who had worked out his entire life looked back at him. This seemed to please him. He lay naked on his living room floor and stretched deeply for half an hour. Stanis knew if anything informed a person of where they stood in life, it was stretching. The pain, the breathing through it, and the eventual relaxation of muscles afterwards let someone know what they could and could not do. There was only truth in lying on your back and trying to put your legs over your head. It was a simple but telling maneuver he favored doing because, frankly, he could. It would take a few minutes of gentle breathing, but ever so slowly, he would arrive at the intended position, his feet touching the floor behind his head, and life was momentarily complete.

Getting dressed was an event. He wanted to appear casual, yet as always, wanted to be attractive enough to meet someone and perhaps have a life-altering exchange. Fantasies were as much of his daily life as was reality. It was in line with many of his contradictions. He was also alternately as misanthropic as he was social. Simply put, he loved and hated people in equal measure. These were the realities that made life worthwhile. Bouncing between spectrums, as whim or necessity demanded. There was freedom in extending boundaries, vacillating without judgment, allowing for improvisation dependent only upon the situation. No doubt today would be momentous. It had to be. Tomorrow, he would be sixty. How was that even possible? There it was again. Age. Three crooked, malignant letters which augured death. Okay, now he knew he was being dramatic.

Stanis settled on a white shirt to accentuate his calf-brown skin, his favorite pair of jeans, and a bright-colored vest he hadn't worn in years. Noticeable without being comical. Today, he would still be young.

Stanis had lived at or by the beach for most of his life. It wasn't planned. Like many things, it simply came to be and now it was precedent. As he walked out of his apartment into the bright sun, a cool April wind ignited him. He was a memory man. The slightest occurrence, smell, or feeling would take him to another time and place. It was déjà vu to the extreme. Presently, he was reliving a spring semester in college. Those days were always marked by a joy which had its own smell. Flowers, pine trees, salt sea ocean, and patchouli oil. These memories came easily, visually. And this cool wind on a sunny April day rendered them cinematic.

He walked straight out to the sand and headed for the ocean, shoes in hand, his backpack filled with distractions. A close view of the ocean's uninterrupted playtime should give him all the humility he needed to approach this day with the proper introspection it required. He stood helpless and happy before the dark blue sheet that stretched past all limits. It rolled and crashed and paid no attention to any rhythm other than continuity. It made him smile to think how beautiful it remained despite all he had heard about its decline. A woman walked by with a rambunctious puppy. Stanis was now grinning at the ocean. Their eyes met. She immediately turned away. *She knows*, he thought. *She can smell my mortality.* This is what it's going to be like. Women were going to be like museums now. Whenever he was in a museum, though he could not touch the paintings, they were his while he was there. It was a lovely consideration in a museum, a rather painful one when adapted to women. For reasons he did not understand, he was slightly amused. One more sip of the ocean air and it was time to continue this valedictory day of youth and discovery.

On his way back through the sand, his phone rang. Not only had he assumed it was left at home, but he neglected to disengage the ringer as well. The caller was one of his closest friends, Nikos.

"Happy birthday, old man."

"It's not until tomorrow."

"I know. Wanted to be the first. Where the fuck are you? Sounds like you're in a wind tunnel?"

"On the beach, man. What's going on?"

"Can you hear me?"

"Yeah, what's going on?

"The party tomorrow ..."

"You mean the surprise party?"

"Should I invite Andrea? I don't want to start any shit on your birthday."

"I'm a have to call you back. Can't hear very much with this wind."

"Big day, baby."

"Yeah, okay."

He wanted to leave his phone at home, but now he might need it for defense. He didn't even want a party. A celebration of something he would prefer to avoid. A recognition that he was in the fourth quarter of his life. Who wants that? He turned off the ringer, and immediately the name of another caller turned up in silence. The appropriately named Eve Palmer. Eve, a legendary temptress, apples in both hands, who was until now, a distant memory. Well, as one ages, memories are more numerous than future adventures. The skill resides in reconciling the two. They had love, brutal passion, and luck in timing. Now they had distance and a past. How many people fell into this category? No. It was too early in the day to become overly existential. Today was the day to fortify himself against all things negative. Negative thoughts sped up the aging process. He unfurrowed his brow. Love and light. That's the ticket for today. Still, against his better judgment, he returned Eve's call. She did not pick up, so he doubled down, leaving a message.

"Hey stranger. Nice to hear from you. It's been a minute. Not sure what to say other than it would be joyous to be in your orbit again. Hope you are giving it your all everywhere."

He hung up, glaring at his phone ... now why the fuck did he say that? Hope you are giving it your all everywhere? Who says that shit?

A text appeared from Eve:

'Today's a big day for you, isn't it? You're man enough to meet the challenge. Big love. E.'

Stanis quickly processed their entire two-year relationship from that text. He came to the same conclusion he had come to in assessing life in general. There was simply too much availability of everything for people to hold on to anything. The world had developed a certain disposable quality to it. He no longer mattered to her except as an extinguished candle does to a wine bottle. The wax drippings were lovely, but the candle often needs replacing all the same. Stanis was culpable of the same behavior, which was why Niko asked about inviting Andrea to the party. The last time Andrea had called Stanis, he too answered with a text. Obviously, he required a good leisurely walk, which no doubt would present with him other sentient possibilities.

He was slowly flooded with disparate images and memories of les temps perdu. Stanis was conversant in the act of being present, but also knew that when it wasn't an option, it was necessary to let his mind unburden noisily without judgment. He was remembering himself as a pre-teen, when stepping outside of his parents' house was cause for celebration. He had a large family, seven siblings who all battled for their independence. He also had a very strict father, which made time away from home the very oxygen he needed. His best friend Carlos had been as ambitious as Stanis in finding something different to experience, and as problematic as all kids who were solely controlled by the curious. This memory was of a night of midnight laundry. They lived in a housing project where clotheslines were strewn in everyone's backyard. He and Carlos would steal the drying, wind-blown panties of the girls in his neighborhood. The simple joys of life ... midnight laundry. It had been decades since this memory had visited him. He remembered Carlos clearly as his twelve-year-old friend for life. He believed Carlos to still be alive while he was certain three of his brothers met untimely deaths in ragged circumstances.

A man on his bike brushed against Stanis, interrupting his reverie. The biker was followed by a skating girl whose butt cheeks leaked out of her jean shorts profoundly. Another man crossed in front of her carrying a sign which read: "Stay present and keep in the divine flow." Following his own advice, the woke man made an about face and trailed skating girl.

Stanis suddenly felt happy to be alive. The sheer randomness of his life was similar to his boyhood existence. As a boy, he never knew what was going to happen on any given day and felt it was his duty only to remain open to possibility. That is the very freedom age tempers. The responsibility to be responsible has handicapped many of those previously marked by their daring. He understood clearly that things had changed as his numbers mounted. What he was experiencing at this moment was one of the most troubling of adjustments he had to make. Women passed by him in a parade of beauty, none of them paying him a moment's attention. He had become invisible with age. Still handsome but no longer young was a poisoned prescription, youth being the most important currency after wealth. The only compensation being his recalling of how even in his studly years, women would ignore him, though it all seemed more personal now. Just then, a woman of import stopped and asked him if he knew the area. She was looking for a certain clothier. He had no fucking idea what she was referring to, but mined the interaction for all it was worth by recommending another store. She gave a smile in a different language and moved on.

He pulled out his phone, which revealed ten new messages. Birthday greetings, he was certain. He redeposited it in his backpack and kept walking in the direction of whatever was before him this day. Propelled by a soft northern wind and tempered curiosity, he moved past musty homeless encampments to a patch of grass, hill-like, and positioned himself lazily on its crest. A view of this convergence of walkways and ocean invited him to sit and ponder life's pageant anonymously. He studied the few locals around him who shared the knoll and noticed he was the oldest person there. This was what he called elevator evidence. For some time now, whenever he found himself in a crowded elevator, he would see where he fit in age-wise. More often than not, he would be the oldest person inside when the doors closed. How could this be? It was most disturbing when he once found himself in a hospital elevator one afternoon and as the doors slid shut, he couldn't help but notice he was the eldest in the space. In a fucking hospital. Soon after, he took only the stairs, avoiding elevators no matter the number of floors he might have to ascend. It was better for his heart, he reasoned.

Sitting out, looking over the populace, wasn't a bad thing. When he was young, all he or anyone else wanted to do was be free enough to sit and watch the world go by. Who wanted to go to work when you could do nothing? It was the same consensus among the middle-aged. Everyone working just enough so they wouldn't have to continue working much longer. Looking forward to a time when they could sit on the crest of a hill and watch the world pass by, participating only when and if one felt motivated. With this consideration, Stanis had already reached the pinnacle of achievement. Well, that was a shit lie. There he was, far from rich but financially stable, watching the world go by and he felt physically, spiritually, and emotionally remiss. He certainly didn't feel like one of life's victors.

A girl was doing complicated yoga exercises directly at the bottom of the hill where it flattened and gave purchase to the bit of shade from a lone tree. There was a tripod with a camera mounted on it, and it appeared she was filming her pronounced flexure. Stanis found it pornographically impressive if not film worthy. Though he was a proponent of deep stretching himself, he also had a deep disrelish of the whole yoga community. He held them in the highest order of hypocrisy. An entire culture that prided itself on peaceful presence and higher consciousness through breathing and movement in ninety-minute segments, except for the fact that this inner peace lasted only the ninety minutes of its continuance. After class it was back to scorching and burning the planet and its people, luxuriating in the supreme knowledge that for ninety minutes traffic they have given up their ego for something more fulfilling. If they had retained their sense of calm afterwards, considering the sheer numbers of worldwide participants, the planet would be an ocean of calm and generosity. That is not the case. Only a few days ago, a woman loaded her mat and yoga paraphernalia into her car, post-class, and pulled out in front of Stanis, almost hitting him with her electric vehicle. Stanis beeped his horn and she responded with an unprovoked profanity laced diatribe, punctuated with an angry middle finger. On her back window were various Hindu sayings. Namaste indeed.

The memory did not compromise his enjoyment of yoga-woman running through various fluid positions on the lawn before him. Now she was squatting, hands pressed together prayer-like, head turned up to face the heavens, still as a drugged turtle. She slowly transformed into another position, which put her on her back, her legs akimbo. Maybe he did like the yoga community. Perhaps his impatience was rooted in his inability to approach someone positioned for all things carnal. He was too old to appeal to her. It would be an insult to interrupt her as she lay herself bare to whatever gods she was summoning. The results would be tragically humorous, bereft of the humor part. If only he were younger, he might have coolly drifted in her direction armed with a bucket of charm and strategy, and gently unlocked her Pandora's box of eroticism. Would he, though? There was some precedent. His freshman year in college he remembered standing in line at the student center behind a girl wearing a wife beater and overalls. She turned to smile at him and without thinking he whispered, "If I don't have you soon, I'm going to perish." Later that evening, they were in a sleeping bag on the forested campus, providing naked answers to every question their hungry bodies could conjure. So maybe it was again this age thing.

As the yoga lady imperceptibly transitioned to a less amatory position, it was not lost on him how most of his concerns regarding aging had a sexual tint to them. He had turned into a horny old man, he opined, which was considered disgusting. Conversely, being a horny young man was just short of sacrosanct. She was now attending to her camera. The show was over, and she began to pack up all things yoga-related, breaking down the set. Stanis rose and strolled in her direction. Why the fuck not? If you can't be brave at sixty, one might as well jump. As she officiously packed her things into a pink sling-bag, Stanis presented her with his most discreet smile, careful enough not to appear leering.

"That was impressive."

"Excuse me?"

"I've never been able to do the splits, and you do them both ways."

She smiled briefly. "It takes a lot of practice.'

"Well, I've been practicing most of my life and it's still a mystery.'

"You're never too old to improve.' This comment scratched at him. He had underwear older than she was and now she was going to manifest her inner Yoda and instruct him in the basics of commitment, process, and result. Or was he reading too much into it? He gently persisted.

"You're absolutely right. In any event, thanks for the inspiration."

"You're welcome. We should all try to inspire one another. Keep stretching. It's life."

"Yes. As is your beauty."

"Sorry?"

"Not objectifying you. Simply appreciating how you have managed to present yourself."

"Okay ..."

Now that he had planted both feet in quicksand, he might as well continue to sink.

"I didn't offend you; I hope."

"How could you offend me? I don't know you."

"Tomorrow is my sixtieth birthday and I'm struggling to find the proper place to put that."

"My dad turned sixty this year."

"How'd he deal with it? "

"I don't know. I haven't seen him for a while. We aren't really that close anymore."

"Sorry. Hopefully that will change ... if you so choose." Her equipment, settled into her pink luggage, the tripod and camera were left on the ground.

"Can I help you carry anything?"

"My car's right here, but if you want to get my camera and tripod ..."

"Of course." They walked the thirty or so yards to her Mini Cooper and deposited her things in the back seat full of empty water bottles.

"Thank you."

"Pleasure."

"So, what are you doing for your sixtieth birthday?"

"I'm having a surprise party thrown for me."

This, too, brought out a smile a bit bigger than her first one. "That sounds nice."

"Don't really feel like celebrating it."

"Birthdays are like funerals sometimes," she offered.

"Hope not."

"I mean, it's not so much for the person who died or who was born. It's for the others to be allowed to appreciate that person. You know?"

"Hmmm."

She walked to the driver's side and reached in. Pulling out a business card, she slid it over the roof of her car where Stanis was still planted. He picked it up gingerly.

"I teach yoga. In case you want to work on your stretching. Happy nativity." She got into her car and drove off.

Fog began rolling in, layered and ominous. Clouds scrambled above and around the sun. Stanis held a large space for weather drama. It was a transcendent phenomenon and always moved him into his sacred place of memory. So many memories. He was overly conscious of age, being chiefly a purveyor of hidden memories. Of the many things lost or diminished as one gathered years, memories only increased bacteria-like, appearing in as many strains.

He was now twelve years old and playing football with his classmates on the muddy banks of a lake. His Catholic school was on a field trip one dreary day, where clouds and fog had turned the air melancholy. He was running through high grass, strangled in mud, laughing. Father Berringer was supervising from a distance, and the usual oppression of all things Catholic brought to the forefront was momentarily abated. Joy was something which was stolen during those days of religious forbearance, and punishment was always waiting in the wings for those who strayed from the magical God of easy retribution. Even then, playing in the mud, though there was no other option, would make him wonder if he was to be shortly punished for such an action. He could still smell the air of that epoch. It was salty. He recalled Father Berringer blowing his whistle to gather the kids for lunch. He liked Father Berringer. When

Father B was ordained, Stanis was one of the altar boys who participated in the customary washing of the feet. He still had the newspaper clipping of his feet being attended to by Father B. He remembered it showed his feet were pointed for some reason. What he didn't know was several years later, Father Berringer would mistreat him badly enough to make him not wish to continue catholic school. Who knew?

The wind shifted and a metallic scent exploded somewhere deep in Stanis.

Now he was in a large bucket under a wooden pier. Another field trip. This was a Boys' Club excursion, and he was on a ride in an amusement park. It was dark and musty, redolent of ocean and wet wood. The ride was etched in his memory for unknown reasons, as there was little remarkable about being in an old tin tub floating under a pier. That said, this was a pronounced memory that visited him often and gave him a sense of tranquility. Some memories were there to add to his life lexicon. Something had happened. His recalling of rendered smells and feelings froze him in a moment which no longer existed. There was sufficient magic in that. He was trying to remember with whom he shared this bucket ride. His childhood friend Carlos, of course. They did everything together.

He fingered the business card yoga lady had proffered him. She admitted to not being in touch with her father. Stanis was a father out of touch with his son. He was reluctant to follow that train of thought. He knew where it led. It had been a few years since he had any genuine relationship with his only son and thinking about it emptied him of happiness. For Stanis, it was more about survival than denial. Attempting to figure out how one could lose the person they loved the most was a fool's errand. After his son turned eighteen, he changed. That was the best he could come up with, far from satisfying, yet having gone over it repeatedly, he accepted this incredibly empty reasoning. There was a time when he was willing to speak with close friends about this unimaginable void. They were always unanimous in their response: Stanis' son was going through a phase. He would come out of it. His son was now twenty-four and the phase had gained speed and elongated into what seemed perpetuity. The finish line no longer contemplated, Stanis worried he had given up and judged himself harshly in accordance. This thought drew him to his phone. He checked his messages to see if, by chance, his son had contacted him for this singular anniversary. Even a desultory birthday greeting would have been cause for reveling. He shielded his phone from the glare and sped through his missives, ending on a poem written by an old girlfriend. Long on rhyme and short on content, it made him laugh and he was thankful for the fleeting respite.

A man and a young boy came toward him. Stanis' eyes fixed on the child. The child was so beautiful, Stanis couldn't contain his joy at seeing their harmony. He offered the child a smile of encouragement, unaware of the raw excitement his smile produced. The presumed father viewed Stanis with a suspicion and held his son a bit tighter as they passed him. Stanis had sometimes behaved in the same manner when someone regarded his son with what he considered too much intimacy.

The moment was broken when a motorcycle announced itself, vomiting the sound of a strangled goat. *Fuck me.* He hated motorcycles on principle. He detested them in practice. Time for a nibble and a glass. Normally, he wouldn't drink in the afternoon, unless he was in Paris, of course, then tout était possible, but this was no normal day, so the standing rule did not apply. He rambled lazily for a few blocks to a restaurant he knew would provide him with a great view, excellent food, and delicious wine, all at a criminally exorbitant price. Though he hadn't partaken in years, he reminisced how a line of pure cocaine afterward would have been his dessert of choice. It made him smile to recall some of the more unsound choices he had made as a youth. It was like smoking, a young man's game. Today he was in search of simple spiritual ablutions, a glass of some supremely fermented grape juice was in order along with something delicious to digest. Admittedly and unashamedly, he considered himself first and foremost an Epicurean.

Entering the establishment of angled glass and polished wood, he was shown to a table giving out to dazzling sunlight and shimmering ocean. The sky was now clustering clouds having been a fog bank only minutes before. More weather drama. It was illegal to be unhappy in these moments and Stanis was nothing if not law abiding. The menu was virtual. He dug into his backpack and extracted one of four pairs of reading glasses always on hand, located his phone, and took a photo of the QR code, its contents magically appearing on the screen. He was getting accustomed to this procedure, though was not certain how he felt about it. He always ordered the seafood salad in any event. A beautiful man came to his table with the physique of Popeye. Before he opened his mouth, Stanis sussed his server was gay.

"Fuck me, you're in shape."

"Hello. Are you ready to order?"

"Seafood salad and a glass of Sancerre."

"Excellent."

"Do you train people?"

The server gave him a long, clueless look. "Sometimes."

"Fair enough." Stanis snapped his napkin onto his lap and glanced around at the half-filled restaurant. The majority of diners were Black folks. This was an expensive restaurant. Mid-day. Mid-week. The white side of town. Perhaps things were changing. His attention went back to his peerless ocean view. In the distance on the sand was a concentration of people standing together like a ginormous cluster of ice plants. Further on, a red lifeguard truck sped in the direction of the throng. Perhaps someone was drowning. A memory resurfaced quickly.

When Stanis was a young ragman, selling clothes at a high-end clothier's, one of his friends and coworkers had a baby. The man was as happy as any new father Stanis knew, not that he knew many at that age. Stevie lived with his wife and child a bit out in the country, where a stream butted his open backyard. His baby was crawling, not three feet from Stevie, when something caught Stevie's attention on the other side of the yard. When Stevie turned around to gather his son, he was gone. Apparently, he'd crawled quickly towards the rushing sound of the stream. When Stanis first heard this story from a common friend, he became numb, bereft of feeling, non-reactive. He mostly spent time attempting to approximate the feeling Stevie must have had when he turned to see ... nothing. It was unimaginable. Stanis had a comparatively fortunate life in that death tales had escaped him by and large. Outside of those who died simply because they were old, he had no experience at that time of the final bell tolling, the disappearance of a loved one. Stanis had no place to put this information. Nothing to hang it on other than shock. His friend Stevie disappeared, and he never heard from him again. He understood this to be a great lesson. Death can never be reconciled. Only accepted. Thinking back to the yoga lady from earlier in the day, he agreed with part of her statement. Funerals are for the survivors. Having been to countless funerals since, he knew this much to be true.

The group on the distant beach was slowly dispersing, the red fire truck heading off in another direction. His salad and wine arrived in silence. Popeye asked him if he needed anything else. Tempted to reply that he would like the man's physique, he took the waiter's tone of seriousness to heart and shook his head. Stanis stared at his plate of the dead fish he was longing to ingest. Crab, shrimp, clams, lobster, who very recently might have been chasing one another in those choppy waves outside his window. Who but an old man would have thoughts like this? He devoured his prey punishingly, then drowned them all again in wine, life and death being masticated in his mouth. Jesus, maybe he did need a line of cocaine. Death was as rich a mine to probe as life. Or so it seemed at fifty-nine.

He would forgo dessert. The postprandial inclination to sleep was already in play and though he was a huge fan of the afternoon nap, there would be no shutting of eyes this day. No turning everything off for a moment of respite. Demons and angels be damned, he would rage against the dying of the light. He paid the bill and once again consulted his phone. Most of his siblings had left voice messages, but like the unopened birthday cards at his house, he would save them for another time. Fucking birthdays. He left sated and a tad somnolent. He passed his waiter on the way out who was engaged in close quarter conversation with another man of similar build, maybe two stones heavier. Their cloaked intimacy made Stanis imagine their sex life. Two Brahma bulls locked in a death grip.

By the time he exited the restaurant, the wind had picked up. He was assaulted by music from a dozen different sources echoing invisibly in the invisible air. A neat trick of nature, to provide such unseen drama. He passed musicians and buskers and jugglers. Serious runners left weekend joggers in their dust. Religious sycophants were selling redemption behind high-volume microphones while Hare Krishnas kept the rhythm tight. Stanis liked the Hare Krishna beat yet knew better than to eat one of the inedible rock-hard cookies they offered. The ocean was a place of collective consciousness. Everyone came there looking for something different or in addition to whatever they already had. The ocean was the source of all things. Even now, with this cacophony of life pulsing through the maddening throng, the ocean crash could be heard as counterpoint to anything man had to offer. A final punctuation. It was the ocean ... followed by everything else.

Stanis decided to thread through the crowd. Normally, he avoided the multitudes, his involuntary feeling of supremacy most evident in these situations. Today, it would be a meagre attempt at crowd surfing. He moved through the throng ant-like, often touching the untouchables. The mix of smells and languages and sounds made him feel like an apothecary of man stuff. He felt both part of the assemblage and distant from everything, and of course, he couldn't help but notice he was older than many. Yet there he was moving through it all, quicksilver-like, as he allowed all observations and impressions to freely manifest. He saw a mound of dyed green and blue hair atop a young girl too young to be concerned by what anyone else thought. Smells of roasted onions and hot dogs left too long on the grill perforated his nostrils to the point of torment. A man was angrily reprimanding his daughter for some unknown reason causing her to respond with a death look of her own. Stanis erupted in uncontrollable laughter after someone detonated a colossal fart. In that respect, he remained a child. Farts and farting were still his go-to for bubbly cheer. Unfortunately, people assumed the man laughing was the culprit. Stanis, fully aware of the veiled attention he was now receiving from those close to him, could not check himself. He began laughing harder at the thought of the guilty person getting away with the deed. Stanis wished it had been him. Just then, a man bumped into him with his hard belly, the size of which could accommodate soon-to-be-born twins. Stanis conjured the comical image of the man attempting to sleep on his stomach and, to follow the theme, what a fart sounded like from a man of those dimensions.

A young man began rapping to an infectious beat. Most of it was incomprehensible, the upshot being that all women were bitches and hos, but he would still spread peanut butter on them. At least that is what Stanis thought he heard. There was also something about guns.

As the crowd thinned a bit, he was able to differentiate, to pick and choose where his attention would settle. Hearing a well-played bass line, he followed his ears and came upon something he found surprising. His home in Venice is in screaming distance from a large homeless community. Stanis often encountered a man who kept his face covered with hair resembling a recently employed mop. This man painted disturbing clown faces on any available flat surface, including his multi-room tent on the beach. He also carried a bass with him at all times. He would relentlessly finger it without the benefit of sound. An electric bass bereft of an amplifier. He played air bass with an actual bass. Stanis had heard him once sit in with a group on the ocean walkway, play a few unfortunate notes, then light the cigarette that dangled perennially from his mouth. This was approximately two years ago. That same man was killing a bass line, holding down the pocket with the help of a seasoned drummer. A lit cigarette hung out of his mouth. His hair was longer, badly braided, but he was undoubtedly a musician now. Stanis wanted to congratulate the man and let him know he had witnessed his journey from mock musician to rock musician. He longed to question him about this unique peregrination. When the song ended and he approached the band, the bassist looked up with dead eyes and sucked mightily from his cigarette, expelling nothing. Stanis left a twenty in the bucket before moving on.

A strip of park ran between the ocean and a busy street cleverly named Ocean. It hung on a cliff where a great mass of nature could be seen from on high. He sat on a bench facing out to the sea and just as he had decided to relax into meditation, a rumbling of excited voices came from behind him. Two young men were throwing haymakers at one another. The energy surrounding them was combustible and others began to get involved, separating into two distinct groups. Stanis involuntarily moved toward the action. It was a good fight, both men fearless and aggressive. Stanis had already deduced the winner would be the first one to land one of those haymakers flush. And just like that, it happened: a pugilist with very long hair walked into an overhand right and was out before he hit the ground. His opponent grabbed the unconscious man by his long mane and continued pummeling him. Stanis cried out for the man to stop hitting, informing him of the obvious, that he had already won. Unaware of what he was doing, Stanis circled the man and grabbed him in a choke hold. The crowd was now yelling at both of them. Stanis let the man go before he lost consciousness and immediately walked away to shouts and jeers. He put some pep in his step but did not run. His pulse was racing, and he wasn't quite sure what he had done. An empty bottle crashed on the sidewalk next to him. He kept walking as police began passing him, running to the scene. They weren't about to stop an old man walking away from violence. He had survived.

"Well, that was stupid," he said over and over until he had put some distance between himself and the craziness of the moment. Before he knew it, he was on the other side of the park. His hands were still shaking when a young bulldog came up to him and began licking them. Stanis returned the favor by kneeling and petting this overly friendly pooch. And this is life. By turns a violent, thoughtless mess and, alternatively, a puppy's love. What was he supposed to do with that? A religious person would have offered it as God's love of the peacemaker. Stanis was anything but religious. His young life of Catholicism had eviscerated any hold religion had on him. He did marginally believe in Karma. The puppy scampered back to his owner. Ah, yes, this is life in all its absurd randomness. What next? He didn't have to wait long to find out.

A man appeared walking a white stunted pony donning a rainbow tutu. Stanis and everyone else within sight of this surreal development paid stunned homage. Sometimes it is best not to require explanations of things one fails to understand. The recent violence, however, had undermined Stanis' ability to appreciate the zaniness of a pony walking the beach sidewalk in a tutu, rainbow colored at that. He had yet to regain his fulcrum. In his fifty-nine years, he had witnessed a good deal of violence, yet never managed to add value to it. It still bothered him profoundly. Intervening as he did in the fight was as normal to him as was his lapse of common sense in doing so. Violence rendered him on autopilot. A reaction developed from an unforgettable incident in San Francisco when he was in his early twenties.

He'd been living in the Potrero Hill neighborhood. He had been stood up that evening and, unable to sleep, felt a nightcap would alleviate his funk. On this late weekday evening, he walked down to the bottom of a steep hill to his local bar. The place was full. About a dozen barstools and three small tables scrunched against a wall were all the bar could accommodate, so Stanis took the one empty barstool and ordered. Next to him sat a hulking form with arms the size of thighs. Stanis' drink arrived, he took a deep pull and turned to commiserate with his gigantic neighbor. Staring back at him was a pair of dark, set eyes, owl-like, unblinking and merciless. It was as if time had stopped out of fear of the next moment. In an instant, Stanis felt his soul abandoning him for a safer venue. He felt helpless to turn away and had no knowledge of how long their eyes were fixed upon one another. He knew only that he was in the company of the grim reaper. Manny, the bartender, smoothly intervened with his practiced pleasantries.

"Stanis, you know Max?"

Stanis remained stunned in silence.

"Max, this is Stanis. Good guy. Good customer. You two should know each other."

Stanis blurted out, childlike, "Let me buy you a drink. Can I buy you a drink, Max?"

Max looked at Manny, momentarily breaking his spell. Manny returned his winning smile, saying something in Samoan, then pouring Max a stiff one. Manny winked at Stanis before attending to another customer. Stanis spent the next twenty minutes staring at his rocks glass, too devastated to show even a hint of life until Max vacated his barstool, which he eventually did. Max rose slowly and walked out of the bar like a man moving through a wall of meat. Stanis couldn't muster the nerve to watch Max's egress from the bar and couldn't look up until he felt Manny's hand resting on his.

"You're good. Don't worry. He's gone. He wouldn't hurt you. He's just, you know ... kinda scary if you don't know him."

Stanis ordered another drink nonverbally. His voice had yet to return. Soon after, he paid his tab, tipping Manny handsomely. Upon following another patron out the door, Stanis stopped just outside to check his wallet when a voice originated from a dark void. The man he followed out of the bar was crossing the street. To his immediate right was the terrifying Max, not three feet away.

Max said one word, "Hey!"

The man in the crosswalk turned just in time to receive an explosion to his head. He dropped onto the street, a mound of wet sand. There was the smell of something burning, something Stanis had never smelled before but seemed somehow familiar. Max's huge arm was still extended, a large caliber firearm in his grasp. It reminded Stanis oddly of the finishing gesture of a basketball player after a successful three-point shot, hand still in the air. The stairs back up the hill to his place were to his immediate right. Stanis made a soldierly right turn and ascended them slowly, unable to breathe fully, tears and nose running freely, imagining himself invisible. One foot in front of the other ... one foot in front of the other ... one foot in front of the other. He bent his whole existence straight ahead, up the stairs slowly, not fully conscious. His fear now was on a cellular level. When he was halfway up the hill, the burning smell of skull, brain, and skin was replaced by that of the shit in his pants.

It's what he remembered most from that night—the smells—and that he walked into his shower fully clothed. This was the closest he had come to death. He was too young at the time to fully grasp the lesson outside of being in the wrong place at the wrong time. Today, on the eve of his sixth decade, the lesson was clear. Anything could happen to anyone at any time. Cynicism coagulates with age.

His memories were ambushing him. Yes, they were random contemplations, but they were also real, readily accessible, and most of them at least partially disturbing. Stanis viewed himself to be, in general, a happy man. That fucking word, "happy." Who is happy without visiting the other side of the ledger? These memories devolved into a free association game with every step, image, and smell. He passed a bush which overwhelmed him with the scent of jasmine. His head became light. Stanis recalled his arrival in Los Angeles so many years ago. He left San Francisco shortly after his close call with the Reaper. He remembered driving the 10 freeway in his Fiat Spyder, top down, his nose filled with the heavy odor of night-blooming Jasmine. He had never experienced a freeway smelling like a flower before. That it was warm and a bit humid in February also came as a shock. He was now submerged in memories he was incapable of stopping or directing. He decided to keep walking.

He would accept this memory ambush, but he would remain mobile for reasons he could not articulate.

He recalled his first apartment on Beachwood Drive in Hollywood. Memorable for, among other things, the incalculable variety and number of amorous adventures which occurred there. Stanis acknowledged his most pleasant recollections were of a romantic nature. Some might call it carnality. He was aware that many would judge his preoccupation with women as obsessive if he were to be candid in his predilections and desires. He often gave this some thought. Was he obsessed with women? Was it dangerous? His answer was always in French ... et alors? His addiction wasn't simply their proximity, though he always sought it. It wasn't that he preferred their company over men, which he did. There was merely the overwhelming contradiction of comfort and unease he felt around them. It didn't matter how brief the relationship was, how well or badly it had ended. It was part of his emotional DNA. Important life material. Men and Women. What else was there to contemplate? When considering his past, he had little regret and no fear of facing an embarrassing composite of youth and its tendencies. These were privately exquisite recollections. Everyone had their ... something. He decided to willingly descend that rabbit hole.

Karen Green was a woman whom he met only once, kissed only once, never saw again, but would remember the rest of his life. A singular response to her, he still couldn't fathom ... this terrible ache for a stranger. Green eyes, dark hair, fair skin, indistinct ethnicity. Everything their young hearts had to give was exchanged on the top of a hill in Hollywood on a sunny October afternoon. Thinking about it now, he wondered at his expression in this moment, wondered what truth it would reveal in a mirror. Wondered if he had ever looked that way before or since.

Deborah, the trainer. Ebony from eyes to feet. The epitome of muscular femininity before it mirrored manhood. He met her of course, at a gym. An aerobics instructor. Cliché now, but at the time, still a novelty. Or at least not yet a redundancy. He accompanied her to her car after a class and launched into a stream of conscience monologue impressive for his being able to sustain it without revealing anything of matter. Whatever he said worked. They ended up at her apartment. One absurd thing led to another until he disrobed and then chased her around her living room as she, fully clothed, laughed and pointed. Although Deborah did finally relent, she also shared the story with various mutual friends, earning Stanis several unforgettable nicknames.

His second menage à trois, which came as a complete surprise, was consummated in that Beachwood apartment. These were more welcome memories he was now experiencing, amorous adventures, his favorite go-to recollections. Lately, these recollections became stuck in the erstwhile. He may never again be afforded the same options.

Stanis arrived at another small bench vacated just as he arrived. He sat and closed his eyes, shutting out the effulgent blaze of sun and ocean. Time to meditate, to be present and see what peace and clarity arrive. The smell of pine and fresh dirt centered him. He could hear the birds in competition with the clamor of the cityscape behind him. This seemed appropriate as he was presently attempting to balance the two. Emptying the mind is not the simplest of accomplishments. There was always so much noise in his head, so many things to be weighed or solved or considered or avoided. The secret to being present is not to judge the uncontrolled thoughts that fight against that present state of being. So, when he couldn't keep the thought of women out of his mind, he didn't judge. Eyes closed, he allowed his mind to drift in whatever direction it wandered and suddenly it was blank. Nothing. He focused on his breathing. He felt the wind kiss him gently. He heard the ocean's call and response. He saw the red bleeding through his closed eyelids. He was now cognizant of the world in total. Everything and all things. Stanis was now a dot in the cosmos, a millionth of a fraction of the size of a proton in a hulking universe of unknowable vastness. Time's importance had evaporated. This was a true feeling of peace. This complete calm created a moment of absolute bliss which Stanis tried to hold on to without holding on to it. Let. It. Be. Out of this state of complete relaxation came a loud, elongated and elevated whisper. It wasn't immediately apparent to him that he had just passed gas. As he grew more conscious of it, he burst into laughter. Opening his eyes, he noticed a couple watching him from a few feet away. They were smiling inappropriately as one might to see an old man lose control of his bowels. He could laugh now, but how much longer before it was no laughing matter? He did manage to achieve a state of presence for ... how long? It didn't matter. He remained fifty-nine and it was just a fart. He hadn't soiled himself. That would be left for another day.

He thought about moving on, but to what? Where was he going to go that would change his circumstances? Whatever he did, wherever he went, there he was and only hours away from entering his seventh decade. He considered descending the lengthy stairs, crossing the bridge over the freeway to the beach, and abandoning his clothes to bathe in the ocean's current. A rebirth as it were in the world's original amniotic sac. There was much restoration to be imagined in the full complement of hot sun and frigid sea. Emerging from the ocean, naked and refreshed on a public beach, he would no doubt be met by the keepers of law and order. This could be a positive as well. Spending a couple of days in jail would prevent him from attending his surprise birthday party. Mid-thought, an oversized man with a face fixed in permanent agony stopped in front of him and waited while his dog relieved himself mightily from its backend. Stanis watched in disgust as the owner retrieved with his gloved hand the estimable offerings of his four-legged friend. As much as Stanis admired animals, dogs in particular, this was the very reason he didn't own one. The man proceeded to wipe the dog's soiled fundament with a tissue. Funny how the most profound personal moments can be interrupted by the basest absurdities. Stanis found the motivation to move on.

The wind had picked up again. Maxfield Parrish clouds formed and reformed themselves steadily. Skinny palm trees bent in obedience and fronds began falling from on high. Nature, Stanis loved its unpredictability. He admired its ability to be both old and new. Earth accommodates all change. It survives. Five mass extinctions, its biodiversity almost destroyed, yet multicellular organisms remained to rebuild the earth anew—Earth, four and a half billion years old and not one doctor's appointment. Pockmarked by volcanic eruptions, brutalized by meteoric attacks, smothered by carbon dioxide for centuries and most recently poisoned by man's carelessness, the earth perseveres. Why is it that people so fragile? They have forty, maybe fifty productive years and then their main concern is securing comprehensive health insurance. Four and a half billion years for Earth, versus eighty years for Earthlings. We hardly deserve the title. What do earthlings even have in common with the planet? Stanis arrived at the conclusion that humans, mortals, earthlings, or whatever moniker rendered, our whole existence was nothing more than fertilizer for future generations. We eat earth's offerings, we die, and shortly return as offerings in the form of compost. Essentially, we are the manure of life. Our entire function is to regenerate the Earth, a sobering thought and one which lends overall existence an unsatisfactory context. It also gives heft to the expression: I feel like shit today.

Bored with empty existential concerns hijacking his last day, Stanis consulted his phone, scrolling through the messages to find someone or something to distract him from himself. Meditation lasts only if one meditates; then you're on your own.

There was a message from an unknown number which read:

Happy born day. I still miss you in spite of everything.

Oh boy. A riddle.

He wrote back: *Who is this?*

There was no immediate response, and he doubted he would receive one. Stanis tried to see this as a positive omen. At least someone was missing him. He dared not call the number in case it was someone with whom he didn't share the sentiment. The qualification, 'in spite of everything,' began to weigh heavily on him. It was accusatory. He went through his mental Rolodex of relationships which ended badly. It was a surprisingly short list. He counted two, both of which he was sure would not have sent him birthday greetings. It must be someone with whom he shared a momentary dalliance. Now that was a much larger number of suspects, far too many to recount and narrow down with any confidence. The next text message was from one of his oldest friends.

You keep getting older. What's up with that? You need to find and marry someone young enough to be a good caretaker for you. I have some ideas ...

Stanis actually found humor in this message. That his friend was a year older than Stanis probably helped in that regard. He continued scrolling and found a message from an ex-lover, Kamara. She was an off and on sexual adventure which had neither boundaries nor time schedule. They had been recurring paramours for years, though it had been months since they last rekindled the flame.

She texted: *I know we haven't been in touch for a while. I was involved with a crazy man. Nothing bad, I was just overwhelmed when I only want-*

ed to be whelmed. Would love to be in your space again. Happy everything to you, my dear Stanis.

This was a message of interest. Kamara was the woman with whom he shared the longest relationship. Their companionship was Kama Sutra on steroids, but to say their relationship was strictly sexual would be to underestimate the friendship that informed their considerable passion. Indeed, it was their sexual chemistry which launched their friendship. Everything fit. What they did for one another physically answered any questions of trust or merit. Summarily, if people could make each other feel this fulfilled, how could they not be friends? It could be said that his relationship with Kamara limited his possibilities for other relations. He always longed for the same type of non-committed commitment he had with her. She had spoiled him mightily. Stanis, never having been married, didn't understand its relevance. Forever was too long a time strategy for someone who couldn't even plan what he wanted for breakfast. He imagined she had recently called it quits from crazy man. Normally, she didn't wait long after a breakup to contact him. Her timing today was perfect. His birthday. What could be better than a visit with Kamara, spending a few hours with the default love of his life? Yes, there was love. There was always love, there just wasn't forever. Would this be the best way to end his day of self-reflection? What exactly was his objective when he left the house today? Stanis fingered his phone gently, considering this move. He asked himself the stock question: Was he ever sorry for having seen Kamara? Answer: Never. Ever.

He sent her a pithy text. *Free right now. Let's celebrate.*

Her answer quickly returned. *Come over with the candle. I have the cake.*

Stanis was at a loss to measure how much he loved Kamara in this moment. He pocketed his phone. There was no need to see any other messages; none of them could provide more comfort than Kamara's cake. Was this all he needed? Was this all that mattered? An afternoon of diversions and delights with the perfect accomplice? This did not augur well with his belief that he was a complex human being. If a simple bit of cake can comfort all worries, if that was the answer, what the fuck was the question? He still had a good walk ahead of him until he would reach his house. He still had time to ponder sailing ships and sealing wax, cabbages and kings. One of his favorite lines from "The Walrus and the Carpenter." Another memory. As a child, if he didn't attend summer school, his father insisted Stanis memorize a stanza of poetry a day. He still had volumes of classical poems committed to memory. He shared that story with a friend of his when he was still in his forties. The friend promptly told him to call his father right then and there to thank him for this gift. It wasn't until that moment did he appreciate the task his father had set before him so many years ago.

On his way back home, his life tumbled in front of him in images and sensations. He felt nature's talent for life contribute to his own. He was windblown, sun-kissed, and equally impressed by the process. There was a sudden reverence for existence, whatever that was. It didn't matter what had suddenly kicked him into gear. So what if it was the prospect of indescribably delicious communion with someone who shared his passion? Like all things, this too shall pass. It was the commas and parentheses and parenthetical phrases of life which gave him the starts and stops. The paragraphs write themselves despite all. He only needed to enlarge his vocabulary, to keep himself open to new phrasing, to understand the grammar of life is not located in a single language. Whether or not he could comprehend the Joycean constructs that littered his way was a masturbatory attempt at fathoming the unfathomable. There was more. There would always be more, at least for today.

Dark Muse

'Unexpected' is a word which often belies itself. "The weather was unexpected." Doesn't the weather normally behave with irregularity? "She gave the man an unexpected reply." One can imagine a panoply of questions which would receive a response falling outside the realm of the desired, men and women being who they are. But why would any response be expected in the first place if there was indeed a genuine question? Or is that the literal example of begging the question? These were the thoughts which multiplied and pestered Leo as he held the phone to his ear as if it were a newly realized appendage. The caller, Marianne, had hung up after delivering the message a full minute ago. In movies, one will see an actor receive news of significance, perhaps life-changing, and their actions would differ dramatically from Leo's. One actor will convincingly slam the phone down, perhaps smashing it to pieces. Another might pull the phone away and stare at it profoundly, a dangerous foreign object in the palm of one's hand. And yet another actor might choose to let the phone hang down from their side, looking off in the distance, conceivably contemplating eternity. These were also the things which passed through Leo's mind as he realized he was even now, still holding the silent phone to his ear.

That he was out in public writing jokes minimized his response but did place the news in sharp relief. News of the death of a friend while scripting humor was, without doubt, a singular event. He did not, however, entertain the word unexpected. Marianne had called him as he sat in this, his local coffee shop and told him, after sharing some minor details, that his friend had died ... unexpectedly. Those were her last words before she rang off. Leo was a comic, and he had a comic's mind, so he initially came up with the beginnings of a joke regarding unexpected death. Earlier in his life, he would have been scandalized to find immediate humor in tragic news, but he no longer judged himself along those lines. He was a comic and that was where he lived, between the blurred lines of comedy and tragedy. That said, Marianne saying Leo's friend's death was unexpected initially troubled him. Was Leo expecting this tragic occurrence? Of course not. His friend had been in good health as far as Leo knew. Leo took umbrage with Marianne saying this, as if that apprehension, that tenuous grasp on the circumstances, somehow shed light on the situation. 'Unexpected' or 'expected' were two words which should have been meaningless given the situation, yet somehow weren't. He'd work through this eventually, he knew, and after having given it ample scrutiny, he felt the cloud of reality descend. His friend had just died ... unexpectedly. There was nowhere for him to go at this moment, so he ordered another coffee. It would be best to experience this second wave of feeling surrounded by this din of strangers. Ambient human hubbub would keep Leo buoyant for the time being.

Marcus Leonard Perry—Lenny to some, 'Tri' (for trinomial) to others—had been Leo's best friend for a decade. Almost ten years ago to the day, they had met and established a friendship based initially on their love of food and wine. Marcus was a closet chef. Leo was an out-of-the-closet eater. There existed no real conflict between them when it came to gastronomy. There were, of course, lively discussions regarding wine vintages and sourcing local ingredients, but they both knew it would all end up being digested. As Leo sat in the café, he reconciled the fact that there would be no more three-hour meals shared with someone who had taught him the meaning of feasting. No more plans to save up enough to visit France, drive through the country, stopping at several Michelin-starred restaurants, with the only objective being to eat as two twenty-first-century pashas. This was never to be. That was a word which had heft: never. Nothing unexpected ever follows the word 'never.' Leo was beginning to experience the first stage of grief. He was in denial. There were still no tears from a man whose eyes would water at the beauty of a dripping candle or at the randomness of a leaf floating in the wind. Conversely, he could find humor in a car wreck.

Although Marianne had spoken briefly about Marcus' death, she neither revealed how he died nor did Leo inquire. What was the point? This had come at a time when Leo was in the throes of writing a new stand-up routine. Always an anxious time for him, he was stuck in the self-appraisal mode. Was his stuff any good? Was he funny? Could he come up with another routine worthy of an audience? And now, how would the death of a friend affect his work? Again, a selfish response: wondering how someone's death would affect his work. Leo attributed that consideration to his being in denial. He then wrote a quick sketch about someone reading their own obituary in the newspaper. It was humorless except for the part where the death survivor was more upset about the photo they'd run of him in the paper than the news itself. He'd work on it.

Marianne also told Leo she would keep him informed as to where and when Marcus' 'celebration of life' would take place. Because of COVID, she wasn't sure it would be a public event. Marianne was Marcus' sister. She would know what's what. Surely Leo could find humor in a Zoom funeral. Leo hated that term celebration of life. He found it wholly disingenuous. You simply can't have a celebration of life for a dead person because ... well ... they were dead. Leo made a mental note to get some comic mileage out of a celebration of death.

He stopped writing and looked around at all the real celebration of life in his café. His perspective had changed since the phone call. The thirty or so customers, some feigning work, others lost in who they were, all of them suddenly seemed offensive to him. They were in no way affected by the death of his friend. In an instant, he understood in part the reasoning behind mass shootings. It was time for him to change environments.

The next morning, he woke up on the floor of his living room, naked except for his socks, with a disgusting taste in his mouth. His throat was sandpaper and his mouth, desert dry. It slowly occurred to him that he had drunk the better part of a bottle of mescal the previous night. As he stood in his bathroom unleashing a world-class piss, he remembered coming home, watching some Dave Chappelle, and filling glass after glass with that liquid agave. That he used a glass instead of drinking straight from the bottle gave him hope. Maybe the only thing he did was get pass-out drunk. More importantly, he had managed to stay home instead of searching the bars for the first woman with the least resistance to creative copulation. Leo checked his phone. There were several messages that he ignored and, instead, went to his contacts.

Marcus Leonard Perry was still listed. Of course, he was. He would stay that way. There were several contacts who were no longer celebrating life, who remained listed. He refused to delete them. That would be untoward.

Walking into his kitchen, he stubbed his toe on a chair which had been upended. His cry of pain was cut short. The appearance of a dildo on his kitchen sink superseded all. Leo was not in the mood for absurdity but needed to process this information. Yes, it was his dildo. A couple of years prior, Leo had met a woman for whom toy shopping was foreplay. He no longer entertained this woman, but he wasn't about to get rid of the odd toy he had purchased on her behalf. To his surprise at the time, those gadgets were pricey. Still, the question remained: what was the dildo doing standing erect on his sink next to a bowl of guacamole? It should have been stored, always cleaned with a dousing of alcohol in the event he ran across someone like-minded. The pain in his toe resurfaced cruelly. He figured last night he must have been looking for a way to put the dildo in his act. That's what drink will do. Maybe that was it. What else could it have been? He didn't attempt to situate the guacamole in the equation. The possibilities were frightening. He did, however, take a quick photo of this marriage of mescal and guacamole. The visual could be revisited another time for comic inspiration. Then for some unknown reason, he was compelled to smell the dildo. Having passed the sniff test, he tenderly put it back in its secret place with the few other erotic effects.

Leo had a full-length mirror in the short hallway which barely separated rooms. He stood in front of it clad in nothing but mismatched sox. The tall, brown man who looked back at him featured an inert penis recently manscaped. He was rocking a soul patch these days and, in this moment, felt he resembled a blues musician. There was a pleasant, subtle sadness leaking from his gaze. Leo was a preternaturally handsome man.

This he knew. He had been so his entire forty years and had often been told as much. He also felt it was meaningless at this point in life. He was certainly grateful for being blessed with good genes, but if you asked him, it presented its problems. People assumed certain things about him before he ever opened his mouth. He was often assumed to be vain or stuck up or disingenuous or privileged. A lot of alpha men simply wanted to kick his ass, calling him "pretty muthafucka" in venomous tones. His looks had in fact been a deficiency early in his career. He came up with a whole bit about how difficult it was to be accepted as a comedian if you weren't somewhat peculiar-looking. Being fat was good. Ugly was also cool. If you were someone funny-looking, with oversized ears or irregular features, it could be enough to lubricate the audience before the first joke was shared. This poor-handsome-man bit didn't ever go over too well. It was like a rich person telling an audience how difficult it was to be flush. He knew this could be the response, and that was his strength as a comedian. He didn't care what anyone thought because it was the truth. Fat people tell fat people jokes. Cancer survivors tell funny cancer stories. People of color tell colored people jokes. He always followed the truth, and most of the time, the truth, in the right context, often turned out to be dangerous. It risks alienating the very audience it's attempting to engage—Witness Pryor, Carlin, or Chappelle, his holy trinity. So, he told attractive people jokes at his own peril.

Looking at himself in the mirror, naked as a dolphin, he predicted there would be some death jokes in his immediate future. And maybe some manscaped dick jokes as well. Now it was time to sneak up on his phone and painfully subject himself to the calls of grief. He received a new text just as he picked up his phone.

Outside your building. Can I come in?

He replied.

I'll buzz you.

It was Marcus' girlfriend, Isol. She'd been over with Marcus many times for meals and the occasional drink. Marcus was very open with Leo about his love life, and it was sometimes a challenge to forget how effusively enthusiastic Marcus had been when he spoke of his and Isol's sexual congress. Leo knew there was a pretty good joke in there somewhere. But not today. Today, he was puzzled as to why she had turned up alone at his apartment. This was a first. Leo threw on some doctor's scrubs, his go-to in emergency situations. Props for having a brother who was a surgeon.

Upon entering the apartment, Isol walked past him without really looking at him. She landed in the middle of the living room and turned to him, her face, an agonizing challenge. She began speaking, all the while pacing rhythmically. She was a speaking, moving metronome.

"He called me. Right before. I was in the shower. He didn't leave a message. So ... I assumed ... I didn't assume anything. He just didn't leave a message. I was in the shower! Did he say anything to you? Lately? Anything that made you think something was wrong? He really loved you, you know. I just want to ... jump out ... of my skin. I want to ..."

Isol was Mexican, stunning, and quite short. She had a strong accent even though her command of English was comprehensive. Isol was also a poet. In this moment she was devoid of all poetry and Leo was wondering if she needed to be sedated. Her voice was screaming in its calmness. She was imploding and it all remained below the surface like a volcano on the precipice of spewing. She had stopped talking but continued to pace. Leo gently, wordlessly, offered her a seat. She, also wordlessly, told him she didn't need a fucking chair.

"Marianne called me and told me yesterday. I hadn't seen Marcus in a few days. I don't know what's, you know. What's going on? What happened? She said he died unexpectedly. I didn't...I don't really know what to say ..." Isol stopped pacing and fixed Leo with an expression that literally interrupted his breathing. Not knowing why, Leo sat. He placed his hand in his lap, resembling a reprimanded child awaiting instruction. Isol continued. "You don't know what happened?"

Leo had no reply. He had only fear and nausea. Whatever was coming next was going to supply him with unwanted context. Up to this point, there was only loss, which he refused to acknowledge fully. As Leo watched her, he saw so much emotion roll across her face he thought she might be having a stroke.

"He rented a car. He drove to a public parking lot. Top floor." She began her metronome dance again as she spoke. "He was all alone. At the top of this ... with a view. He did it there."

"... the fuck did he do?!" This leapt out of Leo in his highest register, shocking them both.

"He shot himself ..."

"No. No. That's not possible ..."

"Security guard found him. She heard the music. He had his stereo on blast, and she went to tell him ..." There was a long pause. "Leo ... he shot himself in the heart."

She sat directly across from Leo, enervated, but already practiced in counterfeiting a painful nonchalance. She watched Leo process this information and realized she was back where she was when she entered his apartment. Looking for someone to translate the untranslatable. There was no release in this exchange, but there was hope. A hope which comes in the abstract form of shared vulnerability. They were now meeting at a place where words were extraneous and even knowledge was functionless. But they could meet. There were no barriers now. This is as much as she knew she would accomplish. Isol was a little ahead of him in the game. He imagined it brought her a perverted satisfaction to watch him squeeze all that he didn't have into angry tears which flowed unwillingly. They both were now sharing the awesome power of death together. Leo and Isol were attached at the eyeballs, both searching for something they would be unable to reconcile for eternity. Their eyes blazed, incapable of moving off one another until Leo finally stood up and screamed. It was a sound so raw and uncontrolled. A jagged, beautiful piece of his soul had detached itself, and Leo knew in that moment it was never to return. Isol did not flinch. Leo was now in the anger stage of grief..

Three days later, Leo was leaving a comedy club. He had been invited to do a set but decided to remain an audience member. If he could laugh ... if he could laugh ... that would help. The previous days were filled with empty comments of sadness and people devoting prayers and such. Leo found none of this useful. People were disturbed by Leo's dismissal of their attempts to placate him during this time of tragedy. His addiction to truthfulness was not solely witnessed in his comedy. Some folks would approach him and begin their spiel of concern, wherein he would cut them off without listening and move on. It was generally considered rude on his part. Leo didn't care. He did not want his days and nights to be filled with the discourse of sorrow. Enough time had passed for him to understand he was beyond consolation. Consolation was incompatible with this reality and there was nothing he could do to change his circumstances. With this truth, he had made a tenuous agreement with himself and had reasoned to fill his days with something other than grief. Anything other than grief. He settled on edibles. He popped them like candy and spent many hours flying solo. Being high took the edge off and didn't make him sick the next day like mescal. It was also more efficacious. He was high when he went to the comedy club and the jokes somehow seemed funnier. He made a note to encourage audience members to partake in edible eating before seeing his shows. Those three days of being euphoric served their purpose. Again, they took the edge off. They also made him forget names, dates, places, and more often than not, where the fuck his phone was. He needed to try something else.

The next day, he went to the movies. His favorite arthouse was showing *The Godfather*, also one of his favorites. He figured there would be a long line and got there early. When he arrived to buy his ticket, not only was there no line, but only two other people were seated in the theatre. COVID was good for something. He immediately thought about humor possibilities, the positive effects of COVID, and just as quickly let those thoughts disappear. Surely someone had already mined that vein.

There was something healing about being in a large, empty, dark room. He had not been in a movie theatre in over a year, and he had misplaced the power of cinema. It was almost overwhelming. The sound was loud enough to vanquish most of the noises in his head and render him complete observer status. He was able to lose himself in the film. Mission accomplished. Do something which is entirely outside of the self. There was safety in being in the hands of so many talented actors. There was comfort in taking the familiar ride with the Corleone family. There were crosses and double crosses just as in life. There was a wedding, infidelities, family meals, unimaginable demonstrations of loyalty leading to warring strategies, funereal pondering, and an immense body count. Some people were strangled, some run through with knives, but mostly they met their demise from a bullet. Leo watched these various assassinations attentively, without feeling personally involved. His head, emptied of thought, his heart in cold storage, Leo wasn't sure if the experience was joyful, but it certainly hadn't been painful. He sat through *The Godfather* three times that afternoon.

The next day, Leo learned, through a text from Marianne, that a date and time had been established for the upcoming celebration of life. Whomever was in charge decided to ignore the plague and hold the event in a public space. It was to be in four days' time at Elevation, a non-denominational sacred space. For his part, Leo was just glad it was not ecclesiastical. Marcus was neither religious nor spiritual. He was pagan beautiful through and through. Leo remembered going with Marcus to a church funeral for someone who was about as religious as a spider monkey. They both ended up feeling like two priests invited to an orgy. Marcus had often trumpeted his belief in the universe and how little humanity mattered in its continuation. God was never in the details. One of his favored maxims was: "Life is short and hard. Somebody's got to decorate the motherfucker" Not exactly Shakespeare, but the notion was clear. If there was a God, he'd have to settle his debt with Marcus in the afterlife because he was doing this one solo.

Marcus did allow for a kind of spirituality, although drug-induced, into his purview. Leo and Marcus once travelled to Thailand together, and at Marcus's request, Leo was to get high with him on Ecstasy while there. Leo travelled a great deal in the states as a touring comic but had never been out of the US. Marcus had been so many places it went without saying he was an excellent travel companion. Leo agreed to explore his other dimension, as Marcus put it, and they ended up in Koh Samui for ten days. The first day they rented motorcycles and rode around the island getting massages and mud baths and eating fresh fish in outdoor restaurants overlooking the ocean. Early the second day of their stay, Marcus woke Leo up with a roguish smile and two tablets of Ecstasy in his hand. "Let's do this." he said. They had rented a double in a run-down hotel which barely provided the basics, but it was on the beach, a football's throw from the water. There would be no motor biking that day, he assured Leo. Leo was reticent only because of all the drugs he had consumed in his life; Ecstasy was not one of them. He had no idea what to expect. So be it.

Leo was hungry, but Marcus didn't want to diminish the drug's effect and told Leo not to spoil it by eating. They downed the pills on empty stomachs with a liter of water, grabbed towels, and went to the beach in front of their hotel. Leo spread out next to Marcus, whose smile was radiating with the sun. Leo drifted off to sleep, for how long he didn't know. Upon waking, the edges of his skin, perhaps his entire being, felt like it was whispering. He was lighter and suddenly felt supremely happy for no apparent reason. He turned to Marcus, who was grinning silently, having the best of waking dreams. This made Leo even happier, if that was possible. Leo lay back down and watched the show of clouds and wind engage with a cobalt blue backdrop, seeing these colors as meaningful metaphors for happiness.

A snorting sound emerged in the distance. Leo wasn't sure if this was imagined or not. He was deeply feeling both the physical and mental effects of the drug. When he raised his head to search the origin of the sound, he was sure he was hallucinating. He called out Marcus' name three or four times before he got a response.

"What, motherfucker? What?"

"Look at this shit." Marcus rose on his elbows.

The largest bull either of them had ever seen was rumbling down the shoreline, twenty feet away. It was a massive, scary creature with defined musculature, wielding deadly, looping horns. Leading this moving monstrosity by a rope attached to the ring in its nose was a small boy. He couldn't have been more than ten years old and was probably small for his age. Leo and Marcus were experiencing this with an added dimension of drug-induced incongruity. Now this ... this could be qualified as unexpected. Both were twinned in their positions, supported by their elbows, watching this miracle of madness until the two were comfortably out of harm's reach. They regarded one another at the same instant and laughed. For two minutes. Straight. No interruption. This was the first and last time Leo ingested the magic pill. It was also one of his favorite and most recurring images of Marcus. Laughing on the beach, under the influence of some drug, in a foreign country for the first time. No, neither of them was religious ... God would not have approved of that moment.

Marcus had a friend who was, in Leo's eyes, some type of faux shaman. Leo couldn't remember his name. It was one of those improvised names that are lame attempts at provoking either curiosity or fealty. Red Risings, Red Sunset, Red something was all he could remember. When Marcus introduced Mr. Red Whatever to Leo, the man had identified himself as a soul healer. Never one to miss out on a joke opportunity, Leo told him he had an old pair of shoes which could use his attention. Mr. Red had accompanied Marcus on numerous mind-expanding trips, which Marcus later would recount, replete with graphic descriptions of friendly phantoms and misshapen succubi that may or may not have appeared. Leo was never worried about Marcus completely falling off the road to reality. It seemed to be more the occasional experiment for him than perennial practice. Marcus' curiosity was unrestricted, not destructive. Still, with Marcus gone, Leo wished he could have taken more trips, psychedelic and literal, with his fallen friend. Perhaps he could have prevented ... something. At the very least, he would have had a few more minutes of uninterrupted laughter to remember. Without acknowledging it, Leo was deep in the throes of the bargaining stage of grief. It was ... if only this, and what if that? Staying away from phone conversations and discussions with mutual friends, he had few options to relieve himself of his grief.

Eventually, he turned to the internet. This he could do anonymously. He sat for hours and excavated the chats and memes and photos and dedications and remembrances of his friend that were populating the virtual world ad infinitum. Red River Solstice. There he was. Another trinomial. Marcus Leonard Perry and Red River Solstice. One of them had three first names and the other was just fucking nuts. At least that was the conclusion Leo had come to after reading Red River Solstice's dedication to his "soul traveling friend." He had posted:

"In the membrane of life, we float unassisted through many realities. Often it is an uncomfortable journey, but the destination is clear. We are free-falling into our own separate destinies. We are fully awake and conscious enough to experience that we are at the end of this existence and have moved on to another dimension previously unknown. Let us all exalt in Marcus' arrival."

The only thing that made Leo sicker than being subjected to this drivel was reading the commensurate fawning comments that followed.

So beautifully captured!

River, my friend, you run so deep.

Finally... *Consciousness is all we have. We are merely conduits.*

Leo's absolute favorite response was:

Consciousness says ... Wakey. Wakey.

There was also a personal note which Leo took to be a not-so-subtle advertisement for River enterprises, or whatever it might have been called. Red River Solstice was offering his studio for a special chanting session for all those interested in remembering Marcus by incanting gibberish for an hour. Donations would be welcome. Although Leo considered this stuff comic gold, it was too soon to fully appreciate the nuclear madness of the world at his friend's expense. He did, however, take a few screenshots to preserve these comments. He had a special file labeled *Dementia* in which he dropped them all before abandoning his computer.

His mail from the last few days sat on his desk unopened. He moved through it aimlessly, using the letter opener Marcus had presented him after his return from Sierra Leone. It was a beautifully made, slender piece of ebony wood with a noble African head for a handle. He was appreciating the letter opener more than he was paying attention to the mail until he arrived at a postcard which had three delicious looking tacos covering three quarters of the card. Thinking he might have been offered free tacos, he chanced reading the script floating discreetly in the margins. In block print at the top of the spiel was: **Everything you need to know about cremation**. Leo reread it a few times, imagining it to be one of the greatest advertising fuckups of modern time. As unbelievable as it seemed, he realized he was being solicited to attend a seminar on cremation. It was to take place at one of the more popular Mexican restaurants, where all participants would be awarded free tacos for their attendance. There was also a list of topics to be discussed, the most interesting being: 'Why you don't want your children or heirs to make your arrangements for you.'

It was moments like this Leo felt being a comedian was sheer redundancy. How could he be funnier than cremation tacos? Perhaps real comedy could only be found in the advertising and publicity world. He couldn't help but imagine what the meeting was like when the execs decided combining Mexican food and cremation was a thing of genius.

Hi fives all around. Breaking new ground without breaking ground. And so on ...

He was feeling better now. The rest of the mail was either bills, requests for more donations from charities he had already supported, or more advertisements ... none of which were as captivating as cremation tacos. The other advertisers obviously needed to step up their game. In an instant, he'd been supplied with comic gold. As soon as he could get out from under this cloud, he had some work ahead. Now it was all about surviving.

Leo had an improvisation class he taught twice a week over Zoom. It was a lucrative gig. He had twenty-eight students who paid him a handsome monthly fee. Ninety minutes twice a week was all he needed to stay afloat until he went on the road with his comedy. Tonight was personal improv night. One at a time, he would give his students a word or phrase and they would be obligated to vamp on it to wherever it led them for three minutes. It doesn't sound like much, but Leo was all too familiar with this type of free-fall. He knew it was as exciting as it was perilous. From his vantage, there were very few things more emotionally painful than bombing on stage. He also knew the unbridled joy which came with triumphing on your feet. He immediately thought of Marcus' celebration of life. In tonight's class he would give all his students related topics to explore.

'Death approaches. 'A friend's funeral.' 'Walking through cemeteries.'

'To carry a casket.' This was a partial list.

There was one student who was noticeably more gifted than the others. Leo thought he might do well with something like Cremation Tacos but decided to leave that one for himself. A strange thought came to him as he was wondering what to have for dinner. It must have been the cremation tacos that triggered it. He decided to add another topic to the improv class: 'Cooking for the dead.' It made no sense, which was what he found most persuasive about the notion. Or perhaps it did make sense. He and Marcus had cook-offs once a month where they would prepare the same dish and compare. Last month, Marcus outdid himself with a garlic and sea bass pasta. The category (because they treated it like a game show with commentary) was seafood pasta. It was Marcus' crowning achievement. Leo's delicious Bolognese with shrimp instead of meat took a distant second. Leo's commentary, waxing eloquently over this gastronomic achievement, cemented the meal as one of the most memorable. They ate until they were sick, with Leo calling the meal like a sports announcer.

Yes. Cooking for the dead ...

A year or two ago, Marcus and Leo went to a wake. A true wake. The body was there at the house, laid out on a table uncomfortably close to another table bedecked with food. The visual was disturbingly hilarious. Neither of them was close to the deceased; they had come as a show of support for a mutual friend. It probably wasn't the best decision for them to fire up a blunt beforehand, but once it's in the system, you go with what you know. Marcus was in his element. He knew how to be high in public. Leo on the other hand, couldn't stop snickering. It was one of those, 'everything is funny' highs for Leo. When Leo wasn't fighting chuckles, he was eating, all the while giving the nearby corpse the side eye. Marcus stayed busy being overly cordial to the several dozen people who passed in and out of the house on that **funereal** day. Leo kept to himself. He didn't know many people and he was paranoid of being found out. He settled for pleasant walks around the grounds, which were vast and lined with animal-themed topiary. He played with two Labradors who seemed not to care that he was high. He returned inside and found himself in an empty room where he passed the time staring smilingly at an elaborate lava lamp. When the time had come to leave, he found Marcus in the living room leaning over the body of the deceased, motionless. He was fixed in place and Leo wasn't sure what was transpiring between corpse and man but couldn't help thinking about the dementors from Harry Potter and how they could suck the life out of people. He grabbed Marcus by the arm and ushered him outside with some haste.

"You, okay? What was that? Communing with the dead?"

"I've never really spent much time with a dead person. It was surreal. I think I saw him breathing."

"Shut up."

"Well ... I definitely smelled his breath."

"Let's get the fuck out of here."

Marcus agreed, and while they were walking away, he stopped to light up again. He offered a hit to Leo, who declined.

"I gotta take the edge off." Marcus puffed. "Do me a favor. If I die before you and somebody wants to put me on a slab next to a table of rare roast beef, tell them to go fuck themselves."

Later in the evening, while making dinner, Leo wondered how Marcus would feel about his own upcoming celebration of life. Marcus loved a good party, but Leo had never experienced a party-like atmosphere at one of those things. The space, Elevation, was a multi-use building. Now that he had time to think about it, he remembered Marcus had invited him to Elevation another time. It was for one of those sacred dance events with music playing, people dancing, and incense smelling up a cavernous expanse. Leo declined. He saw those affairs as a gathering of rhythm-proof people moving to scary music only heard in yoga studios and ashrams. He did a full fifteen minutes of his impressions of these places in his standup. It was one of Leo's better-received bits while on tour. He killed.

Leo set his dinner table. He had just finished making a Caesar salad the old Mexican way. He'd recently heard this salad, the Caesar, originated in Mexico. Who knew? At least it's what they claimed over the internet. One of the ingredients lost on those outside of Mexico was the jigger of tequila in the dressing. Not Leo. He added the tequila, egg yolk, Worcestershire's sauce, garlic, mustard, and, of course, anchovies to the long leaves of romaine. He ate with relish for the first time in days. Sated, he began pondering the possibility of this celebration of life turning into some dreaded sacred event replete with spooky music and even spookier dancing. Leo might have to turn up to this celebration high, on the one hand, to honor his friend, and on the other hand, to self-medicate.

Marcus had shot himself in the heart.

This was still an unfathomable act. It was grossly incomprehensible. On top of that, try as he could, Leo could not help considering the dexterity and intent required in such an undertaking. The event itself was now revealing itself in waves. Leo would be fine, going about his day. He would busy himself with whatever it was that had a calming effect, when suddenly his life would stop and imagination would manifest itself, cinema-like. He could see Marcus in the car, perhaps listening to music. That sounded like a Marcus move. Getting in the mood to call it forever and a day. Some of that scary yoga music in the background might do the trick. Some whispery chants in a made-up language would certainly put Leo in the starting blocks. Besides, you don't kill after listening to someone like Marvin Gaye ... unless you're Marvin Gaye's father. There was no note, so he would have had time to listen to something. He had time to think, perhaps question the madness which was about to take place. It had to be an unequaled moment of loneliness. It would also have been an inexplicable instant of decisiveness. Even the drive to the parking lot had to be monumentally sinister. In Marcus's mind, he was on his way to what, where? What could he possibly have been thinking in those penultimate moments? Leo simply couldn't untie the strings to this mystery. He never had any inclination to end his own life, though the thought of ending the lives of others had occurred with random frequency.

Leo had previous experience with suicide. The first was when he was six years old. One of his neighbors shot his wife out of jealousy and then turned the gun on himself. Leo knew them both. He had been inside their home. They were a young couple who had lived directly across the street from his family. The soon-to-be-dead wife would kiss Leo on his forehead whenever opportunity presented. Her husband, the double murderer, had often played catch with Leo. Leo's parents tried to hide the news from him, but his young friends shared all the gory details. Shot in the head. Blood all over the walls. Screams. From a six-year-old's perspective, it was partly fascinating, partly distressing, but mainly incomprehensible. There was no context. He had no understanding of life yet, so how could he reconcile death? Thinking about it now, Leo did remember the moment with some disturbing exactitude. There was a foreign smell which came to him as his friend recounted the story in his parents' backyard. It wasn't something Leo could recreate, but it was locked somewhere in his sense memory. Not a memory which resurfaced often, but that it was still accessible after thirty-some odd years spoke to its power to sustain.

The other suicide he recalled was that of a friend severely compromised by drug use. Leo was ahead of the game on that one. He had expected no less. This was back in the days of attended funerals, which he did not. The deceased was a perennially troubled friend whom Leo felt was not built to withstand freedom of choice. Too many options. In other words, neither of these experiences remotely prepared him for the death of Marcus. Sounded like a play: The Death of Marcus. It would not have been the traditional four acts, but it would have had a surprising and tragic ending. Leo could feel exactly what was transpiring within his whole being after eating his Mexican Caesar salad. Even he had to resign himself to the fact that he was falling into the depression stage of grief. He needed air. He needed company. He even considered locating some of Marcus' magical ecstasy pills. Unfortunately, that would have meant contacting the charlatan shaman, Red River Solstice. Better to lather himself in honey and lie in a colony of fire ants than subject himself to that.

There was always the option of losing himself in the throes of some random female. The more random, the better. He didn't want to involve himself even peripherally with someone familiar, someone who was au courant with the tragedy. Pitiful is not an adjective he would have precededing sex. At this point, he doubted he could pull off what was needed to entice any woman to spend a vulnerable hour or so in his company. He might end up in tears. Adding to the fact he was not feeling particularly carnal himself, he worried he had the smell of death about him. It was a good time to go for a run. The park would be busy, but the runner's path would be clear and with any luck, he could air his soul out.

A half mile into the run, his head was somehow emptied of the detritus of death and replaced by the quotidian sounds and sights of the park. His nose was pleasantly assaulted by the powerful scent of Eucalyptus resin. He considered it to be 'the' California tree. A tree whose odor held his childhood identity. Its smell could and did transport him to a mass of memories grafted to his unconscious. It begged his memory to unleash layers of time stacked in some remote corner of his person, enabling him to literally run through his life feelingly. These were fleeting images, familiar yet just out of reach. His deep breathing, encouraged by effort, was all he could hear. Even in a peopled park, he was alone. He often ran to clear his head or to imagine his body chemistry running rampant while he was moving through space. He liked to read up on the human body and the ridiculously complicated functions his body performed, even at rest. He knew while he was running, his heart, lungs, and blood were performing the incomprehensible with ease. This knowledge centered and humbled him the same way contemplating his place in the universe did. He would sometimes gaze up at the stars, the planets, and instantly reconcile the obvious. His life was less than less when it came to considered history or anticipated future. This was noticeably helpful. He was having a moment of normalcy, which felt strangely amusing. Runners seldom smile, but he could feel a goofy grin steal up on him. Marcus also made an appearance in this Déjà vu experience fleetingly, phantom-like, and always laughing. Effortless memory occupied him until he was weightless. He ran past a lake, which seemed too beautiful for contemplation. Everything, every damn thing, was a suggestion of something else.

There was a time when Leo loathed running. He would observe runners passing him and shake his head almost as an affront to this labored activity. Where the hell were they all going? A poet friend of his in college, Robert Sawyer, introduced him to the sweaty art. They were walking by a track, when Robert suggested they 'do a few laps.' Leo cringed at the thought of it but couldn't say no; it was such a stupendously distant notion that it made sense. Leo managed to get halfway through the first lap before his stomach rebelled.

"Just breathe. Slowly. Deeply," Robert told him. Leo took his advice and finished the half mile. He became a runner from that day forth.

Leo suddenly had a remembrance of a long-ago run which produced happy tears. Marcus and he were in Martinique on one of their last minute out of the blue adventures. The day they landed, they went for a run outside the city center. Halfway through, a thunderstorm broke out, drenched them in warm droplets, then disappeared. At that precise moment, they rounded a bend where a cemetery appeared. Behind it, at the edge of the property, was the water. The dead were bequeathed an ocean view. Only in what's considered a third-world country would they be given this type of real estate. In America, Leo and Marcus would be looking out at a block of condominiums instead of this verdant field of age-stained headstones. They held this exacting conversation with no more than a shared glance. The dead had rights. Leo imagined Marcus being buried by that sea—the view of life ... in death.

Normally, Leo was a three-miler. He had done this circuit twice, which meant he had run six miles this day, an achievement motivated by a supreme sadness and fear of the same. For the moment, he basked in this accomplishment. Leo found a bench that would serve to accommodate a deep stretch. It was in this action Leo had his most profoundly naked feelings surface like a football-field-sized-submarine. Finally. He found himself stretched to his maximum, weeping uncontrollably. It was the full on, snot producing, gasping for breath, ugly faced, release of sorrow. He was now without questions or answers. There were only bodily functions gone amiss. He anticipated publicly expelling from all orifices if he didn't leave the park immediately. It was not lost on him how deep stretching can release more than muscle tightness.

Leo sat in his bathtub, soaking in steamy water augmented by some crystals Marcus had given him, which he swore by. They were supposed to administer inner peace. Leo had never used them before, but thought if not now, when? Besides, Marcus was correct about that little blue Viagra pill he had once sent him in a birthday card. Leo sported a hard-on for two days. This evening, Leo had candles going and even turned the ringer of his phone back on. He'd spoken briefly to a fellow comedian who shared a couple of new jokes he had written, which were funny as shit. Leo, paying the highest comedian-to-comedian compliment, admitted he wished he had written them. He had just drifted off into a place of absolute peace when his phone rang. He was lucky enough to have it next to his tub. A rarity. The caller was a blast from the proverbial past. Dara and he had been a hot item until she graduated from med school, at which time she immediately moved to Boise. Why anyone would move to Boise, bumfuck, Idaho, remained a mystery to him. He supposed people required doctors in Boise as much as anywhere else. She was checking in after a two-year absence.

Things were good in Idaho, but she missed him.

"Really?' And so, it began. There he was, soaking in a tub after a miraculous run, pondering all things dead and gone, and now having thinly veiled phone sex with a doctor. Life was a thorny, funny little thing. His privates were not so private anymore, sticking out of the water like a flagpole of pride. Before the cherished moment of finality, he unleashed a torrent of flatulence, which caused him to drop the phone in the tub presently teeming with a sea of bubbles. All was not lost, however, as he knew this was more comic gold. There was much to catalogue recently. Damaged humor ... damaging humor ... what did it matter? If he could just make it through tomorrow, it would all settle itself. Yes, he could clearly see life was a strange, unpredictable journey with an unforeseen comic likelihood.

The day of the 'Celebration of Life' announced itself with an exuberant display of sunshine. It was no surprise to Leo. By this point, ironies had become the rule. It was to take place today, coincidently on a Sunday, which as a bonus would align it with the hidden drama of all things church-like. Leo still was not certain he would attend. The recurring thought of Red River Solstice turning Marcus' departure into an infomercial for his chanting dynasty gave Leo tremendous pause. It would be unlike Red River to miss this opportunity to spread his incense scented wisdom. What better place than a celebration of life on a supposed holy day. No, he wasn't sure he could make it through such nonsense without inadvertently screaming. Or attacking. He did have his clothes selected in the event logic failed. Casual. Cool. The same way Marcus would have dressed if the coffin were fitted for Leo. One thing Leo knew for certain was he would have to arrive at the last possible moment if he was to avoid the rush of death small talk. He had been successful at isolating himself for the most part since that dreaded day. He'd returned a few texts and phone calls, limiting his responses to mutterings in the affirmative to whatever people were saying. It was clear they wanted to speak and the easiest thing to do was let them. He no doubt would be a person of interest when he arrived, by default. Leo had not been available and there were many who would want to ... catch up.

When he arrived at Elevation, the carpark was overflowing. He was obliged to park three blocks away. It was a three-hundred-meter trek. On the way, he attempted to empty his mind, knowing it would be filled with the horrors of anticipating what he would find upon arrival. A dog was chained to a fence, barking with menace as Leo passed. Another bad omen. He felt the gravel through his shoes in this unincorporated part of the city, bereft of sidewalks. The sound was malignant. He was crunching time with every step. It was not often he sauntered with his head down, watching his feet do what they always do, but today he could do nothing else. A strain of unidentifiable music could be heard briefly, then it ended strangely. With the door a few feet away, there was still time to turn around. He seriously thought about it, then laughed. That might be the ticket. Enter this circus with a sense of humor.

As he opened the door, he was struck by the crush of the multitude. It was standing room only space. There were people pouring out of everywhere. A thrust stage was set up, with people on three sides. Entering the front door left him facing the stage behind several others standing in front of him. No one noticed his entrance. A man whom Leo did not know was waxing eloquently about Marcus, something about his character being unique. *This might be manageable*, he thought. Leo leaned on a wall for support and, if needed, the door was directly behind him in case an emergency exit was required. Several people wandered up to the stage to expound. They all moved with reverence and purpose, and they all said basically the same thing. 'Marcus was this. Marcus was that.' Many told the tale of how they met or how long they had known him. It was a history class for strangers. A few attempted humor in their panegyric and received polite laughter. In a comedy club, their comments would have been greeted with aggravated silence. That's when Red River Solstice moved his shaman ass to the stage. It was a dramatic moment, at least it was clear Red River thought as much. Upon arriving on the stage, he turned around and took in the audience with a silence he surely mistook for profundity. He stared out at the gathering for a full ten seconds before speaking. Leo turned around to ensure the exit door remained within reach. To his great surprise, Sir Solstice didn't have much to say. He appeared truly overwhelmed by the passing of his partner in highness and had trouble getting the words out. As much as Leo hated to admit it, he was moved by this brevity. Or perhaps he was simply overjoyed that he would not be subject to an incoherent monologue of spiritual drivel. Red River needed to be helped back to his seat. Well of course, he did.

Several others spoke. And so it went until Marcus's sister came to the stage. She was wearing a peach-colored dress, which accented her full figure, leaving not much to the imagination. Marianne was always forthright in who she was and what she felt. In many ways, she mirrored her brother. Leo and she always got along. This could be interesting. Marianne spoke of Marcus as a child. He was curious in mind and behavior. She told of his adolescence. He was always honest, mostly to his detriment. She extolled him as a man. He was a true friend to all those deserving. When she talked about what he was as a brother, she meandered here and there and ended with an apology to all her women friends. She said her brother had asked her to hook him up with several of them. Her stock reply was "None of her girlfriends were worthy." The best line so far elicited chuckles.

Marianne looked out over the crowd searchingly, silently. This went on long enough for Leo to wonder if she had mentally wandered off. It would be understandable if she had. The crowd waited patiently in supreme quietude. Suddenly, Marianne spoke out with unnatural force. She inquired loudly over the microphone if Leo was present? Leo turned to the door which was now completely obstructed by newcomers. Slowly people looked around to see where this person Leo was. Some undoubtedly wanted to know who this Leo person was. It was premature of him to think his trip from his car to the venue was to be the longest walk of his life. He was now faced with passing through a gauntlet of bulging eyes and the strangely inverted smiles landing on him as he made his way to

Calvary. He thought of women walking in beauty pageants being ogled by lecherous judges. He was reminded of the time he was elected class speaker as a lark—a joke. No one really wanted him representing them and it was revealed how little they felt about him when he rose to speak. Leo seriously would have preferred to be chanting with Red River than going up there and saying ... what? He noticed himself moving, again watching his feet do what they do. A strange phenomenon at present. He would never again take the simple act of walking for granted. Someone reached out to touch him on the way. He moved back to the center of the aisle to ensure it would be the last time that would happen.

Marianne was patiently awaiting his arrival. When he stood next to her, she took his hands in hers. Their eyes met painfully, secretly, in public. She hugged him and whispered. Whatever was exchanged was going to be a real secret. That's to say, a secret never told. She left him there.

It took a moment for Leo to face this community of Marcus' acolytes. When he found a sliver of composure, he faced the crowd. His eyes landed on Red River Solstice, who was giving him some type of shaman hand greeting. It was a complex, exaggerated movement of both hands. Leo couldn't turn away. Obviously encouraged by the attention, Red River began embellishing. His hand movements became more dramatic. He had locked onto Leo, and now he was taking flight. Silently, at first, he rose. Standing in place, his head lulled in circles, rhapsodic, trance-like. Leo was mesmerized. This was some crazy shit. Red River caught the attention of others who politely allowed for this display of spiritual possession. Leo had no notion of what was happening, but whatever it was ... it was some funny shit. He began to chuckle. Red River picked up on his chuckle and joined him, without missing a beat in his gesticulations. He wasn't chanting aloud, but his body was now an orchestra of chants. He turned to face the crowd. There was a chorus of titters slowly building. While Leo may have been laughing at Red River, the audience seemed to be laughing with him. Leo was now convulsed with laughter. He now had to step away from the microphone. He could barely breathe for laughing. The moment was now completely out of hand. Marianne reached over and pulled at Red River's belt of talismans. He sat down as happy as he'd been in life. Leo had, in turn, reached the final stage of grief. Acceptance. Comic gold.

Juveniles

The park at Palais Royal sits hidden across the street from the Louvre, and directly behind the great French theatre, La Comédie Française. Because it is surrounded on all four sides by buildings, it is a quiet couple of acres in the middle of a busy section of Paris. In late June, when daylight intrudes into the night, people gather around a generous fountain that anchors the park. Barry Davies, part time therapist, full time adventurer was seated there, shoes and socks beside him, feet dangling over the fountain's lip, watching couples kiss as if they were alone in their bedrooms. He didn't allow his feet to touch the water, as it was beige, fetid, and a little stinky. The minor stench didn't seem to dissuade the locals' passion, so Barry stayed and observed the ways of the French until the smell was no longer cute and then moved on to his destination. Just on the other side of these buildings, a restaurant waited and, he hoped, an evening of promise. As he laced his shoes, he recalled his good fortune.

Earlier in the day, he had had a chance meeting with a 'friendly Parisian stranger.' He revisited the phrase as he put on his shoes. 'A friendly Parisian stranger.' An oxymoron if there ever was one. A woman of physical gifts too numerous to ignore was seated next to him, alone in a café. Barry gambled and asked her for directions to Quai Branly, the city's newly opened museum. From her blank response, he assumed correctly that she understood no English. He had no alternative but to assault her with his horribly corrupt French. Surprisingly un-offended, she produced her Paris map and traced the route to the museum with her finger. No wedding ring on an expressive hand. Poitrinée ... he understood this word to be slang for having breasts. And she did. They were elegant mounds perfectly positioned to take advantage of the afternoon sun's highlights. She spoke. Barry waited until he found a word that he understood to jump in. Tour Eiffel. Eiffel Tower. He got that. It was near the Eiffel Tower.

"Do you know a good restaurant? Un restaurant pas cher mais bon? J'aime bien le vin français."

She answered him in a rapid stream of consonants and vowels, engaging sounds, yet completely unfamiliar. French, French, French, French was all he could hear. With much difficulty, he understood the name of the restaurant to be Juveniles, and she was to eat there at nine p.m.

"On mange ensemble?" he asked her.

She stopped and cocked her head to the side, regarding him as if she had just noticed a mouth growing out of the side of his face.

"Vous est Americain?"

"Oui, je suis Americain."

"Beatrice. Je m'appelle Beatrice."

"Well, hello, Beatrice. Je m'appelle Barry."

"On mange ensemble. À neuf heures. À bientôt." And she left.

Five hours later, after his stop at the fountain, he found himself seated at a corner table in the recommended restaurant, waiting patiently for his date. Beatrice, an interesting if not necessarily pretty name. Beatrice ... a compound of bear and actrice. Which made no sense at all but thinking about it allayed his nervousness. What if she didn't show? What if she came with a friend, her boyfriend, for example? Arriving with a girlfriend would be more encouraging. Ménage à trois was a French term after all.

She had given him perfect instructions to locate the museum, but by the time he arrived, there was a line around the block. This prompted a notation in his diary: 'a new museum attracts visitors. It is an event. Arrive early.' In retrospect, this turned out to be good news. The prospect of his relating a museum experience to Beatrice in French seemed painfully comic. If previous experiences held true, having dinner with her would be much less difficult. He found that French people so loved to talk, he needed only point her in the direction of an interesting topic, and she would proceed. His job was simply to look enchanted by what she had to say.

When Beatrice arrived solo, Barry was well into his second glass of a Chenin Blanc from Languedoc. She almost kissed him on both cheeks, then ordered a glass of the same from the waiter. And so, it began. French, French, French, French. He listened attentively, and when there was a pause, he would act as if he were deeply considering what she had said, then reply, "Oui, mais bien sûr."

He was absolutely content to sit there and quietly watch her lips swell and pucker in the strange formations necessary to produce French sounds. With enlivened eyes she spoke about the politics of America referring to several American Presidents. Quite a feat, he thought, being able to make politics sound sexy. He noticed she had added something to her blouse, a colorful vest that stopped at her ribcage. Additional clothing notwithstanding, she appeared more naked than before.

The waiter took their order, flirting with Beatrice shamelessly. Food followed in waves. Barry's French improved dramatically. Or was it the wine? At any rate, he was doing quite a bit of talking, vaguely aware yet unconcerned that he was savagely murdering the French language. He used the wrong tense, gender, word, and often all in the same sentence. Beatrice appeared undeterred, listening, smiling, and from time to time, touching herself for dramatic effect. She ate with an energy usually reserved for famished chinchillas. Sponging up sauces, deftly removing all meaty remnants from a string of baby lamb chops, matching him glass for glass.

They worked leisurely through a second bottle of a delicious St Joseph, while enthusiastically emptying their dinner plates. A moment of silence would creep in, Barry would try to look thoughtful, the penny would drop, and she was off again, French, French, French. It poured out of her mouth like liquid glitter. He scanned the table between them. The paper tablecloth was littered with breadcrumbs, stained by red wine and blood from her lamb. She's a lovely carnivore, he thought as he fingered a demitasse discolored by thousands of espressos. Ah, now this, this is Paris, this instant intimacy, this mixture of sensuality and civility. It charged his imagination and set into motion all his fantasies. Anything was possible. Barry acknowledged his good fortune. A meal with a beautiful woman in a foreign city. A foreign restaurant. A foreign language. Since they shared no history, there could be no expectations, therefore no disappointment. He was free to fantasize at will, and being a therapist, fantasies came effortlessly. Their very proximity provoked intimacy. He could smell her from his seat a breath away, and when she ate with such relish, he felt as if he could taste what was in her mouth.

And still she talked. Barry wondered if she talked in bed. Of course, she came in French, but was her orgasm accompanied by the French National Anthem, or did she simply repeat, 'Oui, Oui, mon dieu?' So many possibilities. The therapist in him advised him to remain fixed in the moment. This may be it, he thought, so it must be everything. The best fantasies live in the heat of possibility, when the prospect of physical contact still existed.

Suddenly, Beatrice stopped talking and pointed at Barry. It immediately dawned on him that he had left some of his dinner on his face. He reached for his napkin, which was no longer in his lap but had fallen out of reach under the table. Beatrice moved back and brought the table slightly with her.

"Vas-y," she told him.

Barry squeezed his head underneath the table. He snatched his napkin and saw her skirt was set back on parted legs and try as he could, he could not help noticing a sheer G-string that exposed a patch of black sable. A sound of wonder escaped from somewhere deep inside him. As Barry reemerged from underneath the table, he banged his head. Beatrice tried not to laugh. Rubbing the pain away, he wondered whether she knew of the joy that could be gleaned from a flash of flesh and colored cotton, if she knew how unfair her power was, to be able to cloud a man's mind and fire him with need in one effortless gesture while remaining unaffected herself. It was fucking unfair; however, it in no way interfered with his sense of gratitude.

"Ça va, toi?" he responded. He remembered to wipe his mouth and when he went to replace his napkin, he thought he had felt her foot in his lap. It was not her foot, but rather his appendage, disfiguring his pants.

By the time the lavender ice cream arrived, they were comfortable even in their silence.

The waiter brought them chocolates and a round of champagne on the house. Barry had cultivated a growing distaste for the waiter. When he had excused himself earlier to go to the toilette, he noticed the waiter arrive at his table and stay until he had returned. Barry was inclined to introduce the waiter to a little old-fashioned American violence, but reason prevailed.

Two bottles of wine and four after-dinner drinks richer, Beatrice and Barry made their way out of the restaurant. A taxi flew by them. They began walking. At the top of the road sat a large-scale statue of Molière fitted like a dashing musketeer. They stopped to admire it.

"Did you know Molière died on stage performing?" he asked.

Beatrice smiled.

"You don't speak any English, do you?"

"No English," she said, unapologetically.

"It's okay. Je parle anglais et tu parles français, okay?"

"Oui. Okay." She began to fiddle inside her purse.

"I look at you and I can't help but think you must taste like caramel and apples, yum." Barry waited for a response. She offered him a cigarette.

"Caramel, apples and Gauloises, I'll bet you taste like that, yum, yum."

Beatrice shrugged, took a deep drag off her cigarette, and blew a piece of tobacco off her lip.

They walked on through the streets of Paris, past the Ritz Hotel, up the Rue du Rivoli and turned right in front of the Hôtel de Ville. Parisian life purred around them like a fat, happy tomcat. Beatrice led and he followed, the alcohol clearing slightly from his head. He wondered from time to time if she was even aware that he was following. She finally came to a stop as they arrived at a big stone bridge arcing the River Seine.

Beatrice turned to face him, her back against the railing and her arms open wide to interpretation. She fixed him with a look that was foreign even to a therapist.

Does she want to fuck me or kill me? He was amenable to either choice as she drew him into her, her arms winding tightly around his waist. His body was fully attentive, stuck against Beatrice with a concrete rail behind her. To his left in the distance sat Notre Dame, behind Beatrice was the Eiffel Tower, and below them was the River Seine. It all seemed romantic and medieval. He wondered if he was worthy of the moment and knew it called for bravery. A courageous man would fall to his knees, pull her skirt over his head, and kiss her until she ran out of secrets. That thought must have been communicated because with a slight movement, Beatrice offered him her lips which did taste of wet sweet caramel and apples and Gauloises, and brought chills to Barry and reconfirmed his belief that women were what made everything else important and that if he died right now, in this moment, with Paris all around him and Beatrice pushing into him, if the last sounds he heard were her short breaths and quiet moans, if his mouth would stay dripping from the moisture of hers, then midnight could come when it would.

Behind Beatrice, the Eiffel Tower erupted in flashing lights. It was midnight in Paris.

Turkey Day

It was the first Thanksgiving dinner without Mom. Their father had passed a little over ten years before, and all the children focused the balance of their parental love on Mom. As in many families, Mother was the purest recipient of their love. With her gone now, they considered themselves orphans. It would be the first time all six of them would gather since the funeral eight months prior. It was to be decidedly sibling exclusive. The presence of husbands, wives, and/or children was not requested. In that particular arrangement, they were all in agreement. Decorative handmade invitations were assembled and mailed with tiny reflective turkeys strewn inside the envelope. This touch was a nod to Mom who regularly sent her children festive cards with holiday appropriate confetti poured into the envelope. Messy magic.

Baron, the eldest son, took responsibility for the mailers. He insisted everyone RSVP, though it had been previously discussed ad nauseam for weeks. He left numerous voicemails on everyone's phone. Baron habitually saw things through, if often to the point of absolute tedium. From his tiny bungalow in Topanga Canyon, he would handle the who and what of this family gathering. The siblings accepted this display of authority without argument. Baron took control of family matters by default. He was admittedly controlling by nature. Many believed he would have made a splendid Nazi, but Baron was simply a good guy who had no off switch. Red lights and stop signs were mere suggestions to him. He avoided the hurricanes of life because more than his full throttle drive, he possessed killer charm and an epic ability to fabricate on his own behalf. Also, being the oldest sibling really meant something to him.

Thanksgiving dinner would take place at the home of the youngest daughter, **Lizzie,** and her affluent husband in Sherman Oaks, California. A tony neighborhood in the dreaded valley where Lizzie and her husband Bill had built a mini fortress. The three-story with basement house was anchored in front by a sizeable working fountain replete with pissing angels. It must be added that these plaster heralds were noticeably well-endowed. The first test upon arriving chez Lizzie was to survive the entrance. Lizzie's brothers and sister often failed this test, and no visit was without comment on the angel's lavatory in the front yard. Lizzie's response never varied: "Mind your business." Being the youngest girl in a large family gave her a pedigree that included subtle lifelong benefits. She was granted certain passes similar to the ones her brother Beau received, though he was biologically the youngest. It appeared being born female, and the youngest girl at that, was a definitive case for merit. Or so she believed, and she showed no reluctance capitalizing on it. Lizzie's voice was seldom less than declamatory, her opinion stream of consciousness. Lending her consideration to any situation, Lizzie assumed the posture of oracle. That she, the youngest sister, and Baron the oldest brother got on so well remained a mystery to the rest of the family. They both drove the same lanes brakeless.

Of the six, only two had to travel some distance. **Quentin** (Q) would drive down from San Francisco. Quentin and Maya, the oldest sister, were fraternal twins. Q presented himself as a successful graphic artist, though a good deal of that success originated in his ability to score a fabulous apartment in the city with not only rent control, but an uncommonly humane landlord. He had held onto that apartment in Upper Clayton for the past ten years. Q detested Los Angeles and identified the San Fernando Valley as the devil's scrotum. His ex-wife grew up in Encino.

Quentin was the brother unfairly considered the least intelligent. At least, he thought it unfair. Sure, he would confuse things like secular and non-secular or salted and unsalted butter. He could never remember whether non-secular meant religious or not. In all fairness, its definition is somewhat counterintuitive. As for salted or non-salted butter, in his words," What the fuck?" He also had a habit of making scores of notes to remember important things, then often forgetting where he put these notes. However, it was his choice of wife that placed him squarely in the category of the supremely unenlightened. He met a woman of extravagant beauty, and after a month of bliss, married her, divorcing her three weeks afterward. This was a failure of intelligence none of the family could embrace. That he was also considered the most artistic member of the family lent a mote of balance to their appraisal of him. As for the subject of his paintings, the themes changed yearly almost to the day. His current subject matter was homeless people relieving themselves in and on iconic buildings. Again, in his words, "Art and comedy are the only two places you can breach etiquette with impunity ... and I ain't no comedian." Quentin did impress by making a living selling his paintings, but even that success was marred by questionable thinking. He had been audited ten years running.

Julian, AKA Jules, flew in from New York. As much as he adored NYC, a trip to warm southern Californian weather was always a welcome respite from the familiar chaos of the city. Jules was an emergency room doctor who, by his admission, disliked a good portion of his patients. 'Too many problems, not enough responsibility.' Julian began as a painter. He wasn't bad. Quentin was much better. Julian moved on to math, which he hated, but it turned out to be a subject he could master effortlessly. This, along with the desire to make a substantial living, led him to med school. He knew of no doctor being food insecure. Med school was a laborious stretch of his life, and he often wondered how he would fare when the initials MD appeared after his name. His outlaw tendencies didn't align with the professional responsibilities expected of his field. He was prodigiously tattooed, resembling a traveling fairground carny, more than an emergency room doctor. Although he kept current with the new medical information, discoveries, and techniques, he opted out of most doctor conferences, which put him at odds with his superiors.

Jules worked at a teaching hospital, which meant he would instruct interns and resident doctors on what to expect at work in the emergency room. In that domain, he reigned supreme. It wasn't that he was popular with his students, which he certainly was, but it served as a joyous release from the day-to-day lunacy experienced in an emergency room. He had many anecdotal tales to frighten and/or entertain his disciples. Like the time a patient high on PCP became so combative he had to be subdued by half a dozen nurses and EMT's, yet still broke one of their jaws. Or when, after being deloused and given new clothes, a raging patient stood up from the gurney and a shower of dead lice fell from his beard and hair, littering the tile between them. And of course, there was always the possibility of being vomited or shat on by a patient for any number of reasons—fun times in the emergency room.

Julian arrived in LA secretly a couple of days in advance so he could enjoy the beach before the holiday dinner. This time out, he encountered a public interest lawyer who also took pole dancing for upper body strength. She had an autistic daughter who was spending the holidays with her father. He liked her complications, which were on par with her fitness. In their initial meeting, she eagerly informed him she was a Scorpio with some such and such a thing rising. All of which is to say he didn't emerge in any substantial way from his Airbnb for forty-eight hours after meeting her.

Maya was the closest geographically, maintaining an apartment in Hollywood. She had recently moved in with her man, who was twenty years older and struggled mightily with English, having grown up in Mexico City. Maya spoke negligible Spanish and felt the communication deficit was the key to their happiness. That, and he was useful around the house. Her man worked in construction. Their love was as much mutual agreement as passionate exchange. Their biggest disagreement in the five years they'd been together was in her explaining why he wasn't invited to this year's Thanksgiving. He normally went home to Mexico during that period, and this was the first time he was to remain in Los Angeles, He simply couldn't factor why he wasn't invited. Maya was the easiest to be around. Her disposition was steeped in her appreciation of life and family. She could take your breath away with her kindness. Lizzie once described Maya as 'a sad song that always promised a happy ending.' Maya had a grown son living in Santa Fe, New Mexico, tending to a restaurant he had built from scratch. Maya was thankful for all things and considered both good and bad happenstances to be blessings. She belonged to a universal church whose name none of her family members could ever remember. Her church affiliation was her most meaningful touchstone apart from her immediate family. How could it not be? Her reality existed alongside those who experienced the most misfortune, and she was adroit in that territory. Where others would ignore or qualify what's unattractive in humanity, she demonstrated the patience and curiosity people normally reserved for personal advancement. Her family nickname, half in seriousness, was Saint Maya.

Beau was the youngest sibling. He had recently turned twenty-one and had discovered drinking to augment his love of cannabis and phone addiction. His nickname used by all was 'that Gen Z brother.' Beau was always busy but seldom worked. Or if he did, not for any length of time. He was heavily into hip-hop culture and dressed as if he were forever auditioning for a rap video. He might have been. No one really knew what he was up to or where he was until he landed on someone's doorstep in need of familial assurance. He was also the go-to if someone needed IT assistance. Beau was deadly handsome, and no one ever saw him with the same girl twice. He was and always would be the baby. After his mom and dad had five children, Beau might well have been called a parental afterthought, if not a mistake. His entire existence could have been a fortunate (for him) accident. Wholly unintentional. He was old enough to process this probability, which he frequently did, chiefly at family gatherings. At these turn-ups, his stories, his concerns, his very dreams often fit outside the paradigms of the rest of his siblings. He felt unique in his comprehension of the world and his age had much to do with it. In the family fold, he was the wrinkle. He had been born into a world of phones, internet porn, virtual reality, and data addiction, not to mention some of his youth being stolen by a worldwide plague. Conversely, his siblings actively protected their memories of dial-up phones and playing outside until the streetlights came on, against the onslaught of this new, unrecognizable world. When his brothers and sisters were young, they could do serious jail time for a nickel bag of weed, whereas Beau enjoyed VIP customer status at half a dozen cannabis collectives. There was an avalanche of unspoken polarity visited upon their contrasting worlds. It was harder for his brothers and sisters because, to put it bluntly, they were living in his world now. And to extend this plain speak, Beau was enjoying the shit out of it.

The Wednesday before Thanksgiving in southern California is always a day of crowded everything: streets, stores, freeways, restaurants, and, weather permitting, maxed out beaches. To use one of Beau's terms, it was a time to 'Git in where you fit in.' The entire Noble family was doing just that. Julian, the emergency room doctor, had reluctantly released his pole dancer, Lola, from his Airbnb and was focusing on his last day before the family get-together. He loved his family dearly, but in appropriately small doses. Earlier that day, he was walking around his place wearing Lola's panties on his head, crown-like, and singing Bob Dylan's, *Like a Rolling Stone*. He would sing full out as if he were in concert, then turn to his image in the mirror to adjust his crown. Life was a beautiful thing. Before he went out into the madness of festive LA, he called a friend to score some blow for Lola. He had promised to provide her with a bit of nose candy, and she had promised to return later that evening attired in different lingerie. Win-win. He then put in a call to Beau, the family member with whom he felt closest. Beau picked up first ring.

"What's up, doc?"

"Hey, baby brother. You good?"

"Chillin' per usual. You in town? You coming tomorrow?"

"Yes, yes."

"How's work in the ER? Shit must be lethal in the Big Apple..."

"... tryin' to save 'em all, even the idiots. Vicious cycle. You working?"

"Gettin' in on that sneaker joint. Buy low, sell high. Got a lead on some Kanye West shit. Ya feel me? That's the new stock market, tennis shoes 'n shit."

"Well, okay. I have no fucking idea what you're talking about, but git in where you fit in."

"You see? That's what I'm talking 'bout. Man, I gotta move on somethin'. See you tomorrow, yeah?"

"Okay, Beau. Easy does it."

"If it ain't easy I don't even think about doin' it."

Jules understood this last comment to be an unfortunate admission, but he and Beau got along fine because neither he nor his baby brother was overly judgmental. After hanging up, Jules stood admiring the panties on his head before folding them neatly and placing them in his pocket. He opened the curtains for the first time in two days, letting in some LA almost-sunlight, and noticed he had a lovely view of Echo Park and its putrescent pond. Many years ago, he had attended a Cuban festival there with his brother, Quentin. Q had met his ex-wife there, who had been at the festival dancing as if she were possessed. It turned out that she was, and Q's marriage and divorce could have been source material for many a horror story. Jules warned him early on and more often than Q could appreciate, which is why to this day, they have a complicated love for one another.

Thanksgiving Day was sunny and chilly in Sherman Oaks. The smell of burning firewood smoldered in the air and gave off a hint of winter, the best it could, being a mere fifty-eight degrees. Inside the home of Lizzie and Bill sat a large table garnished with extravagant place settings. It had a friendly pumpkin theme, orange being the dominant color. Everything on the table looked edible, even the plates and silverware.

Lizzie was a perfectionist whose anxiety allowed for nothing less. She was taking photos of her table setting and Bill was taking photos of Lizzie taking photos. He had hundreds of similar photos. It began as Bill's way of proving to her she took too many pictures. Now it was his favorite photographic subject, wife with camera. They then sat quietly at the table, holding hands, surveying their prandial artistry. Lizzie leaked a tear.

"I just hope the little millennial or Z, X, Y, whatever refrains from getting high before he gets here. I can't stand to see that dumb look on his face."

"You mean the glassy eyes?"

"I mean, the 'nobody's there because I'm high as fuck' dumb look. If Mom was here, he wouldn't do that." The doorbell rang.

"It's Baron."

"I'm sure."

Wednesday, the day before Thanksgiving, Baron the presumptive Nazi was high in Topanga Canyon. Not high like Beau, but from a hike high up in the mountains with Valerie, his sometime lover. Baron had met her on a dating site and their inchoate relationship was predicated upon long hikes followed by food and ending in sex. Baron was a life coach who enjoyed considerable success offering behavioral tips to confused couples. A closet criminal, he managed to stay off the radar while he charged people a small fortune for his services, convincing them to pay in cash. Consequently, online dating was a gimme to someone with Baron's conversational skill set, and although he found Valerie on a site, she had become his longest relationship in recent memory. Admittedly, she was changing him, even so, he kept his online dating lifeline current without meeting any new prospects. They remained in the always accessible pipeline one click away. It was his safety valve. Recently Valerie had become less available. Which meant she wouldn't let him tie her up, or do any of their fun role playing, both activities introduced by Valerie. Baron thought the nice trifecta of hike, food, and sex during this holiday time might get her back on track.

On this day before the feast, they were investigating rock formations and hidden caves. At least Baron was. Valerie sat on a smooth boulder, fixated on a distant vista, silently conversing with the horizon. Baron joined her. She had tears in her eyes, which threw him completely. Whatever was going on inside her was about to come out in smoldering waves.

"I'm pregnant ... I'm fucking pregnant."

Baron heard it the first time but failed to respond. He was frozen. Colors emerged. His breathing grew labored. He felt faint but was unable to move enough to lie down, which was the only thing he wanted to do. He needed to lie down and maybe cry for an hour. Or scream. The vista before him became blurry. His heartbeat sped up. He successfully stood up only to slump back down on a nearby boulder. He repeated this action several times until Valerie smacked his ass resoundingly, the only part of him she could reach. Baron buried his head in his hands and after a moment of saturated silence, he whispered softly, "Whose is it?"

Valerie's scream could be heard for miles.

Maya was very involved with her church. This time of year, she did volunteer work getting food to the rampant homeless population in her Hollywood neighborhood. On this Wednesday before Thanksgiving, she was finishing up organizing a pre-cooked meal for hundreds of destitute drifters when she received a call from her son in New Mexico. The restaurant's name, Salt and Wine, popped up on her screen. Her son was calling from work, something he rarely did.

"Hi, baby."

"Happy Thanksgiving. What are you doing?"

"Setting everything up for our Thanksgiving dinner for the homeless. It's all done. What about you?"

"Prepping. Doing a special dinner tonight. Completely overbooked."

"That's so good, baby. Wish you were here."

"Me too ... can you talk?"

"Is it ..."

"Yes, Mom."

"K, baby. Hold on."

Maya went into a makeshift office on the multipurpose church grounds, locked the door, and stretched out on a tattered secondhand sofa. It was here she would listen to her son reveal all his misgivings about his life, his purpose, and the world. These sporadic conversations always began with...

"Mom, it's all feeling so crazy again ..."

Maya disbelieved her son was suicidal. She had had too many conversations like this with him over the years. Without ever openly admitting it, she had been his therapist for a large part of his adult life. She would receive this call two or three times a year where her son, Amos, would open up in stream of consciousness. Unquestionably, COVID, Trump and George Floyd had added a certain bitterness to everything he was feeling of late, and then the holidays were especially revealing for everyone. Maya lay on the couch listening without interruption.

"... and that's' how everything is. The world is a cruel shit bomb and everyone in it is just trying to get theirs. I'm trying to ignore some of it, but it attacks ... you know ... and then I don't want to act like stuff isn't happening because that's no good ... I breathe and try to stay present but ... but what's happened to us? To people ... friends ... that girl ... you remember her ... we don't speak anymore, was I disposable and how come I didn't catch that earlier? A love affair going bad happens but it's like … it's where everyone is now. It's not even about that. It's money, money, money, and people treating kindness as weakness, and everyone is so fucking rude and selfish and entitled as fuck. I check myself all the time to see how far wrong I've gone cuz ' it's a culture this disease and I know I'm affected too … everyone is so disingenuous which is just a polite way to say everyone knows they're lying but they can qualify any behavior and tell themselves they're telling the truth and here I am … what am I doing … I'm cooking. That's all I'm doing about it. Man! That's fucking crazy. Isn't it?!"

This went on for a good twenty minutes. At times he would gain speed and incoherence while his brain was attempting to catch up with his divergent thoughts, his emotional responses. She could tell he was seeking somewhere soft to land.

"You know I don't have that God thing like you do and for sure it would be easier if I did. I could just say that it's his way and eventually it will all work out, but I don't believe that shit. I know … I know you have all that faith … and I'm sorry I can't but … but … I'm trying. You know, I'm trying. Without the Holy God thing …"

His torrent of words would eventually exhaust him, and he would abruptly turn silent. His emotional arteries opened, he'd bleed a while, and then fall into an anemic quietude. Amos was done. This was how it went. The storm was over, and Maya was the calm thereafter. The phone would turn into a silent vessel of hope, both innate and animate.

Maya was fully aware the world had changed in every recognizable way since she had grown up. The how and what to do, the options available, the problems and solutions and most tellingly, social discourse had emerged as a weapon. The social network had not, as promised, brought people closer. She also knew life remained on a continuum of change, which now was working at warp speed. No introduction, pause, or reset. Maya herself had difficulty making any sense of its trajectory. The beneficiary of twenty-nine years more experience than her son, she was painfully aware the challenges Amos faced were foreign to her as well. Her antidote was always steeped in her world, one which she inherited from her mother. A world which no longer existed.

When Maya intruded on their silence, her voice was composed and confident. She unflinchingly alluded to some of the problems Amos had divulged. It would have been disingenuous not to. Speaking of God would also have been counterproductive but speaking of the love she felt from her beliefs was something she could portion faithfully. She spoke to Amos of the joys of life. The beauty of possibility, or rather the possibility of beauty, in spite of the obvious. She layered in maxims, 'it doesn't matter what the situation is. Only your response matters.' She told him again the story of how, when he was born, she was deathly afraid of being accountable for a child's life. She felt so woefully inadequate and unprepared that she wanted to die at one point. It was what defined Maya's approach to life. But mostly, Maya's conversation led with love, not failing to include its discontents. Yes, even love was baffling. However, she insisted, love was still the hammer and the nail which kept all things together. He'd heard it before. 'It's simple, it's just not easy.'

Maya went silent. Her response was pithy yet gentle. A life passed between them, muted and weighty. Her son was her dream made reality. Locked in him was her faith in the world, her faith in God. She waited patiently.

Amos' voice sounded husky, deconstructed. "I'm making cornbread ... tastes like magic in your mouth ..."

The first words Quentin uttered as he pulled off the Los Angeles 101 freeway were, "This fucking place ..." The drive from San Francisco to LA turned into eleven hours of uninterrupted mental torture. He despised driving. Back home, Q used the Bay Area's public transportation almost exclusively. At the driver's wheel, he experienced only terror. The closer he got to LA, the more traffic deteriorated into unadulterated vehicular madness. He had arrived three days early, hoping to avoid this holiday mayhem. It was early Tuesday afternoon, for Christ's sake. How could the freeways be jammed on a Tuesday? Weren't most people working from home during these COVID days? Q couldn't decide if the people in Southern California were the worst drivers on the planet or the most inexcusably selfish. Driving here was to focus on how many ways one could either die or end up paralyzed by one of these errant fuckers. This trip solidified the choice for his next art subject. He would paint unhoused people defecating in luxury autos.

Quentin turned off on Coldwater Canyon, pulling into his favorite burrito place on the side of the freeway. It was a painful challenge expelling himself from his car after this last unrelieved four-hour stretch of driving. Empty bags, bottles and cans littered his car like the stadium floor following a home game. But it was his back that worried him. It was completely inflexible. A car accident many years ago resulted in compression fractures on a couple of vertebrae, and the doctor warned it might develop into arthritis years down the road. If Quentin stayed seated for any extended period, he would lock up in excruciating pain until it released him. Resembling Gumby as he exited his car, he was barely able to close its door; any other movement was agony. All he could do was swear, which he did with proficiency.

"The fuck you lookin at?"is how he addressed a rather large, suited man who had parked next to him. The man was guilty of smirking. Quentin was spread out over his car, stretching. To the innocent bystander, it could have appeared strangely erotic. This was LA, after all. Q was framing his body against the car in every possible position in order to free up his back. Q walked gingerly to the takeout window and ordered. The suit from the parking lot was waiting for his food, ignoring Q, three feet away. Q was not a physically threatening presence. During his early years Quentin was the recipient of multiple ass whippings for the simple reason he was in fact, no threat. This forced Q to learn Jiu-Jitsu. These days he was a more than a competent practitioner and always ready to make someone tap out, whether it be in the dojo or on the street. He couldn't give a fuck. He would randomly assess people and imagine what critical damage he could inflict on them. Q had an anger problem he was combating and on occasion, was mildly successful. Their food came out of the window at the same time. They mirrored one another, walking back to their cars. The suit turned to Q and smiled.

Q returned in a voice barely audible through his rage, "Say one fucking word ..."

Beau was in bed on Wednesday afternoon. On the surrounding floor were dozens of boxes of new athletic shoes and cellophaned shirts and jackets. His business was spilling from everywhere. Above his king-sized bed was a painting of a couple locked in complicated congress with the caption: Kama Sutra Candle Dance. He was attempting to replicate this portrait with the two naked nubiles who were jockeying for position. Beau, hip hop to the bitter end, sported only a Raiders T-shirt and a backwards NY baseball cap while he moved smooth black bodies into advantageous arrangement. The scene was more comic than erotic, and the two girls gave up, deciding to smother Beau, providing themselves with their own amusement. Beau knew there were one or two things more satisfying than sex, but at that moment, he couldn't recall what they were. Happily smothered, he thought whatever he was to accomplish in life, it would have to be something which advanced his amorous lifestyle. He couldn't give a shit what anyone else thought about that. His brother Jules and he were similar that way, with the exception that Jules also found meaning in hard labor. Beau, on the other hand, was certain the evasion of effort in the job place was nothing less than genius. So far, this philosophy was working out for him. He bought and sold the newest fashion, some of it cleverly appropriated over the internet. He made money and spent it. Life was grand.

The three of them sat on a pile of soiled sheets and pillows, passing a joint from a tube labeled 'nuclear fission.' The girls exhaled into one another's mouths as Beau waxed dreamily on the future of drugs, explaining how the world has not even touched its 'getting stoned' potential. One day, he predicted, you will be able to take a drug for whatever fantasy you could conjure. And ... still go to work the next day. Not that he wanted to go to work, which he had made supremely clear. They laughed and coughed, lying spread out on the bed, an advertisement for nonchalant nudity. Beau remained in his cap and the Raiders T-shirt. The remote was accidentally fingered by one of them and when the music sounded, Beau leaped out of the bed and danced. It was a floor show, with Beau giving it all, dangling in the wind while keeping time. The intertwined girls made for an exuberant audience. They understood this to be his gesture of thanks. Such a wonderful way to begin Thanksgiving.

There was an unfriendly pounding on the door loud enough to overtake the music. The three looked at one another, stoned, while they mutually and unsuccessfully willed the knocking to subside. Beau stepped into some five-hundred-dollar sweatpants he was to sell later that afternoon before leaving the bedroom and arriving at the door.

"What the fuck?" flew out of Beau's mouth as Baron entered without preamble.

"Get a doorbell." Baron stood on the inside of the threshold, looking around. He and Beau embraced aggressively and released quickly. Beau knew his brother and understood something untoward might be in progress.

"Can you talk?"

"Not now. You heard of phones?"

"You remember Valerie?"

"Your Tinder girl?"

"She's pregnant."

"Whose is it?"

At that moment, the meaningful part of the menage à trois appeared in the hallway, fascinated. They resembled a Van Gogh portrait, manic eyes opened wide and focused with questionable intent on the viewer. Baron was stunned into silence. As no one seemed motivated to reveal, Baron mumbled a tepid request for the ladies to leave. Beau gently whispered they were his friends and as such ... it would be disrespectful. So ... no, they were not leaving. Baron's head rotated back and forth between Beau, who was adamant, and his paramours, who now viewed Baron sympathetically. Baron shrugged and walked slowly between the girls, hands in pockets, crumpling onto the couch. Beau offered drinks to everyone.

Bill and Lizzie had been married for nearly ten years. Their communion was strongly supported by like-minded ideas of comfort and shared revenue streams. They had both advanced in corporate enterprises and amassed an enviable nest egg in savings and properties. It was Bill who brought the most to the table, having been prodigiously successful before they met. Lizzie came to the relationship with nothing more than an infectious vigor and in short time became something of a curator to Bill's investments. This proved more beneficial than he could have imagined. And ... she kept her job. It was often said by her siblings, 'Bill does the work, but Lizzie gets it done.' Bill was also a closet chef. He's always loved to cook, and Lizzie knew if she married him, she'd eat well the rest of her life.

Bill was not terribly close with most of his own family. He preferred to live vicariously through the dramatic vagaries of Lizzie's tribe. There was much to discern in her family of now six. Bill also benefited from being the favorite in-law. He was the only in-law. One of the conversations which never failed to turn up during family gatherings was the scarcity of its married members. They all would philosophize about why, the men especially, could not settle down. Maya at least had a stable relationship with someone. Lizzie, being the youngest, also appeared the most mature in matters of relationships. Her ten years with Bill trumped everyone else's and gave her a satisfying feeling of advantage. This was manifested in her tendency to speak without censorship. She, the youngest of them, was also the most outspoken and the least corrigible. Witness the piss fountain.

Bill had a son from a previous marriage who was a criminal attorney in Philadelphia. Lizzie had a daughter from a previous marriage who did social work in San Francisco. The secret Lizzie and Bill concealed was that their two children were, in fact, a long-distance couple. Paramours. It was not a point of pride for either of them, and they both shared hope that the distance would eventually dissolve the romance. In any event, it would not be a welcome conversation at the dinner table with the likes of her disparate-thinking family. It remained a point of raw discomfort, especially for Lizzie. Bill was less troubled about it but honored Lizzie's sentiment. He had provoked her on occasion by simply admitting his lack of apprehension regarding the relationship with their children. They were not, after all, related. Lizzie would grow cold at the mention of this before launching into a rearview moral diatribe about family being sacred, community perceptions, and how everyone was obliged to accept certain cultural standards. A response Bill neither understood nor could figure into Lizzie's normally logical sense of propriety. He knew Thanksgiving was not the day to revisit those positions.

Quentin had finally arrived at his destination. Mercifully, his back was feeling better. He was unpacking and hanging up his clothes in the tiny guesthouse of a property rented by his ex-girlfriend, Sasha. They had been off-and-on lovers for many years, which ended abruptly two years ago. She was now in a serious relationship with a man whom he had yet to meet. Her new man traveled extensively for work and was presently in Istanbul, which afforded Q's stay in the back house. Q called her about his Thanksgiving visit on a lark and she told him as much. He would be welcome. Quentin looked around the place at the photos of his ex and her man assembled throughout every room. They apparently traveled the world together and were enamored with selfies expressing repetitive smiles of wonderment. Having not physically seen her in some time, he searched for what he thought would be the most recent photo to refresh his memory and divine how much she had changed. Quentin settled on a picture of the couple at a beach. She stood ankle deep in water, bathing suit clad, in which she remained a solid testament to womanhood. Her man wore a loose T-shirt and shorts, not enough to hide his paunch. Not impressive, but perhaps an equally valid statement about manhood. Women worked harder than men. Quentin was most attracted to these quarters because they were central, and he had little need to use his car. He was also painfully curious about Sasha's new love.

She had availed him a mountain bike with a basket which stood just outside his doorstep. Quentin was looking forward to investigating the neighborhood on two wheels. Through the screen door, he was surprised to find a dog glaring at him a few feet away. There was no sign of a dog when he had arrived. This full-sized canine was of mixed breed with more than a dash of Pitbull in his DNA. Q latched the screen door for precaution. The dog rose from his seated position as the latch clicked. His tail stiff, his eyes alarmingly wide.

"Hello doggie ..." This tepid greeting was as short and empty as the space between the two and equally as troubling. No movement meant doggie didn't speak the same language. He doubled down and unlocked the screen door, slowly exposing himself, managing to get half his body outside before the animal rose and snarled in Q's direction. *What the fuck was this? What the fuck was this?* Momentarily, the dog's ears went up and his tail fluttered as Sasha walked through the gate.

"Bodie's funny around strangers. But he won't bite."

"Good to know."

Q and Sasha moved into the house proper. Q sat on a puffy, royal blue couch while Sasha was in the connected open kitchen preparing tea. The whole place had a strong *Architectural Digest* touch to it. Colorful hassocks and throw pillows for comfort, carefully selected modern art on the walls to impress. The entire ceiling was fixed in flesh-toned wallpaper from which hung a chandelier Napoleon might envy. Bouquets of flowers were strategically placed. Even the air was redolent of some tropical fruit. Why was everyone Quentin knew doing better than he was? Sasha watched him nervously fiddle with some figurines on the table in front of him. He was particularly taken by a rainbow-colored skull.

"What do you think?"

"... it's a bag of confusion ... Transgender Pride skull?"

"It's from an AIDS march."

"I see."

She brought out the tea and poured. They sat in silence. Q was not super fond of teas of any type, and she had chosen chamomile, his least favorite. He thought it tasted of tepid piss.

"How do you like the back house? Comfortable?"

"It's great. Thanks so much. Nice photos of you guys."

Sasha went to the kitchen and returned with a tray of unidentifiable snacks. In modulated tones, Sasha told him she and her man were going through a rough patch. This came out of nowhere, which is where she wanted to keep it. She smiled too big for the moment. Q focused on the tray, reluctantly choosing the tiniest morsel available. He incorrectly identified what he hoped was a piece of cheese, swallowing it hastily.

"So, are you a vegan now?"

"No, that was seasoned curd. Savory, isn't it?"

"Nice. So, your man is what, in Istanbul? Always wanted to go there."

"He's back now.

Sasha daintily chose something that resembled a prune except it was roseate and chewed it longer than necessary. “He hit me.”

If you can actually cry without producing tears, it’s what Sasha was doing. She focused on the appetizer tray as if it were the forgotten pool of infinity. She was locked in, fragile, and determined not to show emotion. Q could tell Sasha was deeply disappointed with herself for revealing in less than five minutes something she had no plans to share at all. Her disquiet was palpable and for Q, heartbreaking. His soul burnt at the edges.

Someone hit her. Hurt her? He sat there focused on that inedible spread to avoid meeting her sadness with anything other than pure rage. She was no longer there. Q was alone experiencing a full-blown violent fantasy. Bereft of any real knowledge of this man, it was the photograph of him at the beach with Sasha, with his fat paunch and his oily smile, which yielded Q the object of his enmity. Q wanted to do bad things to this man, and he wanted to do them now. His voyage into hell was relieved slightly when Sasha touched his hand. He returned a difficult smile. She couldn't possibly know what he was thinking when she informed him her ex was on his way home.

Eloy was the name of Maya’s man. When they met, she had him pronounce it several times, thinking she had misheard it. It was a name she felt uncomfortable not understanding, so she Googled it in the middle of their introduction. Maya discovered the name had a slightly complicated history. Derived from the Greek name Eulogios or Latin name Eligius or from the Hebrew, meaning high, being a version of Eli. Trying to explain this to a man who spoke severely limited English proved to be accidentally romantic, not to mention comical. To be sure, romance and comedy was not only a memorable beginning but their recurring theme. She was younger than he was, but had been recently dating younger men, most of whom had disappointed her on various fronts. So, his age was not really a concern. Maya considered herself a catch for the same reason she was often not considered such. Maya was a genuinely nice person. Even Maya recognized how kindness in this current culture was terribly undervalued. By her admission, men preferred bitches. Eloy was kind. The first thing she registered in their initial meeting was the kindness unhidden in his eyes. He looked at her without agenda. She felt his immediate openness without the usual searchlight that came with it.

Eloy had the body of a man who used his body. She also liked that. For her, however, the soul of his masculinity rested clearly in his hands. He had a man's hands. Not so large, or defined, but beautifully expressive. Since they were communicating through mutual foreign languages, his hands literally came into play. It didn't hurt that he was genuinely tactile. When he shook her hand for the first time, he held onto it. Such a curious moment for her, in that it seemed natural. She allowed her hand to rest in his. He wasn't trying to prove anything. He seemed authentic to her, sincere. Very hard to come by, that.

It took several weeks for the relationship to develop for the simple reason that they couldn't understand one another clearly. He spoke Spanish to a Mexican crew all day on his construction sites, and she was not interested in learning another language. Full stop. Counterintuitively, she had no problem struggling mightily to explain either the most basic or most important things to her man. As she would tell her family, who had no idea how this relationship worked, Eloy loved her more than anyone else ever had. Communication sacrifices were negligible. It was in a word, different, being with him. In her previous relationships, she had the distinct feeling she was being repurposed by men, without the purpose part.

That Maya didn't invite him to Thanksgiving (again, it was the biggest argument they'd had to date) didn't stop Eloy from keeping his promise of accompanying her to church today. Eloy, a fallen catholic, found church, any church, an endless source of sadness. Raised on Christ hanging from a cross, murdered saints, and the nonstop need for sacrifice, his disagreeable position regarding the holy institution was fixed at an early age in Mexico City. He would attend services every Sunday with his nana and tia, both devout Catholics easily given to deep shows of emotion during Mass. Their tears and occasionally frightening moans placed a terrifying accent on the Blood of Christ sermons. The stifling celebration of incense didn't help either. Whatever was going on, he wanted no part of it. To this day, whenever he passed a church, he made the sign of the cross, not out of reverence, but out of fear of having left the church so completely. He was hedging his bet.

The church Maya belonged to wasn't physically a church. It was a large, drafty, barn-like edifice owned by one of the parishioners, if that's what they called themselves. The meetings were unapologetically casual, helped along by the unremarkable interior of the structure. A stranger would be hard-pressed to recognize it as a place of worship. There were quite comfortable chairs on an elevated platform, and usually food was provided. Eloy particularly liked the food touch. A few dozen lit candles were the singular ritualistic ingredient. Walls were unadorned. There was no altar. The windows were not stained. Nor were there any statues of elevated idols. Dogs were allowed inside. Eloy wasn't sure if cats were not welcome, or the presence of dogs made them scarce. There were about a hundred people scattered around the room, standing as well as seated.

One person at a time came to the microphone, spoke until they were done, then someone else would step up. Eloy understood little, but it seemed very civilized to him. There was neither the Blood of Christ nor manifestations of the devil's hellfire.

What was lost on Eloy with his poor English was the unending show of optimism that occurred. People took turns coming to the mic and explaining what wonders God brought into their lives of recent. It was a harmless celebration of the positive as well as a fervent show of gratitude. The structure of this denomination was as amorphous as the God they were extolling. For them, God was everything and everywhere. The devotion lay firmly in how one simply appreciated the goodness squeezed out of life. There were slight ceremonial touches in the handing off of the microphone gestures, but these were lost on Eloy as well. In every chair was a printed manual styled after a hymnal, like the one Eloy was fingering. Its cover read ... *Be As One*. That, Eloy could read. He didn't go any further than the cover. What Eloy took great pleasure in was examining the structure of the place and imagining how he would figure in its reconstruction. There were spaces dying for free-standing walls and perhaps a staircase to a loft. There was certainly plenty of height to accommodate a number of improvements. A skylight and the odd elliptical window overhead would change illumination for the better. Eloy believed it was the simple modifications in a remodel that mattered.

He was reimagining an entryway when he heard a familiar sound. A woman was at the microphone relating joyously how she had been given another healthy grandchild by her only daughter. He understood every word. She was supremely ecstatic over this development, and it was all expressed in Spanish. Initially, he thought he was experiencing a translation miracle.

Maya watched Eloy plug into his native tongue. He held her hand tightly, allowing Maya to feel the casual vigor that so attracted her to him initially. When the woman finished speaking, Eloy turned to Maya. She had subtly motioned for him to go to the microphone and share his common joy in the language of his heart. He instead kissed Maya so deeply she failed to suppress a solitary moan. He then looked straight ahead with a renewed interest in the speakers. Still reeling from his kiss Maya, recalled an instance when she tried to explain her love for this 'non-English-speaking-dude' to her family. She told them, "Sometimes I don't feel like kissing him. But he can always change my mind. No matter what mood I'm in. Always. No one else has ever held that kind of power over me. Can you understand what that takes? When a man can ..." They never asked her anything about him again.

Unlike Quentin, Jules loved driving around LA. In New York, he always traveled by subway, underground, moving through the bowels like rats. Bereft of the visual journey, he was forever arriving somewhere with no appreciation of the voyage. In LA, above ground, there was always the sun, the views. Even the crowded freeways were of interest to him on some mysterious anthropological level. This was understandable. He worked inside an enclosed emergency room and had his fill of humans in close contact. Sick, complaining, smelly, and needy patients obligated Jules to meditate an hour before each shift in order to deal with the exhaustive nature of his profession. Consequently, cars and freeways were strangely welcome in his orbit. From a vehicle, he could see trees and houses develop into distinct neighborhoods. This being LA, there were always more cars than houses. Cars parked in driveways, sitting at curbs, and a few resting on front lawns. This was somehow comforting. The absence of people was in evidence. Not so in New York City. There were, of course, cars in the city, but people remained the leitmotif.

Jules pulled up to the curb of a large Craftsman home in Mid-City. It had the works, pitched gable roof, elevated porch, sturdy columns, a house as horizontal as the sea. After admiring the row of mature magnolia trees straight lining the street, he bounced up the four stairs and rang a doorbell which resounded in bell peals. *California. Gotta love it.* When a laughing man opened the door, the reek made it clear he either housed a family of skunks or someone was blazing inside. California, home of the midday high. Jules entered.

The interior was a luxurious, darkly paneled room with couches occupied by half a dozen people. The curtains were closed, the place was illumed by artificial lights. Half a dozen people were taking turns sucking on the business end of a complicated vaporizer designed as much for style as efficiency. It had a massive dragon's head at its mouth. The man who answered the door, Doctor Mike, was still laughing. He placed a heavy hand on Jule's shoulder and led him out of the dark living room to a private room.

Doctor Mike was no doctor, though he was not averse to making house calls. He was awarded the moniker for his stellar connections and the pure quality of his product. If it got you high and, more importantly, if you were cool, for the right price, he would arrange the merriment. They met the previous Thanksgiving through Beau. Jules continued his relationship with the good doctor with the proviso that Beau was not to be privy to their occasional meetups. Jules didn't want to set a bad example for a baby brother who was already the poster boy for bad examples. So here he was, scoring a gram of coke for Lola in a darkened Craftsman house in midtown LA the day before Thanksgiving. There was some sick poetry in that. It was a quick exchange of cash for a small gram-weighted white envelope.

Walking back to his car, Jules was aware of being deeply redolent of robust marijuana. He didn't partake in grass himself, believing it only made one dumber. He decided to take a stroll down the lovely, canopied block and walk the smell off. It was another countless day of sunshine and there was a hint of the Santa Ana winds to come. He arrived at the end of the block and savored the strong scent of jasmine. When he turned around, a woman was pointing in his direction a short distance away. There was a parked police car from which an officer emerged to join the woman. Jules felt for the envelope in his pocket. The officer and the woman were now mobilizing in his direction. The woman looked fearful, her arms folded securely in front of her, a protective step behind the officer. The policeman had one hand at rest on his gun. Jules' mind was off to the races. He removed his hands from his pockets and attempted a look of casual alarm.

"How are you doing this afternoon?" the officer greeted him. Jules' response was quicker than his caution. "That depends ..."

The officer turned to the woman. "Is this the man?" Her grip tightened around herself. She paused. "I'm not sure."

The officer had Jules hand over his identification. There was no protest.

"New York?'

"That's correct.'

"You staying in this neighborhood?"

"Visiting."

"Who are you visiting?"

"The neighborhood. I stop at beautiful streets and walk them. It's a different planet here ... LA ... New York."

"Mmhmmm."

"Can you tell me what's going on?"

"Hold on a minute." The officer walked back to his car, the woman trailing him, and called in Jules' ID. Jules was feverishly searching for a moment he could discard the gram of coke into one of these lawns thick with succulents, but the woman wouldn't refrain from eyeballing him. From a distance, she appeared sinister. He had no idea who this woman was, but he was quite sure he hated her.

The two calmly strolled back to Jules, providing him with an unexpected revelation that police never seem to be in a hurry. Remove the uniform and he could be going for a Sunday stroll. The woman was holding herself so tightly Jules thought she might accidentally strangle herself. The policeman spoke leisurely.

"You're a doctor."

"Emergency room."

"New York City emergency room ... must be pretty busy these days."

Jules felt it best not to respond. He was aware of the LA attitude towards NYC, there was a competitive element and Jules didn't want to challenge the policeman's bullshit idea of superiority. We love LA and all that. The officer reluctantly returned Jules' driver's license, resting his eyes unblinkingly on Jules. Jules couldn't discern if the officer was using his poker face or the more often applied look of unused power. Void of subtlety, the officer scrutinized Jules.

"How'd you get here?"

Jules pulled out his key fob. His car chimed a two-note melody. The officer located the car, looked to the woman's flattened blank face, then returned to Jules.

"There have been some daytime robberies in the neighborhood, and someone was in this woman's backyard. We're checking things out."

Jules waited.

"Same size. She thought it might have been you."

"Well ... it wasn't."

The officer afforded a half smile. "Have a good day, Dr. Noble."

When Jules finished the long perp walk back to his car, he was shaking. He guessed his heart rate at about 200 over 90. He didn't want to chance making a turnabout and was obligated to pass them in his egress. The officer was still scribbling notes. The woman glared disapprovingly at Jules as he drove by them. Jules, beyond disturbed, fantasized about one of those big magnolia trees collapsing on her in its entirety.

He drove circuitously through several neighborhoods, which instantly differed in tax brackets. Realities morphed quickly in Los Angeles. He was now passing through a more modest zip code where trees were sparse and windows barred. About a mile away, he pulled into an alley and beat at his steering wheel, screaming "fuck you!" over and over until he felt hoarse. After exhaling deeply several times, he opened his white envelope and had a quick bump.

Baron sat forlornly on Beau's couch, ensconced between the two girls, now partially clothed. Beau sat facing his eldest brother, thoughtfully taking hits off a joint. That Baron was comfortable being gently consoled by his paramours was not lost on Beau. They each had a hand on a shoulder. Beau had a contentious relationship with his brother in particular. Baron was the eldest, a fact which came into play in most of their interactions. Beau was both amused and confused to see Baron sharing his cataclysmic situation with the brother whom he had the least in common.

"I had an abortion."

Baron wearily lifted his head, looking at the girl who spoke as if she had magically appeared.

She took her hand off his shoulder and continued. "I thought I was in love with him. It was a few years ago. I was eighteen. He was twenty-five. Too much was going on. He was scared of me having the baby and changing his life. He had a good job and made lots of money, he thought I would take. He was scared of me having an abortion, too. Worried something could go wrong. It didn't matter what he thought because I knew that having a child at that point in my life wasn't the choice I wanted. And, in truth, his reaction showed me that the man I thought I loved was not the person I thought he was, because he cared more about how it would affect him than me. The abortion isn't really the issue here with your girlfriend, Baron, it's how you support her and her choice."

Baron looked flushed and fascinated. He noticed for the first time she had half a dozen earrings in the ear closest to him. She also had a boxer's scar above her eyebrow. She looked as tough as she was striking. Her gaze was forthright, unrelenting, but devoid of anything accusatory. It was a genuine question.

"Who are you?" he replied gently.

"I'm Tara." The other girl spoke up.

"I'm Latecia."

Beau was predictably high and could not help but snicker at this exchange. Beau shook his head and a very long and sibilant "... shiiiit ..." escaped him, shrouded in smoke.

While Quentin and Sasha waited for her man to return, they held hands. Sitting close together, their heads turned in opposite directions, a photograph dying for a caption. Neither of them required language. They were experiencing communal déjà vu. There was no other woman with whom he had been more intimate. Their affection was their relationship. Physically and spiritually in sync, their pleasures were near unspeakable. This human couplet was interrupted a dozen times over the years as one or both endeavored to pursue serious alternatives. There were many reasons they were unable to remain a couple. She wanted children, which was anathema to Q. He was unconvinced of any service children might provide the world outside of helping to populate it. Children were spoiled examples of spoiled examples. This thinking amused Sasha since she felt Quentin was the definition of spoiled. He wanted to do whatever, whenever. They both benefited from time away. They would meet when they could. During those random reunions, they would redefine their intimacy, an intimacy which somehow found more depth with each rendezvous. 'Rendezvous,' the safe term they used to avoid any semblance of true love. They were on the same page, in the same book, rewriting chapter after chapter. Without understanding how or what this was, their passion never diminished. No one else could ever match their comfort level. Of this, they were both assured. They were also convinced they could never be a conventional couple. What they were objectively was the most literal example of an affair. If such an unending thing can be considered an affair. Yet here they were again.

The metallic sound of keys spoke loudly. Quentin, who had mentally dismembered this man the moment she revealed he'd struck her, was prepared. There was no more conversation to be had. He still hadn't been apprised of her ex's name. Quentin appreciated Sasha for not sharing it. Quentin couldn't give a fuck what his name was. It was all he could manage not to ask specifics. Quentin stood up, rigid as an oak, emotionally salivating. Sasha remained seated, her arm lightly brushing his leg. Her sense of strength was in her calm resolve. That was always her superpower, an uncanny ability to navigate madness without participating in it.

Matt, that was his name, came in the door and Q was immediately underwhelmed. Quentin's initial thought was, why do so many women downgrade when they move on? Matt was a large man resplendent in all-white jogging attire. The shoes matched as did his headband which held back shoulder length hair. He didn't look anything like someone who jogged. He looked like someone who enjoyed a good bag of potato chips. A portion of Quentin's malice melted as Matt stood stuck there, smiling. Admittedly, he was handsome and might resemble a rockstar archetype. To achieve this status, he would be obligated to learn two words: I'm full. Whatever credit Q was willing to give him diminished when Matt spoke his first and only words.

"Well, hello there. Is this a bad time?"

Anyone who has ever been the instigator of a truly violent act is familiar with the telling moment beforehand. The fraction of an instant when consequence and logic smash atomically. Whatever transpires, the aftermath is going to be unsatisfactory. If it ends in death or mutilation, there's always a terrible price. If someone is let off the hook, granted a reprieve at the last minute, even this act of forgiveness can torment in the extreme. Though Q had death lurking in his eyes and malignancy flowing through his veins, he erred on the side of life. Perhaps he thought blood all over the white tracksuit in Sasha's home would be untoward. Quentin walked to Matt, took him in for all he was worth, then jabbed his index finger into Matt's forehead in the most delicate show of deadly intent. He needed to do no more. It was as if Matt's soul exited through the door, followed by his remains. It was anticlimactic and inexplicable, yet vaguely satisfactory. Matt was gone, vamoosed, removed from Sasha's life with a single digit. Sasha never moved from the couch. Never changed expression. Quentin sat down next to her, arms firmly crossed, hands locked under his pits, shaking noticeably.

There are countless maxims about how the best laid plans are sabotaged by the unexpected. The most common being, 'Man makes plans—God laughs.' It's unsure who would be laughing, but Turkey Day did not resemble in any manner what Lizzie had come to expect. And that's taking into consideration Lizzie's more than generous tendency to expect the worst while hoping for the adequate. She certainly couldn't blame herself for this family mess of a mess. She oversaw the location, which, in all fairness, was San Fernando Valley palatial. The food? Restaurant excellent and holiday abundant. It was the guest list which had detonated. No, it was the conversation. Yes, it was the guest list and all that came with it.

Before getting involved with Bill and business, Lizzie had halfhearted designs on becoming a science teacher. She developed the habit of processing information and situations in scientific terms. At this moment, sitting at the dinner table, she wished she were a photon. A photon travels at the speed of light and is not susceptible to time. At the speed of light, time stops. Einstein's dictum, 'the faster you go, the slower time goes.' She wanted time to stop so she could process what was happening at her dinner table, preferably in nonscientific terms. The table had been extended to meet the demands of several more guests.

Baron and Beau had arrived with two excitable women in tow, Tara and Latecia. Before answering the door to receive them, Lizzie heard Beau finishing a conversation through the open window.

"Well shit, if I'm the only brother in there I know I'm in the wrong fucking place." Soon after, Maya entered arm in arm with Eloy. Lizzie made the common gesture of speaking louder to Eloy in the hope of being understood by someone who doesn't speak her language. Eloy bowed his head and placed his hand gently on his heart in thanks, which frankly terrified Lizzie. She responded with an awkward hand gesture of invitation.

Julian arrived with Lola and before Lizzie could greet them, Julian announced, "Cops here are worse than New York City. You should warn a brother."

Sasha was at least a familiar face. When she and Quentin were doing whatever it was they were doing, they had occasionally met by chance. Lizzie remembered Sasha because, against all norms when it came to her brothers' lovers, she liked Sasha. They were the last to arrive. Now instead of eight dinner guests there were twelve. To a person her siblings casually pleaded that their dates had nowhere else to spend the holiday. Lizzie had no place to put her discontent, no time to react rationally or otherwise. She busied herself with the enormous task of improvisation. She steadied herself with the business of serving, entertaining a moment of regret for not having hired someone to help. Tara and Latecia appeared in the kitchen magically and silently. They began to work as if on the clock. Lizzie's place was turning into a co-op.

Maya remained seated, nuzzling happily with her boyfriend while Baron and Beau whispered back and forth intensely. Julian and Lola, whom Bill had whispered to Lizzie was a lawyer and a pole dancer, shared beatific smiles while their hands investigated one another's laps underneath the dinner table.

Lizzie backed away from the kitchen and witnessed all this unhappily. What were all these strangers doing in her house on the first Thanksgiving without her mother? These people who had no idea of the significance of the moment. No understanding of the magnitude of the loss or the family's attempt to reemerge as one unit on this special day. She wanted to hurl the food on the floor and scream. She wanted to be a particle collider smashing protons. She was seeing quarks and leptons. It was all quantum mechanics to her now. Lizzie wanted to stop time and perhaps bend it a bit, back to when Mom was still here to hold the family together the way only she could. She would often tell people without exaggeration that her mother was the finest human being she'd ever known. This was the kind of person she was honoring with today's meal. Lizzie really didn't give a fuck about Thanksgiving. For her, it was all about this family ritual that their mother would elevate to something supremely human. She was realizing loss on a continuum. Her husband watched her impassively, knowing better to interrupt the internal monologue he knew she was undergoing. Nothing good would come of an intrusion. So, he waited as she processed whatever it was she was processing and then finally joining the rest of them at the table. When she did so, there was the silence of reckoning. All eyes were on Lizzie as she bowed her head and, without prelude, began to say grace.

THANKS

I would like to thank Jeff Johnson, who on top of being a terrific writer, was indispensable in this book's entire process. He offered editing, general advice and moral support every step of the way. Everyone needs a tough but gentle literary angel and he was mine. I would like to thank my parents and family for their unconditional love and belief in me. The Staff at the Rose who allowed me to spend countless hours writing in their restaurant even though I would only order a glass of iced tea. All my friends in Paris who have given me life and love for these many years. Jon Lindstrom, a good friend who introduced me to my agent, Liza Fleissig of Liza Royce Associates. Tina Beier, my editor, Alexandria Brown and the rest of the staff at Rising Action Publishing who got it all done.

A few friends I would like to single out who've inspired me: Nicholas Frangakis, Tommy Panos, DM, Paul Verdier. My son, Amari, who made my life comprehensively more interesting and loving. The dozens of people who read early drafts of the stories and provided both genuine and entertaining feedback. Apologies and thanks in advance to those I may have missed.

ABOUT THE AUTHOR

Dominic Hoffman received his BA in English Literature at UC Santa Cruz, and his formal training at American Conservatory Theatre, LAMDA and NYU Film School. He is the author of numerous plays and screenplays, including the double Ovation Award winner (actor/writer) for *Uncle Jacques Symphony* and NAACP Best New Play Award Winner *Last Fare*. Dominic is an award-winning narrator of dozens of audiobooks, among them James McBride's *Deacon King Kong* and *The Heaven and Earth Grocery Store*, Homegoing by Yaa Gyasi and Percival Everett's Audio Book of the Year, James. He works as an actor in theatre and television. His latest film role was in the independent feature, *Henry Johnson*, written and directed by David Mamet.